Complete Book of Throws

Jay Silvester

Editor

Human Kinetics

Library of Congress Cataloging-in-Publication Data

Complete book of throws / Jay Silvester, editor.
p. cm.
Includes bibliographical references and index.
ISBN 0-7360-4114-1 (soft cover)
1. Weight throwing. 2. Javelin throwing. I. Silvester, L Jay.
GV1093 .C64 2003
796.43'5--dc21

2002002351

ISBN-10: 0-7360-4114-1
ISBN-13: 978-0-7360-4114-0

Acquisitions Editors: Todd Jensen and Ed McNeely; **Developmental Editor:** Laura Hambly; **Assistant Editors:** Alisha Jeddeloh, Dan Brachtesende, and Kim Thoren; **Copyeditor:** Patsy Fortney; **Proofreader:** Julie Marx Goodreau; **Indexer:** Bobbi Swanson; **Permission Manager:** Toni Harte; **Graphic Designer:** Fred Starbird; **Graphic Artist:** Tara Welsch; **Cover Designer:** Robert Reuther; **Photo Manager:** Dan Wendt; **Photographer (cover):** Andy Lyons/Getty Images; **Photographer (interior):** Human Kinetics, unless otherwise noted; **Art Managers:** Dan Wendt and Carl Johnson; **Illustrator:** Tim Offenstein; **Printer:** Versa Press

Human Kinetics books are available at special discounts for bulk purchase. Special editions or book excerpts can also be created to specification. For details, contact the Special Sales Manager at Human Kinetics.

Printed in the United States of America 10 9

The paper in this book is certified under a sustainable forestry program.

Human Kinetics
Web site: www.HumanKinetics.com

United States: Human Kinetics, P.O. Box 5076, Champaign, IL 61825-5076
800-747-4457
email: humank@hkusa.com

Canada: Human Kinetics, 475 Devonshire Road Unit 100, Windsor, ON N8Y 2L5
800-465-7301 (in Canada only)
email: info@hkcanada.com

Europe: Human Kinetics, 107 Bradford Road, Stanningley, Leeds LS28 6 AT, United Kingdom
+44 (0) 113 255 5665
email: hk@hkeurope.com

Australia: Human Kinetics, 57A Price Avenue, Lower Mitcham, South Australia 5062
08 8372 0999
e-mail: info@hkaustralia.com

New Zealand: Human Kinetics, P.O. Box 80, Torrens Park, South Australia 5062
0800 222 062
e-mail: info@hknewzealand.com

Complete Book of Throws

Contents

Preface

The *Complete Book of Throws* is a labor of love. The authors love the events they have written about and share the expertise they've acquired over years of competing and coaching at the highest levels. This book is a valuable resource for coaches and athletes who wish to improve their ability to coach or perform in the throwing events. It contains detailed technique instruction, training suggestions, and drills that will benefit coaches and athletes at all levels—from beginning to elite.

Few books cover the four throws exclusively. This book is unique because of the in-depth coverage of each throw, the expertise each contributor brings to the events, and the ease with which the information can be applied to any athlete's or coach's program. Never has a group of authors with more knowledge on the four throws ever been assembled. The techniques and training methods that have proven so successful in their own careers, as well as those of their athletes, are now available to help you achieve your goals. We are confident that all will enjoy and learn from reading this work.

Who can be a successful thrower? As with most human endeavors it is folly to describe limits or parameters too precisely. While we would not discourage anyone from enjoying the throwing events, the physical characteristics that enable success at higher levels in the throws can be generalized.

Discus thrower—Relatively large, reasonably tall, powerful, lithe, quick, and explosive.

Shot-putter—Rather massive and powerful, quick, and explosive. The rotation or spin technique allows powerful individuals of modest height to compete at world-class levels.

Javelin thrower— Lean, lithe, fast, flexible, and very explosive. Size is much less a concern than in shot put and discus, although reasonable height may be of some advantage.

Hammer thrower—Powerful, agile, great balance, very quick, and explosive. Hammer throwers need not be tall.

At the junior high and high school levels the smaller, earlier maturing, quick person will frequently be a very good performer in the throws. Often the larger boys and girls do not have adequate strength relative to their size to create the force necessary to throw far. The relative lightness of the implements at these age levels (17 and younger) also works in favor of the smaller person. As the larger youth mature, they frequently develop the strength, quickness, and power to compete effectively later in their high school years and thereafter. Successful throwers at the collegiate and postcollegiate levels are generally not small in stature.

What is the best way to proceed when learning and teaching the throwing events? Should you start with biomechanical principles, a discussion of levers and forces? Should you consider the throws from a more rhythmic, artistic perspective? Or should you approach the throws from a mechanical perspective, carefully considering the positions a thrower should go through while progressing from start to finish? We present all of these techniques in this book in the hope that by doing so we may more definitively convey the concepts we consider most important.

Obviously the methods a coach of a 10- to 13-year-old beginner uses would be different from those used by a college coach of a reasonably successful performer. Nevertheless, the principles taught should be the same.

The technique chapters of this book cover each event carefully. We have organized the material in such a way that beginning coaches and athletes will understand and be able to readily apply the techniques. However, the models for all of the techniques and conditioning programs result from studying the techniques and conditioning programs of the most accomplished throwers in the history of the sport. Therefore, while the information is understandable and useful for the beginner, it is no less useful to the more advanced or even elite athlete.

The chapters in this book are designed to address concepts that are essential to one who would embrace throwing either as coach or athlete. Chapter 1, the biomechanical chapter, addresses the major challenges of the thrower—those of developing momentum and then transferring as much energy (force) into the implement as possible. In this book you will learn the techniques necessary to create as much force as possible in the movement area and how to transfer that force to the implement. Chapter 2, the strength and conditioning chapter, provides the unabashed truth about strength and conditioning for throwers. You will learn the exercises, the frequency of doing the exercises, and the length of time normally required to reach various levels of strength and power appropriate for successful competitive throwing.

The event chapters provide brief histories of the events followed by detailed discussions of the techniques that produce excellence in movement and thereby long throws. As we discuss each position in the full movement, we note possible errors and suggest how to correct those errors. Generous illustrations will enhance your visual understanding. Our most carefully crafted written descriptions, coupled with sequence illustrations and diagrams, represent the best we can portray in a book. These chapters also include additional strength and conditioning specifics for each event.

Some refer to the track and field throwing events as the classical throws since many originated in ancient (classical) Greece. The discus and javelin throw, for example, were contested as part of the Olympic Pentathlon. We contend that these events stand as classics in terms of their historical longevity, their demand for precision of technique, and the requirement for thorough attention to all aspects of conditioning.

The movements of a throwing event are far too complex, unified, sequential, rhythmic, and demanding of precise summation to capture verbally. While we may not be able to accurately portray in writing a beautiful throw in any one of the throwing events, we will take you as close as possible to sensing how it happens.

We have done our very best in producing this book. We have every confidence that those who give themselves to throwing for a season, whether as athlete or coach, will learn the concepts, feelings, and movements that will help them better understand, perform, and coach the classical throws.

chapter 1

Biomechanics for Throwing Techniques

Jay Silvester

© The Sporting Image

The objective of this chapter is to focus on the basic essentials of throwing from a biomechanical perspective while clearing away most, if not all, of the complicated details. Essentially, we will focus on three concepts:

1. Developing kinetic energy, or momentum (these terms are synonymous in this chapter)
2. Stretching elastic tissue prior to the delivery phase
3. Transferring energy (force) to the implement

It is not uncommon for a coach to work with a thrower for years without discussing the principles that are presented in this chapter. When throwers begin to view themselves as human beings developing as much kinetic energy as possible with the attendant problem of controlling that energy and focusing it into the implement at release, they have a clear view of the essence of throwing. Successful throwing technique includes movement characteristics that

1. facilitate high levels of kinetic energy propagation of both the body and the implement,
2. produce significant stretching of elastic tissue to enhance range of motion and release velocity, and
3. transfer significant kinetic energy (force) efficiently from the body to the implement just before release.

Throwers who are aware of these biomechanical concepts have a clearer picture of the problems they encounter and are better able to focus their workouts.

Developing Momentum in the Run-Up Area

All four throwing events are contested within what we refer to as a "run-up area." Far and away the most liberal run-up boundaries are in the javelin throw. The javelin runway is 30 to 36.5 meters (98.4 to 120 feet) long and 4 meters (13 feet) wide. The most restrictive run-up boundaries are found in the shot put and the hammer throw: 2.135-meter (7-foot) circles. The discus throw is also contested in a relatively small 2.5-meter (8 feet, 2 1/2 inches) circle.

One might wonder who decided on the dimensions of the run-up areas and why. Why don't we just throw the implements from a standing position? Obviously, run-up areas, although very limited in three cases, were designed to allow for the development of additional momentum to apply to the implements, thus propelling them to greater distances than are possible from a standing throw.

How is this momentum generated? The movement of the human body is powered by muscle contraction. Contracting muscles are fueled by the expenditure of chemical energy. Contracting muscles pull on a system of levers in our bodies (skeletal system), creating mechanical energy that moves our body parts. When mechanical energy moves a human being, the human being in motion possesses kinetic energy (KE). The degree or amount of kinetic energy depends on the mass of the person and the velocity of that mass:

$$(KE = 1/2mv^2)$$

Small changes in velocity markedly affect kinetic energy. Another term that is very similar to *kinetic energy* is *momentum* (M). Momentum is the quantity of motion of an object. As mentioned earlier, these terms are used synonymously in this chapter.

Kinetic energy never truly becomes a force until the body with kinetic energy contacts another body or object. Force can be described as push or pull, but it is more precisely defined as the product of mass and acceleration. When a thrower creates angular or linear momentum (kinetic energy) and then applies that momentum to the implement, force is the result. Obviously, then, when a thrower grasps the handle of a hammer or grips a shot, discus, or javelin and starts moving, some force is being applied. With that application of force and the movement of the implement not only does the body have a quantity of momentum but the implement itself also has some momentum. The hammer, because of its mass and velocity during the turns, would possess far greater momentum than any other implement during the run-up phase.

The distance the implement flies depends on the total amount of momentum created by the athlete–implement system as well as the efficiency of the transfer of energy/momentum/force from the thrower to the implement. A human being creates the greatest KE or M when the highest velocity is achieved ($KE = 1/2mv^2$). Successful throwers must be quick and powerful, capable of very rapid acceleration. Slow, ponderous individuals may succeed at the beginning levels of throwing, that is, at the youth, elementary, and junior high school levels. But if they do not develop good, even great, power, their lack of ability to accelerate very quickly (create high levels of KE or M) in a very small space will generally preclude success at the high school or college level.

Muscular Power

As mentioned earlier, the KE or M created by the thrower results from muscle contraction. A thrower who has a more powerful muscular system than another would, all other things being equal, throw farther. The nature of conditioning is such that if an athlete with reasonable body size is motivated to work hard and consistently on a well-designed strength and conditioning program for a few years, he or she will develop strength and power levels comparable to elite throwers. Muscular power is one critical determinant of momentum or energy production and thereby long throws.

Stretch of Elastic Tissue

Another very important determinant of throwing success is the ability to stretch elastic tissue and produce a forceful and fast shortening of the stretched tissue. This crucial concept is seldom given adequate attention in throwing discussions. Successful throwers must develop significant stretch on elastic components of the body (muscles, tendons, and ligaments) just prior to beginning the delivery phase. Once stretched, this elastic tissue must then shorten with a very powerful, even explosive, return to pre-stretch length.

Good flexibility has been noted as an advantage in countless athletic activities. However, if the quality of the elastic tissue is such that there is a minimal or slow response to stretch, it is of little consequence to the aspiring thrower. Conditioning programs for throwers must produce strong and very responsive elastic components.

To summarize this brief discussion on the importance of stretch, there are two concepts that throwers should attend to:

1. Conditioning the body to maximize the stretch response
2. Developing technical competence at putting various body parts on stretch just prior to delivery in a manner that derives the greatest benefit from the stretch response

Technical Efficiency

Technical efficiency refers to developing high levels of kinetic energy in the run-up area and delivering a significant portion of that energy or momentum into the implement during the delivery and release phase of the throw. While

Muscular power and technical efficiency determine how much momentum is created, how much is transferred to the implement, and therefore how far the implement flies.

I suggested earlier that with proper effort and time athletes will develop very high strength and power levels, the results of working hard and consistently for a few years to develop "great technique" are by no means as predictable. Working to develop efficient technique will certainly lead to improvement. In fact, it is *the* most important area for gains in performance. Whether this improvement will result in *elite*-level performance is less certain, however. Careful attention to the concepts discussed in this text will help you develop the elusive "effective technique."

Transferring Energy From the Body to the Implement

In each of the throws the crucial moments are just before the implement leaves the hands or fingers and the actual launch. The challenge to the thrower is to move at very high velocity (possessed of great KE or M) in the run-up area and move and control the body and the implement in such a way as to enable as large a portion of the developed energy as possible to be transferred into the center of mass of the implement while launching the implement at the proper angle (all four implements) and attitude (discus and javelin) into the atmosphere. This efficient transfer of energy or force to the implement takes place not only at delivery but also throughout the entire run-up. This means that the implement must be positioned carefully at different stages of the run-up to enable a successful transfer of force in the moments just before and at release.

The concept of the thrower becoming one with the implement is an absolute requirement for high-level performance. Becoming one with the implement suggests two important concepts:

1. Positioning the implement throughout the run-up, delivery, and release phases so as to allow the most efficient application of force
2. Smoothly accelerating the implement over a maximal range so as not to jerk the implement

Ultimately, all accomplished throwers must become successful at what is arguably the most difficult, complex, and demanding achievement in all sport: a true *maximal summation of forces*. It is relatively simple to rather beautifully coordinate a submaximal or easy throw. However, when a person tries to move at the absolute highest velocity with each body part sequentially contributing maximal force until the arms, hands, and fingers add their last maximal force, the potential for error increases dramatically. Throwers will experience thousands of "missed throws" in the process of becoming successful at maximal summation throwing.

Most coaches of beginning throwers pay considerable attention to mechanical positions. Initially, these positions must be taught statically and with slow movements. This approach is certainly defensible. Young athletes need to learn the feelings associated with correct positions. Rather quickly, however, these athletes should learn to push themselves to move as fast as possible while still delivering the implement properly. *One of the most important principles of throwing is to move as fast as possible without causing a breakdown in throwing efficiency.*

Maximal and Submaximal Summation of Force

A rather classic question frequently asked by those in the throwing events is, Can an athlete learn to do maximal summation of force throwing by doing submaximal throws? In my experience, the answer is no. It is impossible to learn maximal summation movement at submaximal levels of effort. That is not to say that submaximal throws do not have a place in the initial stages of learning and even in the training programs of elite athletes. Maximal summation of force throws place great demands on the body's nervous and muscular systems. How many maximal force throws are possible during a workout? Certainly not many, if they are truly maximal force throws. Therefore, most elite athletes engage in throwing workouts that include a number of throws that are characterized by careful attention to correct positions and rhythm without maximal summation of force. This is more true of javelin throwers, who use light implements with very fast, even violent, movements, than the other throwing events. In fact, many elite javelin athletes have a low percentage of maximal throwing in their training. The basis of world-record holder Jan Zelezny's training, for example, is a very high volume of submaximal throwing. In general, however, I think practice sessions should include a reasonable number of maximal attempts. The most significant truth in all throwing is that the athlete who delivers the implement with the greatest release velocity, other things being equal, wins. Athletes might win while moving at velocities below maximal; this would depend on the competition. Additionally, if an athlete cannot perform successfully while attempting to move at maximum velocities, he or she should throw at submaximal speeds. Ultimately, however, successful throwers must master maximal summation throwing.

The movements of an accomplished thrower are pleasing to our natural sense of symmetry and rhythm. Great throwers are very strong and powerful athletes who have learned the ever elusive techniques of creating great KE or M during the run-up phase and transferring a very significant portion of the KE or M (force) into the implement during the delivery and release phase. Thus they become one with the implement, accelerating their bodies and the implement while transferring developed energy to the implement in a maximal summation of force that is at once graceful, precise, and breathtakingly explosive—and results in a long throw.

chapter 2

Strength and Power Development for the Throws

Jay Silvester

© The Sporting Image

Perhaps most important when conditioning young throwers are programs that concentrate on developing good health and overall fitness. Teaching injury prevention during training and developing physical qualities that reduce the possibility of injury while competing are also crucial aspects of conditioning programs. While there are no conditioning routines titled "programs for injury prevention," good conditioning programs produce athletes that are highly resistant to injury.

Once a basic fitness foundation is in place, workouts should focus on the development of higher-level physical qualities that result in superior athletic performance. Throwers who typify these higher-level physical qualities are strong, powerful, quick, explosive, fast, and flexible. Size (mass) can help, but at junior high and high school ages it is often not very important.

In general, the desirable fitness characteristics for throwing are no different from those desired for football, basketball, or many other sports, with the exception of long-distance events such as running and swimming.

It is no secret that the basis of all conditioning programs for throwers today is strength and power training. Before the 1950s, weightlifting was thought to cause a person to become "muscle bound." Track and field throwers were the first athletes in the United States to challenge this concept by using weightlifting as an aid to performance. The proof of its effectiveness was in how far those athletes were able to throw. In general, they were able to throw much farther than those who did not lift weights. Today, athletes in most sports use strength training as specific conditioning for their muscular systems.

The athletes involved in sport today are brought up with strength training. To them it is simply part of their workout experience. Some of us who trained for years without strength conditioning and then started strength training were pleasantly surprised at the very helpful effects.

Principles of Strength Training

The principles that guide strength training, and indeed all conditioning, are as follows:

- Progressive loading (overload)
- Specificity
- Recovery
- Variability
- Individuality

Progressive Loading

Progressive loading refers to progressively increasing the resistance, thereby requiring the body to adapt by increasing muscular strength and power. There are many progressive loading systems, and some are presented later in this chapter. In any progressive loading program it is important that resistance not be added too quickly, especially when working with young athletes. Adding resistance carefully is appropriate for anyone, but it is particularly relevant for the novice. Too much resistance or too many repetitions can result in injury and chronic joint problems.

Specificity

We will focus on two forms of specificity. The first is physiological specificity, which relates to the general strength and power of the muscular system. The second is technique or event-specific training, which involves loading the systems in ways similar to, if not the same as, how they are loaded in a particular event. This type of loading is believed to produce better results than general loading.

Physiologically Specific Strength Training

All athletes need to be physically strong and powerful to perform at peak levels. The process of increasing the strength and power of the major moving muscles of the body (calves; leg flexors and extensors; adductors and abductors; hip flexors and extensors; abdominals; back muscles; chest muscles; shoulder, arm, hand, and perhaps neck muscles) is what we refer to as physiologically specific strength training. We use the term *physiologically specific* to suggest a general physiological effect (strengthening) without regard to any particular sport. Increasing the strength and power of the major moving muscles of the body is very important to throwers. No conditioning activity is more effective in producing positive results in athletic performance than a general strength conditioning program.

Event-Specific Strength Training

Classic examples of event-specific strength training include throwing over- and underweight implements and wearing weighted vests or leg or arm strap-on weights during throwing workouts. Another example is any resisted exercise that is designed to emulate a technical throwing movement.

Adding weight to the torso, arms, or legs of an athlete while he or she is engaged in throwing practice has not proven helpful. The added weight appears to interfere with the precise movements required to achieve the proper rhythm, timing, or sequencing at high velocities. The demand for neuromuscular precision appears to outweigh any benefit of weighting the body in practice.

Throwing heavy or light implements in training is commonly accepted as beneficial. The degree of benefit is the question. Normally, heavy implements are thrown during the off season (fall) to increase specific strength and power. The lighter implements are normally used during the immediate preseason and in season to increase the speed at which the athlete can effectively control the technical movement. I advocate occasionally throwing light implements in training during the season. Throwing light implements for fun and diversity is a stimulating neurological challenge. It should also be fun for the athlete. I have thrown heavier implements, but I have not enjoyed doing so. Various athletes with whom I have associated have thrown heavy implements, some without problems, and one shot-putter with very serious problems. This person threw 69 feet (21 meters) as a college junior, trained with the 18-pound (8 kilogram) shot for the fall and winter, and threw 64 feet (20 meters) the next year as a senior. The athletes with whom I have worked in shot put and discus throw have not enjoyed much observable success from training with overweight implements.

There is limited scientific evidence that training with different weight implements produces longer throws than not doing so. The primary benefit of throwing different weight implements may be that it breaks the monotony of repeatedly throwing the same implement and adds to the enjoyment of the athlete. See the event chapters for event-specific, variable-weight throwing activities.

Efforts at event-specific strength training should be approached very cautiously with careful attention to the results. Specific resistance training is useful as long as the fine motor coordination required for excellent performance is not disrupted. To ensure good results, coaches and athletes may want to develop strength and power using conditioning activities that are specific to the *physiological* characteristics that can be identified and improved without engaging in event-specific exercises that might disturb the fine motor skills necessary for technical success in throwing.

Recovery

The physiological adaptations resulting in increased strength and power take place during the recovery periods between exercises, sets, and workouts. Understanding the value of good rest and attaining it are important to any conditioning program. Conditioning programs that do not allow for adequate rest will result in decreases in strength and power, not increases.

Recovery periods allow for energy resupply to the energy-drained musculature and adaptations such as myofibril (muscle) repair or regeneration. The specific recovery time needed depends on various factors—the condition of the athlete, the resistance used (intensity) in the exercise (50 percent, 60 percent, 70 percent, and so on), the number of repetitions, and the exercise. For example, more recovery is needed after a squat routine than after arm curls since much more musculature has been worked. Recovery times between sets when strength training vary from 30 seconds to 5 minutes. Recovery time for core exercises (which are described later in the chapter) is normally from 3 to 5 minutes. Recovery between lifting sessions for the same muscle groups is normally a minimum of 48 hours.

Variability

Research has shown that frequent manipulation of the volume (number of sets and repetitions), load (intensity), and frequency of exercises in a strength training program produces excellent gains in strength and power. This variability in the training routine may be a psychological advantage in reducing strength conditioning monotony. See the periodization section on page 29 for a more detailed discussion of these concepts.

Individuality

Athletes often have dramatically varied maturity levels. The exercises, sets, and repetitions may be the same for the majority of the athletes, but the resistance and intensity levels will be quite dissimilar. All athletes have unique personalities. The conditioning programs of seasoned athletes will differ based on their personalities and their range of experience.

Speed in Strength Training

For at least the past 30 years there has been a question about the speed at which a person should lift weights for the best "power" result. Success in most sports usually goes to the athletes who are the quickest. Raw quickness is simply human power, the ability to move a body or a body part very fast. Quickness in a sport is a combination of human power and skill in the specific sport movements.

How does a thrower maximize power? Research in this area is not entirely conclusive. Strength training of untrained people will always result in improvements in strength. Improvements in strength almost always result in improvements in power. The question is, do those improvements result in maximizing power? Many coaches and athletes say no. Some suggest that strength training must be done at fast rates of speed to maximize power. Try lifting a serious maximum at a high rate of speed. It cannot be done. Research on maximum human power production while lifting weight shows that people who lift weights that allow only 25 percent of their maximum speed generate the greatest power. Does that mean we should find the appropriate 25 percent maximum speed weight for each lift and lift only that? I would not recommend that.

Throwers are always challenging the power of their bodies. This takes place on most throws (if they are done properly) and in most games, and certainly in plyometric exercises. In addition, all of the "quick" lifts require great power output. (The quick lifts include the snatch, clean, and the jerk—either in front or behind the neck.) Therefore, I recommend that throwers include at least one of the quick lifts in each weight training workout, do appropriate plyometric exercises, enjoy good games, and throw hard. Those activities will more than adequately develop the power mechanisms of the body.

Sample Strength Conditioning Programs

Research shows that many different strength conditioning programs produce positive results. Differences are in the following characteristics:

- Exercises
- Resistance level
- Workouts per day and days per week
- Number of sets
- Repetitions for each exercise

The repetitions for best strength gain range from one to eight. Sets may also vary from one to eight. Days per week to strength train range from one to five or six. Olympic weightlifters training at the Colorado Springs Olympic Training Center work out three times per day, six days per week! The strength conditioning programs listed in the following sections are sound routines based on extensive experience and available research. The time constraints of a student athlete will require some adaptation of the workout routines.

We might use many different names to refer to a weight training program: weight training, strength training, resistance exercise, strength conditioning, and so on. For our purposes in this chapter we will refer to these programs as strength conditioning. There are so many variations in workout routines, particularly in the number of sets, repetitions, and the resistance level, that the possibilities become almost infinite. Our purpose here is to present a sample of programs that will, when adhered to, produce improvements in the physical characteristics needed for throwing. Although the exercises mentioned in the following sections are quite inclusive and even exhaustive, you may know or hear of others.

General Fitness Conditioning

Novice athletes will benefit from this general fitness exercise program. Only minimal equipment is needed—jump ropes, dumbbells for walking torso twists, a bar for pull-ups, boxes or benches for step-ups, and medicine balls. This conditioning routine for novice throwers is designed to handle relatively large numbers of athletes easily.

Push-up: 2 to 5 sets of 10 to 30

Burpee: 2 to 3 sets of 10 to 20

Pull-up: 2 to 3 sets of 5 to 15 (Assist beginners as needed.)

Front lunge*: 3 to 4 sets of 10 to 20 (Alternate legs at appropriate fatigue level.)

Crunch: 2 to 3 sets of 20 to 30 initially. Then work up to 2 sets of 50 reps. Raise the torso no more than 30 degrees.

Step-up*: 12- to 18-in. (30- to 46-cm) height. 1 to 3 sets of 10 to 16 steps (5 to 8 reps on each leg). Start with body weight. Add 25 lb (9 kg) at third workout, then 50 lb (19 kg) at sixth workout, then 10 lb (4 kg) per week up to 100 lb (37 kg). Do only 5 reps/leg after 60 lb (22 kg).

Walking torso twist: 1 to 2 sets of 20 to 30

Two-legged jump: 3 to 6 sets of up to 4 jumps

Medicine ball work: All exercises 2 to 5 sets of 10. Choose 2 to 3 exercises per workout:

- Overhead toss
- Side throw (10 on each side)
- Triceps toss
- Basketball chest pass (two hands)
- Straight-arm overhead forward toss (kneeling to partner)

Once they have established a good fitness base, novice throwers should incorporate a beginning strength conditioning workout into their practices. The following is a good three-days-per-week program.

Day 1

Jog: 3 to 5 min to loosen up

Push-ups

Crunches

Lunges

Medicine ball work

Jump rope: 10 min

Stretch: 10 min

Day 2

Jog: 3 to 5 min to loosen up

Pull-ups

---

* Do not do both of these lifts on the same day—alternate days.

Burpees
Crunches
Standing-start single-leg and alternating-leg triple jumps (3 sets)
Medicine ball work
Jump rope: 10 min
Stretch: 10 min

Day 3

Jog: 3 to 5 min to loosen up
Burpees
Medicine ball work
Lunges
Pull-ups
Standing long jump, best into a pit (3 to 5 attempts)
Jump rope: 5 min
Stretch: 10 min

Circuit Training

Once a novice athlete has conditioned for a few weeks, it is appropriate to move to a somewhat more challenging strength conditioning program. Circuit training normally includes many exercises with moderate resistance levels (40 to 60 percent of maximum, 8 to 15 repetitions) and no more than three circuits. Ideally the circuits would be completed three days per week (MWF), but two days is acceptable. The best circuit training setup is to have only one person per station. Using this system, athletes are required to do one set per station and rotate through the stations three times. Rest times between exercises should be from 30 to 90 seconds. If there are many athletes, two or three people can be assigned per station. The circuit training program described in this section requires a fully equipped weight room with appropriate machines and free weights.

Lat pull-down
Pull-up
Bench press
Leg press
Step-up
Seated overhead press
Standing dumbbell press
Hamstring curl
Side lunge
Forward lunge
Twisting Roman chair abdominal work
Back extensions on Roman chair
Biceps curl
Triceps extension
Medicine ball bounce high on wall
Plyometric jump

Core Lifts

This section contains a list of core exercises, those that are most important. You must include a combination of these lifts in your athletic strength conditioning. Notice that all of these lifts are free-weight, large-muscle-mass, multijoint exercises. When you perform, your entire body works in space performing any number of complex movements. Lifting free weights has greater functional application to the athletic movement of throwing than pushing or pulling on a resistance that is directionally controlled by a track on a machine. In most cases effective athletic participation requires repeated explosive power output combined with precise neuromuscular control while moving in space. All of the core exercises require precise control of the weight in space, many require great power (explosiveness), and all are helpful in developing the physical qualities necessary for long throws.

In this section I provide a detailed description of only certain exercises. It is my assumption that most readers will be quite familiar with strength training exercises and therefore do not need further descriptions of such exercises. The ones described and illustrated are chosen for their importance to conditioning for throwers and perhaps, in some cases, their lack of notoriety.

Squats and Lunges

We might refer to squats and lunges as the "core" of the "core exercises"—leg, hip, and back strength are crucial to successful throwing. Be diligent with these exercises.

BACK SQUAT

Place a straight bar behind your neck, just above your shoulder blades. Stand with your feet shoulder-width apart; the inside of your heel should be lined up with the outside of your shoulder. Make sure to keep your weight over your ankles. Bend your knees and lower your body until your hamstrings are parallel to the floor (figure 2.1). Once you've reached this position, straighten your legs back to the original starting position. Make sure to keep your back flat throughout the exercise.

There are also acceptable variations to this standard description. For example, the legs are often wider than shoulder width, the bar is often lower than on top of the shoulder blades, and the depth of the squat might be higher (knee joint to 90 degrees) or lower (top of thigh parallel to floor). Do not move back to a standing position too slowly. Moving reasonably quickly back to an erect position is proper.

Figure 2.1 Back squat.

FRONT SQUAT

The feet are normally shoulder-width apart. The normal depth of the front squat is top of the thighs parallel to the floor. You must learn to protract your shoulders to hold the bar on your deltoids (see figure 2.2). Keeping your hands on the bar requires great arm and wrist flexibility. Folding your arms in front of your shoulders and holding the bar on your shoulders is often easier than holding the bar with your elbows forward and your hands around the bar.

Figure 2.2 Front squat.

JUMP SQUAT

Place the bar on your shoulders just as you would in the back squat. The depth of the squat before the "jump" may vary from one or two inches to thighs parallel with the floor. Most athletes will bend no more than 90 degrees at the knee; many will not go that deep. I recommend no more than a 40-degree knee bend when beginning jump squats. Be careful with this great lift. Do not go too heavy too fast.

STEP-UP

Do 5 to 10 reps with each leg—10 reps with a light weight and 5 with a heavy weight. The height of the benches should be 12 to 18 inches (30 to 46 cm). Make certain the box or bench you step up to is very steady. Be very careful with balance and the amount of weight on the bar. Put one foot up on the box and step up on the box, putting your weight on your "up" leg, then leave your up leg in place and step down and then back up again without dropping your up leg. Do 2 to 4 reps this way, then switch legs. When the weight gets reasonably heavy, it is best to alternate legs on every step.

FRONT LUNGE

This is a great leg-building exercise, but it can be dangerous. Be very careful with the loading and the depth of the drop. Do not stretch too far (drop too low) when doing the exercise.

SIDE LUNGE

Stand erect, lift your right foot, and move it one foot to your right. When your foot comes in contact with the floor, bend your knee to a 90-degree angle, push up, then return to an erect position. Do the same with your left leg. As you become more familiar with this lift, you may move your legs laterally away from your body more than one foot.

Pulls

In all cases of lifting with free weights the resistance is provided by the pull of gravity on the weight you are lifting. In the case of pulls always stand with your arms hanging down from your shoulders, your hands grasping the bar. An Olympic bar loaded with either 15-, 20-, or 25-kilogram (33-, 44-, or 55-pound) weights resting on the floor is 9 inches (23 centimeters) above the floor. To grasp such a bar requires some bending at the hips and knees. One important technical concept associated with this bending is to keep your spine relatively straight or, as is commonly taught, "flat." Keep your head up so your neck is basically in line with the rest of your spine. Initiate the "lift" with a hip and knee extension that begins the upward movement of the bar, after which your back, shoulders, and arms accelerate the bar upward. The bar might come to waist height in a clean pull with heavy weight, to shoulder height in the high snatch or clean pull, or to arm's length overhead in the snatch. If you are going to "catch" the bar, as is the case with the clean or the snatch, you must drop your body very rapidly once you have completed the pull. This dropping under the bar reduces the height necessary to pull the bar, thus facilitating an easier "catch."

All pulls with the exception of the dead lift are commonly referred to as "quick" lifts. That terminology correctly suggests that the proper execution of the lift requires an explosive effort. The behind-the-neck jerk (push press) and the jerk phase of the clean and jerk are also "quick" lifts.

POWER CLEAN

The power clean is an explosive, athletic lift. Proper technique is important. Be aware that racking the bar when doing this lift can sometimes cause problems with wrists and shoulders. "Racking the bar" refers to rotating your hands and shoulders at the completion of the pull so the bar rests on your upturned hands and deltoid muscles.

The proper starting position is with your hands on the bar a little wider than shoulder width; your feet are hip-width apart or a bit less. The bar should be directly over the metatarsal joint of your big toes. Your feet may be turned out slightly. Assume a squat position; your back should be flat and your hips at knee height or lower. Your trunk should be relatively upright and your arms straight. (See figure 2.3a.)

The pull is initiated by a powerful upward drive of your legs and hips. Keep your back very close to the same angle as in the start position until the bar passes your knees. The second phase of the pull begins as the bar passes your knees. When the bar is at knee height, your shins should be vertical. Thrust your hips forward and upward as you violently extend your back. The bar brushes your thighs, then moves slightly forward and passes your hips as you rise on the balls of your feet. Extend your body fully (figure 2.3b), shrug your shoulders, and bend your elbows upward. From this fully extended position with the bar at navel to chest height, drop very quickly into a

Figure 2.3 Power clean.

quasisquat position (figure 2.3c). Rotate your elbows from a position above the bar to a position in front of and below the bar. "Rack" the bar on your hands, deltoids, and clavicles (figure 2.3d).

HANG CLEAN

In hang cleans and hang snatches you grasp the bar and lift it off the floor until you come to an erect standing position with the bar hanging somewhere in front of your thighs. Initiate the lift with a slight flexing of your knees and hips followed by an explosive knee and hip extension and a significant back and shoulder pull upward. As the bar is topping out, drop under the bar, "catching" it in a classic clean position (elbows high, bar resting on deltoids). Use this lift for variety and working on explosive force.

CLEAN PULL—LOW AND HIGH

Cleans have hurt a few athletes' shoulders and wrists. Athletes often do both clean and snatch pulls without catching or racking the bar to reduce the chance of injury and allow them to use heavier weight. When doing clean pulls the bar is not "caught" or racked.

POWER SNATCH

The power snatch is the consummate total body lift. This is a very demanding "long pull" that taxes most of the major moving muscles of the body.

A good way to determine the initial grip width is to extend your arms laterally from your shoulders, then bring your forearms to a vertical position so your elbows form a right angle. Measure the distance between your forefingers and use this measurement for your initial grip width. Experiment with wider and narrower grips to determine which feels best.

In the proper starting position, your feet should be 6 to 12 inches (15 to 30 centimeters) apart, toes turned slightly out. The bar is directly over the joint where your big toe is joined to your foot (metatarsal-phalangeal joint). Squat over the bar, back flat, shins near the bar, with your hips quite low (very close to the same elevation as your knees). See figure 2.4a.

The pull can be initiated from a stationary position or with a bobbing up and down of the hips. The first phase is initiated by the strong contraction of the muscles of your legs and hips driving your hips upward. When the bar reaches knee height, the angle between the lifting platform and the back should be essentially the same as it was when you began the pull. The second phase of the pull begins as the bar passes your knees. Drive your hips forward and upward and pull your shoulders up and slightly back (figure 2.4b). Lift your chest and head and rise up on the balls of your feet, ultimately clearing the platform. In this extended position shrug your shoulders, giving the bar its final acceleration; split your feet laterally to the side, and drop your body into a wide-stance semisquat. Twist or roll your wrists under the bar and lock your elbows, catching the bar overhead (figure 2.4c). When the bar is under control, assume an upright, normal stance posture (figure 2.4d).

Figure 2.4 Power snatch.

HANG SNATCH

Start the hang snatch by standing erect with the bar at arm's length. Grip the bar in a very wide grip somewhere near the collars. Initiate the lift with a slight bending of the hips followed by an explosive pull that pulls the bar high as you drop into a semisquat, catching the bar at arm's length overhead.

SNATCH PULL—LOW AND HIGH

When doing low snatch pulls, the objective is normally to use a large amount of weight to become familiar with heavy poundage. The bar seldom moves higher than the navel. When working on high snatch pulls, the objective is to work with slightly heavier weight than you can snatch and to avoid possible injury to your shoulders and wrists. The bar is normally pulled up to high chest or even shoulder height. Snatch pulls remove the possibility of injury to the shoulders and wrists that sometimes results from catching the bar in the overhead snatch position.

Presses and Jerks

A "press" normally refers to the extension of the arm(s). You may start from an extended arm position, flex your arms, and then extend them again (bench press), or you may start from a flexed arm position and then extend your arms (overhead press). Some leg press movements are done using machines in which the resistance usually runs on a track. There are only two "jerk" movements in weightlifting—one is from the front of the shoulders as in the completion of the clean and jerk, and the other is from behind the neck with the bar resting on the shoulders. This lift is variously called a push press or a behind-the-neck jerk.

PUSH PRESS (BEHIND-THE-NECK JERK)

Stand erect with the weight on your shoulders, hands positioned carefully on the bar. With a very rapid, slight bending of the knees and hips, drop a few inches and then extend your hips and knees and plantar flex your feet, driving your body upward. As the bar starts lifting off your shoulders, continue the acceleration with your arms as your body again drops under the bar. Extend your arms, catching the bar at arm's length overhead.

BENCH PRESS

The bench press is a great exercise for building shoulder and chest strength.

DUMBBELL BENCH PRESS

The dumbbell bench press is possibly better than using a bar for shoulder and chest strength, as it uses more of the stabilizing muscles.

INCLINE PRESS

Some throwers suggest not doing bench presses, only inclines. I suggest that throwers do both.

DUMBBELL INCLINE PRESS

The dumbbell incline press is a great exercise for the shoulders.

OVERHEAD PRESS

The overhead press is no longer an Olympic lift, but it is a great conditioner for a thrower.

LEG TO TOE PRESS

The leg to toe press might be included in a workout routine either as a core lift or as an assistance exercise when other free bar exercises are the "core" for the legs. It is the only exercise in this section that is done on a machine. The machine that I prefer for this lift has a 45-degree angle track. You lie on a padded backrest with your feet above your head on the foot plate. Start the lift by positioning your feet carefully on the foot plate, then extend your legs, taking the weight off the "catches" holding it. Flip the levers that control the weight "catches" so the weight can slide down the track, allowing your knees and hips to be pushed into a flexed position. When you feel adequate hip and knee flexion, extend your legs and hips, pushing the weight back up the 45-degree tracks. At the end of your leg extension, plantar flex your foot into a toe press, assuring that your calves are exercised along with most of the other leg musculature.

As mentioned earlier, there are almost unlimited possible combinations of sets, reps, and weight that might be used in devising specific lifting programs. The strength-building program outlined in table 2.1 is based on the concept that it is more interesting and psychologically palatable to increase the resistance in each set than to complete three or four sets with the same weight. Notice that for each exercise (lift) at least one set is a warm-up or preparatory lift. This light weight set alerts and prepares the body for the demands of the next set.

The sample strength-building workouts in table 2.1 feature twelve core exercises, three for each of the three lifting days of the week. The focus of this and all weight training programs for throwers is to build a healthy, very strong, and powerful body for throwing. Note that Fridays are generally relatively light days. Note also that the resistance levels are written as a percentage. This percentage refers to a percent of maximum weight lifted in that exercise. Young athletes will take some time to determine their maximums. More experienced athletes will have no problem determining the proper percentages (weights) to use. In fact, the best lifting programs evolve when athletes have lifted enough to know what they should be lifting. At that point the workout and resistance levels are based on how the athlete feels, not so much on what is written on the program. Good athletes who are young and to some extent inexperienced in strength conditioning often need to be held in check. They are highly motivated and want to improve rapidly. Injury from lifting too much can set an athlete back many months. Other athletes may consistently wish to lift less than the program suggests. Therefore, the coach needs to know his or her athletes to produce a safe and effective conditioning program. Recovery times between sets will vary from 2 to 4 minutes.

Assistance Exercises

The following assistance exercises will aid in assuring that all of the muscular system is being challenged. The major purpose of assistance exercises is to preclude any weak links in the strengthening of the body. Do two sets of 6 to 8 RMs (repetition maximum).

How much time do you have to train? That is always a question. If you have only limited time, do the core exercises. If you have additional time, complete the assistance exercises three days per week. If you have only time to do assistance exercises one day per week, do them once. Assistance exercises are best done three times per week, but twice per week is adequate, and once per week is better than not doing them at all.

Lat pull-down
Supine lateral raise (fly)
Upright row
Supine triceps press
Toe press
Seated dumbbell press
Reverse fly
Supine bent-arm pull-over
Leg press
Hamstring curl

Table 2.1 Strength-Building Program

Wherever the lifts clean or snatch are indicated, use either hang cleans or hang snatches. Further, if you prefer clean or snatch pulls (high or low), you may substitute them for cleans and snatches.

	WEEK 1 **MONDAY**	
Bench press	**Clean**	**Back squat**
1 × 8 @ 50%	1 × 5 @ 50%	1 × 8 @ 50%
1 × 6 @ 70%	1 × 3 @ 70%	1 × 6 @ 70%
1 × 5 @ 80%	2 × 3 @ 75%	1 × 5 @ 80%
1 × 4 @ 85%	1 × 3 @ 80%	1 × 5 @ 85%
1 × 3 @ 90%		1 × 3 @ 90%
	WEDNESDAY	
Incline press	**Snatch**	**Leg to toe press**
1 × 8 @ 50%	1 × 5 @ 50%	1 × 8 @ 50%
1 × 6 @ 70%	1 × 3 @ 70%	1 × 6 @ 70%
1 × 5 @ 80%	2 × 3 @ 75%	1 × 5 @ 80%
1 × 4 @ 85%	1 × 3 @ 80%	1 × 4 @ 90%
1 × 3 @ 90%		
	FRIDAY	
Dumbbell bench press	**Behind-the-neck jerk**	**Front squat**
1 × 8 @ 50%	1 × 5 @ 50%	1 × 8 @ 50%
1 × 6 @ 70%	1 × 3 @ 70%	1 × 6 @ 70%
1 × 5 @ 80%	2 × 3 @ 75%	1 × 5 @ 80%
	WEEK 2 **MONDAY**	
Dumbbell bench press	**Behind-the-neck jerk**	**Front squat**
1 × 8 @ 50%	1 × 5 @ 50%	1 × 8 @ 50%
1 × 6 @ 70%	1 × 3 @ 70%	1 × 6 @ 70%
1 × 5 @ 80%	2 × 3 @ 75%	1 × 5 @ 80%
1 × 4 @ 85%	1 × 3 @ 80%	1 × 5 @ 85%
1 × 3 @ 90%	1 × 2 @ 85%	1 × 3 @ 90%

(continued)

Table 2.1 *(continued)*

	WEDNESDAY	
Bench press	**Clean**	**Step up 12-in. box**
1 × 8 @ 50%	1 × 5 @ 50%	1 × 8 @ 50%
1 × 6 @ 70%	1 × 3 @ 70%	1 × 6 @ 70%
1 × 5 @ 80%	2 × 3 @ 75%	1 × 5 @ 80%
1 × 4 @ 85%	1 × 3 @ 80%	1 × 5 @ 85%
1 × 3 @ 90%	1 × 2 @ 85%	
	FRIDAY	
Incline press	**Snatch**	**Side lunge**
1 × 8 @ 50%	1 × 5 @ 50%	1 × 8 @ 50%
1 × 6 @ 70%	1 × 3 @ 70%	1 × 6 @ 70%
1 × 5 @ 80%	2 × 3 @ 75%	1 × 5 @ 80%
1 × 5 @ 85%		1 × 5 @ 85%
	WEEK 3 **MONDAY**	
Incline press	**Snatch**	**Front lunge**
1 × 8 @ 50%	1 × 5 @ 50%	1 × 8 @ 50%
1 × 6 @ 70%	1 × 3 @ 70%	1 × 6 @ 70%
1 × 5 @ 80%	2 × 3 @ 75%	1 × 5 @ 80%
1 × 4 @ 85%	1 × 3 @ 80%	1 × 5 @ 85%
1 × 3 @ 90%	1 × 2 @ 85%	1 × 3 @ 90%
	WEDNESDAY	
Dumbbell bench press	**Behind-the-neck jerk**	**Leg to toe press**
1 × 8 @ 50%	1 × 5 @ 50%	1 × 8 @ 50%
1 × 6 @ 70%	1 × 3 @ 70%	1 × 6 @ 70%
1 × 5 @ 80%	2 × 3 @ 75%	1 × 5 @ 80%
	FRIDAY	
Bench press	**Clean**	**Back squat**
1 × 8 @ 50%	1 × 5 @ 50%	1 × 8 @ 50%
1 × 6 @ 70%	1 × 3 @ 70%	1 × 6 @ 70%
1 × 5 @ 80%	2 × 3 @ 75%	1 × 5 @ 80%
1 × 4 @ 85%	1 × 3 @ 80%	1 × 5 @ 85%
1 × 3 @ 90%		1 × 3 @ 90%

Torso Exercises

It is of course very important for throwers to develop a strong torso. The connection between the hips and the upper body of a thrower must be at once very strong and very flexible. Surely many if not all of the core exercises and assistance exercises will produce some strengthening of the torso. The torso exercises described here will improve torso conditioning beyond that developed with core exercises. When doing torso or abdominal work, you should often use "heavy resistance." The torso muscles must be strengthened, and strengthening results from using a resistance that only allows three to eight repetitions. Performing 20 to 100 abdominal crunches or other exercises will result primarily in muscular endurance, but not very much added strength. The following are good exercises for strengthening the torso. You might choose two of these exercises for each of your workouts.

WALKING WITH WEIGHT PLATE

For this exercise you need an area where you can walk forward. Stand erect holding a weight in front of you in both hands. As you step forward with your right foot, swing (gently at first) the weight to your right side, blocking the right hip forward so your abdomen and lower back muscles are stretched and strengthened. Of course when you step forward with your left foot, the weight is swung to the left side, as shown in figure 2.5.

Figure 2.5 Walking with weight plate.

ROMAN CHAIR SIT-UP

Sit on the chair with your legs or feet held by padded supports. With a weight in your hands, lean back, allowing your head to drop well below your hips (figure 2.6a). Lift up when you have dropped sufficiently low (figure 2.6b). Be careful; do not start with too much weight. Increase resistance gradually.

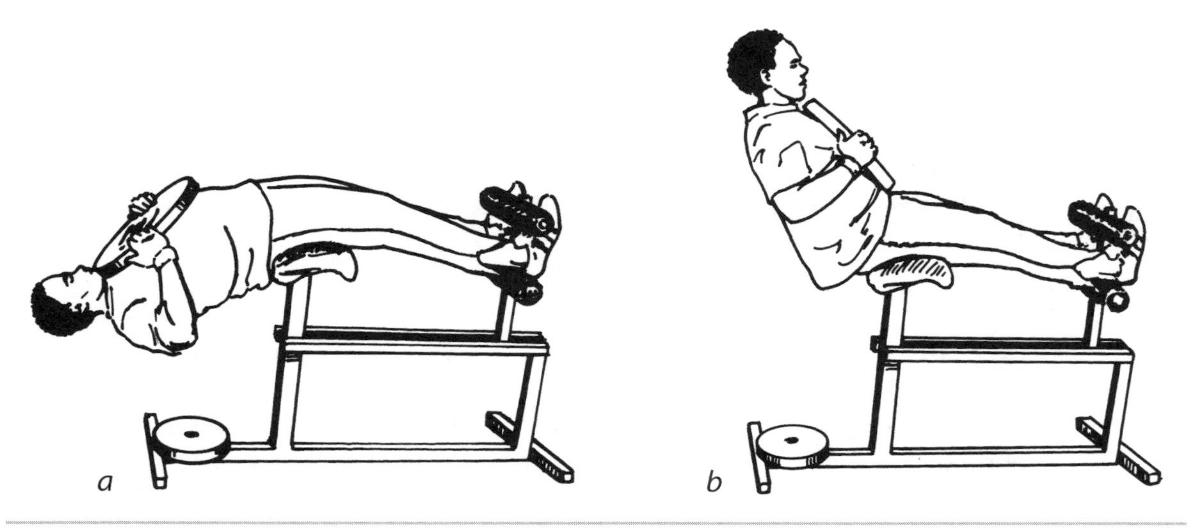

Figure 2.6 Roman chair sit-up.

ROMAN CHAIR BACK UPRISE

Face the chair, lay the front of your hips over the padded part of the chair, and hook your feet in the foot harness. Hold a light weight behind your head, then drop your torso down (figure 2.7a) and return to the parallel position (figure 2.7b).

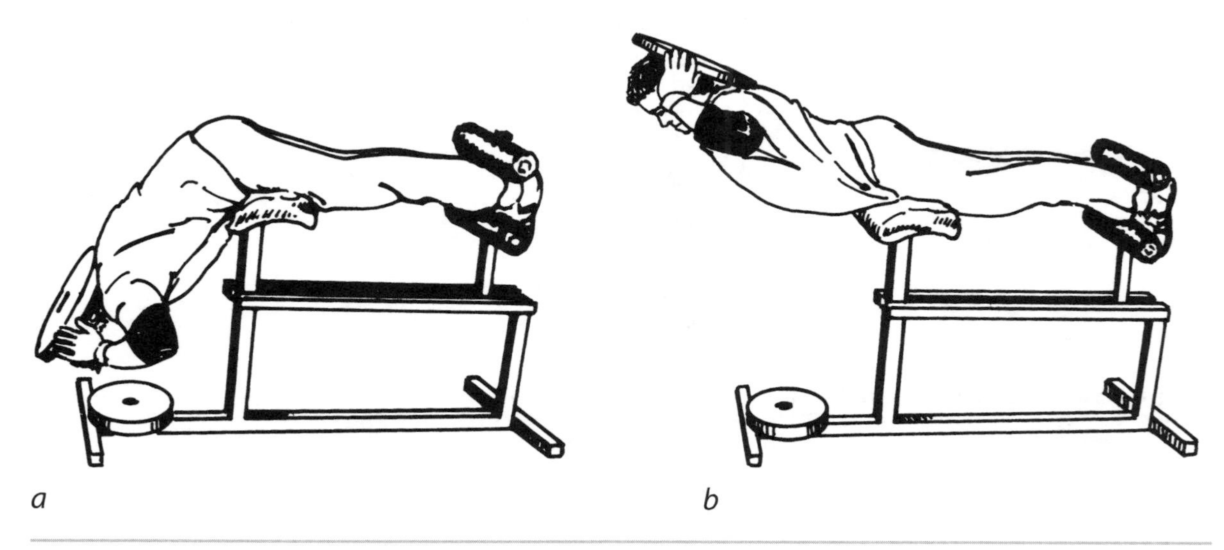

Figure 2.7 Roman chair back uprise.

ROMAN CHAIR SIDE UPRISE

Sit on the chair on one side of your hips and hook your feet in the foot harness so you can drop sideways down toward the floor (figure 2.8a). When stretched adequately, return to a parallel or slightly above parallel position (figure 2.8b).

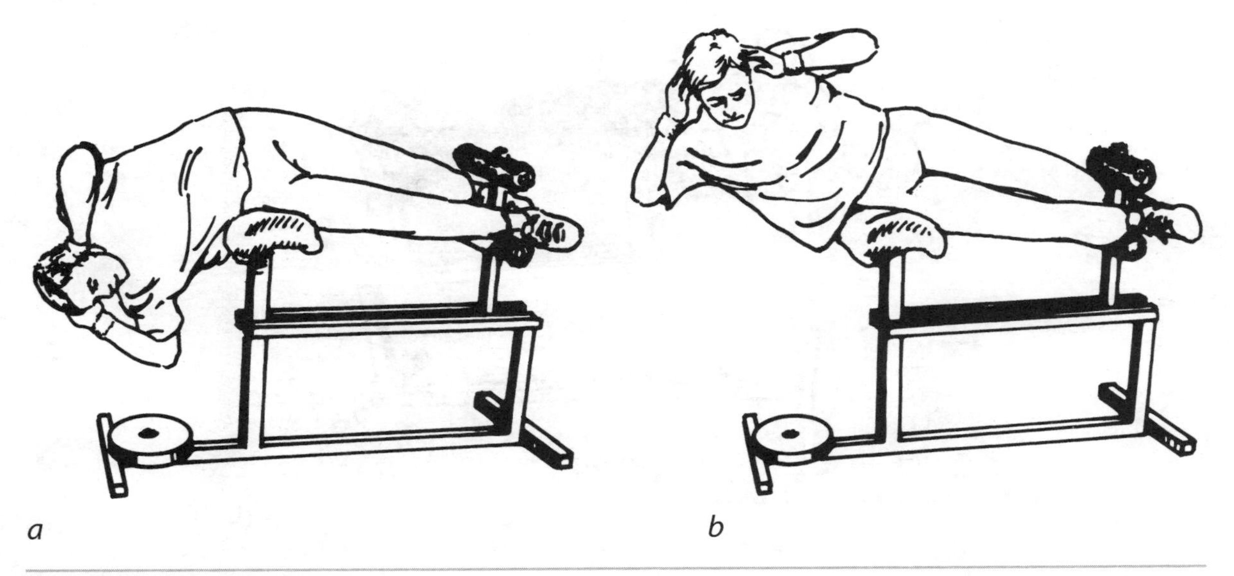

Figure 2.8 Roman chair side uprise.

ROMAN CHAIR RUSSIAN TWIST

Sit on the chair in a supine manner. Holding a weight at arm's length (figure 2.9a), rotate as far right as possible (figure 2.9b) (weight should be hanging down), then rotate as far left as possible.

Figure 2.9 Roman chair Russian twist.

ROMAN CHAIR ABDOMINAL TWIST

Sit on the chair with your feet hooked in the harness. Hold a weight against your chest and twist from side to side until fatigued (figure 2.10), then rest by sitting up. Be careful; add resistance gradually.

Figure 2.10 Roman chair abdominal twist.

INCLINE BOARD ABDOMINAL TWIST

This exercise can be done two ways:

1. Hook your feet under the foot strap, hold a weight in your hands, sit up so your back is off the board, and rotate from side to side until you cannot continue. Rest briefly and repeat.
2. You need a partner and a medicine ball for the second variation. Once you're on the incline board, have your partner toss you the medicine ball from your right side. Catch the ball, do three rapid rotations back and forth, then throw the ball to your partner. Repeat from the left side (see figure 2.11).

Figure 2.11 Incline board abdominal twist with medicine ball.

Plyometric Exercises

The term *plyometric exercise*, like perhaps many terms, doesn't bring to mind a particular sequence of movement. The term *stretch/shortening cycle exercise,* although difficult to say, is much more descriptive of the activity.

In many movements that we make there is a stretch/shortening cycle. Walking is a good example: As the foot strikes the ground, the quadriceps muscle goes through an eccentric contraction, the muscle then holds momentarily (isometric action) before contracting (concentric contraction). If this action is done quickly, the resultant force of the concentric contraction is greater than if there had been no relatively fast eccentric contraction. This sequence of movement is called the *stretch/shortening cycle*. When this action is done quickly, the muscle is stretched slightly and then shortens. The slight stretching stores *elastic energy*. The addition of the elastic energy of the muscle to the voluntary eccentric contraction is one of the reasons given for the increased force of contraction resulting from a stretch/shortening cycle. The other reason is that such stretching also elicits a reflex that results in quicker recruitment of muscle fibers or recruitment of more muscle fibers.

It is thought to be an advantage to engage in strength training followed by plyometric exercises. In general, changes in motor performance are greater when engaging in both in the same workout than when doing either one without the other.

ROPE JUMPING

This exercise is low impact. Rope jumping can be good for coordination and learning to be quick on your feet.

LATERAL HOP OVER BENCHES

The height of the boxes can range from 12 to 20 inches (30 to 51 centimeters). The object is to jump left over a bench then right back over the bench as many times as possible in a predetermined time, normally not more than 20 seconds.

DOUBLE-LEG BOUND

This activity can be done simply by jumping on a cushioned floor (wrestling mats) or by jumping over hurdles or cones. "Flat" (no hurdles or boxes) double-leg bounding is usually done in sets of three to six. The object is to jump as far as possible on each jump. Simply bound as far as possible on each jump, land, gather, and quickly jump again. If hurdles are used, the objective is to bound over a number of hurdles. As you become more competent, carefully raise the hurdles to make the activity more challenging. Bounding up stairs or up bleachers is also a very good exercise.

DEPTH JUMPING

Set up three or four boxes or other very sturdy platforms varying in height from perhaps 18 to 24 to 36 to 48 inches (46 to 61 to 91 to 122 centimeters). The exercise is started by stepping off the lowest box, and then immediately on contact with the floor jumping *onto* the next box. Obviously this exercise can create great stress on the joints of the leg and foot. Be cautious when doing depth jumps.

SINGLE-LEG BOUND

This exercise is similar to the double-leg variety but on only one leg. You might do a series of jumps on one leg and then switch to the other, or you might alternate legs or do two on one leg followed by two on the other. There are many possible combinations.

BOUND UP STAIRS

Double- or single-leg stair jumping is a very demanding stretch/shortening cycle exercise. Coaches should caution athletes to stop jumping before they become so fatigued they might miss a stair and injure themselves.

MEDICINE BALL WORK

There are perhaps fewer stretch/shortening cycle exercises for the arms than for the legs. With creative use of different weight medicine balls, however, you can get good stretch/shortening cycle work for your upper body.

Overhead toss

Side throw

Underhand forward toss

Triceps toss

Basketball chest pass (two hands)

Straight-arm overhead toss (kneeling to partner)

Tossing medicine balls to athletes on incline boards while they are doing sit-ups (see figure 2.11). Athlete catches ball, rotates back and forth, and tosses ball back to helper. Repeat.

Workouts for Nonlifting Days

If table 2.1 (pages 21-22) designates Mondays, Wednesdays, and Fridays as lifting days, that leaves Tuesdays, Thursdays, and Saturdays to concentrate on practicing throws, plyometrics, and agility work. On nonlifting days, you would engage in throwing 15 to 30 throws for each event chosen that day (in the fall, perhaps only one event per day, whatever you choose). As the competitive season approaches, you will be required to practice all events during workouts. Twenty throws per event is adequate when practicing two or three events. After throwing would come sprints: five 20- to 40-yard (18- to 37-meter) dashes. You should also complete plyometric work after the throwing workout if you have not completed it during the previous day's weight training period. Even though plyometric work is perhaps best scheduled after weight training, it is often difficult to schedule during that time. Start with 20 and progress up to 50 ground contacts. Also include up to 50 medicine ball throws to help stretch and strengthen the torso.

Throwers need agility work for mobility and general athletic fitness. A very good agility workout results from 30 minutes to an hour of basketball, soccer, or volleyball. If you play these or other games, you must take care that you do not get injured. If you do not participate in such games, you must engage in agility drills. Obstacle courses and repeat sprints changing from running forward to running backward and sideways are excellent agility challenges.

Periodization of Strength Conditioning

Periodization of strength conditioning is the planned variation of the exercises, load (intensity), volume (sets and repetitions), and frequency of the training stimulus to avoid staleness (plateauing or overtraining) and facilitate peaking strength and power for athletic performance. Three cycles are germane to periodization:

1. *Microcycle*—one week or less
2. *Mesocycle*—normally one to four months
3. *Macrocycle*—a season or a year

Novice athletes may have a *preparatory phase* of lower-load training (1 to 2 sets of 15 to 20 repetition maximum) that lasts from two to six weeks (mesocycle). The objective of this period is to learn exercise techniques and gain initial adaptation to resistance exercise stress. This would be followed by cycling through the five mesocycles of the periodization model in table 2.2.

During the initial or *hypertrophy/endurance phase* high volume and low resistance are again emphasized. The goal of this phase is to adapt to resistance training and to increase muscle tissue mass. The goal of the second or *strength phase* is significant increases in strength. The third or *power phase* is focused on developing significant power. The fourth or *peaking phase* is intended to peak or maximize strength and power. An *active rest phase* follows the peaking phase. The goal of this phase is mental and physiological recovery from the preceding training. Once you have completed active rest (from one to three weeks), you may repeat another training cycle or follow a maintenance program for a competitive season.

Within the past few years a modified, more varied workout system has emerged. This system is a more rational approach to conditioning for most athletes in a school setting or athletes in multiple sports who logically wish to maintain a high level of strength and power during different competitive seasons. Table 2.3 on page 32 presents a possible three-day workout system.

Athletes in season who compete on Friday or Saturday would benefit from lifting only once or twice during the week. If the coach chooses two workouts, use those for Monday and Wednesday. If only one, use the Wednesday workout.

The three-days-per-week strength training routine is ideal for conditioning track and field throwers. After completing the resistance training, you can do a plyometric workout (see pages 27-28) and a stretching session. The entire workout period should not exceed one and a half hours. On nonlifting days you can work on throwing technique and follow that with sprint work and flexibility conditioning. An agility program should also be included. In addition to agility runs, you can use a variety of sports as agility challenges, such as basketball, soccer, racquetball, volleyball, or badminton.

The four-day lifting workout in table 2.4 on page 32 might be used when not competing or between seasons or sports. This routine might be best in the fall when strength and conditioning *may* take precedence over throwing. You will benefit very much from fall throwing, however. You may wish to compare such a four-day program to three-day workouts to evaluate which is best.

Table 2.2 Periodization Model

Mesocycle:	Hypertrophy	Strength	Power	Peaking	Active rest
Sets:	2-5	2-5	2-5	2-5	Light activity
Reps:*	8-20	2-6	2-4	1-3	
Load:	Low	High	High	Very high	

	Monday	Wednesday	Friday
HYPERTROPHY/ ENDURANCE PHASE (2 WEEKS, 6 WORKOUTS)			
Week 1			
Bench press	4 × 8 @ 60%	3 × 10 @ 50%	2 × 10 @ 70%
Back squat	4 × 8 @ 60%	3 × 10 @ 50%	2 × 10 @ 70%
Clean	4 × 5 @ 60%	3 × 6 @ 50%	2 × 5 @ 65%
Week 2			
Incline press	4 × 8 @ 60%	3 × 10 @ 50%	2 × 10 @ 70%
Front squat	4 × 8 @ 60%	3 × 10 @ 50%	2 × 10 @ 70%
Snatch	4 × 5 @ 60%	3 × 6 @ 50%	2 × 5 @ 65%
STRENGTH PHASE (4 WEEKS, 12 WORKOUTS)			
Week 3			
Bench press	3 × 6 @ 70%	4 × 4 @ 80%	2 × 5 @ 85%
Back squat	3 × 6 @ 70%	4 × 4 @ 80%	2 × 5 @ 85%
Clean	3 × 3 @ 80%	3 × 5 @ 70%	3 × 3 @ 70%
Week 4			
Bench press	5 × 5 @ 85%	3 × 3 @ 70%	3 × 6 @ 75%
Back squat	5 × 5 @ 85%	Rest	3 × 6 @ 80%
Clean	3 × 3 @ 70%	3 × 3 @ 85%	3 × 4 @ 70%
Week 5			
Incline press	3 × 6 @ 70%	4 × 4 @ 80%	2 × 5 @ 85%
Front squat	3 × 6 @ 70%	4 × 4 @ 80%	2 × 5 @ 85%
Snatch	3 × 3 @ 80%	3 × 5 @ 70%	3 × 3 @ 70%
Week 6			
Incline press	5 × 5 @ 85%	3 × 3 @ 70%	3 × 6 @ 75%
Front squat	5 × 5 @ 85%	Rest	3 × 6 @ 80%
Snatch	3 × 3 @ 70%	3 × 3 @ 85%	3 × 4 @ 70%

POWER PHASE (4 WEEKS, 12 WORKOUTS)			
Week 7			
Bench press	3 × 3 @ 85%	2 × 3 @ 80%	4 × 4 @ 80%
Back squat	3 × 3 @ 85%	Leg press (light)	4 × 4 @ 85%
Clean	3 × 3 @ 75%	4 × 3 @ 85%	2 × 3 @ 80%
Week 8			
Bench press	3 × 3 @ 90%	4 × 3 @ 75%	3 × 3 @ 85%
Back squat	3 × 3 @ 90%	Toe press	3 × 3 @ 85%
Clean	3 × 3 @ 70%	3 × 2 @ 90%	3 × 3 @ 80%
Week 9			
Incline press	3 × 3 @ 85%	2 × 3 @ 80%	4 × 4 @ 80%
Front squat	3 × 3 @ 85%	Leg press (light)	4 × 4 @ 85%
Snatch	3 × 3 @ 75%	4 × 3 @ 85%	2 × 3 @ 80%
Week 10			
Incline press	3 × 3 @ 90%	4 × 3 @ 75%	3 × 3 @ 85%
Front squat	3 × 3 @ 90%	Toe press	3 × 3 @ 85%
Snatch	3 × 3 @ 70%	3 × 2 @ 90%	3 × 3 @ 80%

PEAKING PHASE (2 WEEKS, 6 WORKOUTS)			
Week 11			
Bench press	3 × 2 @ 95%	2 × 2 @ 90%	3 × 3 @ 80%
Back squat	3 × 2 @ 95-100%	Toe press	3 × 3 @ 90%
Clean	3 × 3 @ 80%	2 × 2 @ 95-100%	3 × 3 @ 85%
Week 12			
Incline press	3 × 2 @ 95%	2 × 2 @ 90%	3 × 3 @ 80%
Front squat	3 × 2 @ 95-100%	Toe press	3 × 3 @ 90%
Snatch	3 × 3 @ 80%	2 × 2 @ 95-100%	3 × 3 @ 85%

ACTIVE REST PHASE (2 WEEKS)

Weeks 13 and 14

Light activity

Active rest suggests being active with activities other than lifting. This means playing games you enjoy: basketball, golf, hiking, walking. It allows you to engage in movement activities that give you a break from the intensity of strength conditioning.

* When doing Olympic-type lifts (cleans and snatches), do not do more than six repetitions even in the hypertrophy phase. Further, only do six repetitions when lifting at 60% of the 1 RM or less.

Table 2.3 Three-Day Conditioning System

	Monday	Wednesday	Friday
Load or intensity zone	8-10 RM (moderate)	3-5 RM (high)	12-15 RM (low)
Number of sets	3-4	4-5	3-5
Rest between sets and exercises	2 min	3-4 min	1 min

Table 2.4 Four-Day Lifting Workout

	Monday Moderate	Tuesday Moderate	Wednesday Active rest	Thursday Heavy	Friday Heavy
Load or intensity zone	8-10 RM	8-10 RM		3-6 RM	3-6 RM
Number of sets	2-4	3-4		2-4	3-4
Rest between sets and exercises	2-3 min	2-3 min		3-5 min	3-5 min

In the four-day workout, Monday/Thursday workouts may include the bench press, clean, overhead press, triceps press and arm curl, abdominal work, and upper-body plyometrics (medicine ball exercises). Tuesday/Friday workouts could include the squat, snatch, hamstring curl, lat pull-down, abdominal work, and plyometric jumps. When working on cleans or snatches, don't do more than six repetitions in any one set. When the weight reaches 80 percent of the 1RM or more, restrict repetitions to three or less.

Macrocycle Planning

Recall that a macrocycle refers to a reasonably long period—either a season or a year of planning. Smaller cycles would normally be mesocycles (anywhere from one to four months). Macrocycles are always made up of more detailed plans called mesocycles, and mesocycles are made up of more detailed plans called microcycles.

Postseason

Most throwers in U.S. high schools and colleges haven't thrown their implements for a couple of months when September arrives. If you are a thrower and like throwing, you will enjoy getting back into it. Fall throwing is great in the sense that it is a time when you can work intensely on improving your technique. It is a time to try different emphases and not fear doing poorly in an upcoming meet. Of course there should be intrasquad competitions and even a Kastarama in which you throw all four implements. (Use decathlon or other tables to determine relative ability.) Fall is a great time to throw for the exacting technique work and for the sheer enjoyment of it. The concept of not throwing for distance is absolutely foreign to a good thrower! You need not measure most throws, and you can take many throws for the sheer joy of making the movement, but you should certainly have a general idea of how far the throws are going. Otherwise how can you know whether a particular emphasis is helping, hindering, or doing nothing? Feelings are indications, but accurate distance measurements are where the "steel strikes the ground."

In the fall, complete a three- to four-month linear series of mesocycles of strength conditioning three days per week. Include plyometric work and appropriate agility activities. You should do short sprints on throwing days—two to three times per week.

For variety and enjoyment have a Scottish Highland Games in October or November. You might have a two-on-two competition in basketball or racquetball. Wrap ankles and enforce sanity during play.

If you believe in throwing heavy implements (and many do), fall is the time to throw them. Various athletes throw a variety of implements including bars, kettle bells, cones, weighted towels, balls, and whatever else may be useful.

Competitive Season

During the indoor season, from January to March, shot-putting and weight throwing are the major emphasis. I do not advocate throwing indoors into nets or screens for experienced long throwers. (A college sophomore is normally an experienced thrower.) If long throws can be taken outdoors, great. Otherwise, stick primarily with the short throws while the winter rages. I advocate throwing 10 to 15 long throws once every week or two during the winter. This is simply a rhythmic exercise to stay connected with the event. Certainly there should be *no intense work* on long throw technique when you cannot determine how far the implement is traveling. My experience teaches me that doing so is very deceptive.

Generally a maintenance program of strength conditioning should be followed during the period of indoor competition. Strength conditioning may take place only twice per week from the beginning of the indoor season until the end of the outdoor season. Young athletes will continue to gain strength on such a program. If you are not competing indoors, you could complete a three-month periodized strength conditioning program. The intensity of the program should vary between *moderate* and *high.*

The intensity of throwing during a season is always high. The volume of throws is generally low. You must learn how to throw at very high velocities (throw far).

You will normally peak for indoor as well as outdoor championships. Peaking consists of backing off on the volume of strength conditioning and maximizing intensity to bring strength and power to a razor-sharp edge. Appropriate nutrition, throwing, lifting, sprinting and agility work, and plyometric work coupled with properly timed rest and recovery will bring you to peak physical condition.

Conditioning Programs of Elite Throwers

As mentioned earlier in this chapter, conditioning programs may take many forms. Among elite athletes there is no question that conditioning programs vary. I competed at international levels for 15 years and never tried to periodize my strength conditioning programs. The program was to get strong in the base lifts (squat, bench press, and clean) and play interesting and challenging games that required muscular endurance, agility, speed, and jumping power (basketball, badminton, and racquetball). Starting with my sophomore year in college I threw in the fall, winter (primarily shot, but plenty of discus if winter was mild), and spring. My throwing sessions started with a few warm-up throws and then they were generally all-out. I tried to perform each throw with as much speed as I could control.

Anthony Washington, four-time U.S. National champion and world champion in 1999 in the discus, does not throw all-out all of the time. He believes a great deal can be learned from throwing at different levels of intensity. His strength training is not periodized. He works on primarily two lifts, the snatch and the jump squat. His strength conditioning workouts are twice per week for one to one and a half hours. He works very fast through the sets and reps with minimal rest. He does a great deal of abdominal work, sprinting, and flexibility conditioning. When in top condition he is hard as a rock, ripped, and very powerful, which means exceptionally quick. About six to seven years ago Anthony worked with an intense coach named Goran Milanovich. While with him Anthony did put in some long, very demanding workouts.

Adam Setliff was the best U.S. discus thrower in 2000, 2001, and 2002. I had the opportunity to observe his training for a few weeks. Adam lifts three to four days per week. He primarily does snatches and squats. However, at least once per week he does a bodybuilding workout wherein he does multiple sets to assure strength and definition. This bodybuilding workout could be considered a once-per-week series of assistance exercises. Adam repeatedly lifted heavy loads in the middle of the day (11 A.M. to 1 P.M.), rested for two to three hours, then went through a hard-throwing workout. Adam enjoys doing 15 repeat sprints up a slope of about 20 degrees. He does not enjoy flat sprinting. Adam jogged to warm up before throwing, then did some stretching, and then threw about 20 hard throws.

Tibor Gecsek of Hungary is the sixth farthest hammer thrower in world history. He has a rigorous training regimen that includes hang snatch and hang clean, mixed with back squats and leg presses. The snatch and clean are performed in a succession of high pulls with the final repetition of each set ending in a catch. Gecsek's personal bests are 160 kilograms (353 pounds) in the snatch and 215 kilograms (474 pounds) in the clean. Gecsek supplements his weightlifting with a wide variety of plate twists and turning drills with weights. Pud throws also make up a large portion of this specific strength training as well. These puds are typically 20 kilograms (44 pounds) in weight and 70 centimeters (2 feet) in length. Running and jumping are also critical for Gecsek's development of explosive power. Short sprints up to 60 meters (197 feet) along with running drills and a wide variety of hurdle jumps, box jumps, and bounds into the sand are performed with increasing regularity as the competition season approaches. In the preseason, he also uses swimming and soccer to enhance and maintain general fitness.

In April 2001 *Niklas Arrhenius* set a new national high school record in the discus throw of 234 feet, 3 inches (71.4 meters). He puts the shot over 64 feet (19.5 meters). Nik lifts Mondays, Wednesdays, and Fridays and throws Tuesdays, Thursdays, and Saturdays. His workouts are presented in table 2.5.

In looking at the year-round training of top javelin throwers, there is a general cycle of training that has different points of focus for each cycle or training period. This training overview is based on what a number of world ranked

Table 2.5 Niklas Arrhenius's Strength Conditioning Workouts

MONDAY				
Clean	**Squat**	**Hang snatch**	**Bench press**	**Incline press**
1 × 6 @ 60-70%	1 × 6 @ 60%	1 × 6 @ 50-60%	1 × 6 @ 65%	1 × 3 @ 80%
2 × 4 @ 70-80%	1 × 6 @ 70%	3 × 4 @ >80%	1 × 5 @ 70%	1 × 2 @ 85%
3 × 2 @ 85-95%	3 × 3 @ 80%		1 × 4 @ 75%	1 × 1 @ 90-95%

Do assistance exercises and torso work, then play 1 hour of basketball in the evening.

TUESDAY

Throws

Good weather: Discus (20-30 throws), shot (15-20 throws)

Winter: Throw primarily shot and weight (15-20 throws each)

Sprints and Jumps

6 × 40-yd dash (may go up to 10-15 sprints)

6 × 6 hurdles (height and number of hurdles vary by how athlete feels)

Depth jumps from 12-in., 20-in., 36-in., 48-in. boxes (no depth jump from 48 in., just jump up to this height from 36-in. box). Some flat double-legged and single-legged bounding, usually triple bounds.

Medicine ball: Tosses for height (6), chest pass to partner (10), side throws to partner (10 each side)

WEDNESDAY			
Squat	**Snatch (floor)**	**Behind-the-neck jerk**	**Dumbbell bench press**
1 × 6 @ 60%	1 × 6 @ 60-70%	1 × 6 @ 70-89%	3 × 8 @ 85%
1 × 6 @ 70%	2 × 4 @ 75-85%	1 × 4 @ 80-90%	
3 × 4 @ 85%	3 × 2 @ 90%	3 × 2 @ 90%	

Do assistance exercises and torso work, then play 1 hour of basketball in the evening.

THURSDAY

Throws

Good weather: Discus (20-30 throws), shot (15-20 throws)

Winter: Throw primarily shot and weight (15-20 throws each)

Sprints and Jumps

6 × 40-yd dash (may go up to 10-15 sprints)
6 × 6 hurdles (height and number of hurdles vary by how athlete feels)

Depth jumps from 12-in., 20-in., 36-in., 48-in. boxes (no depth jump from 48 in., just jump up to this height after dropping from a 36-in. box).

Medicine ball: Tosses for height (6), chest pass to partner (10), side passes (10 each side)

(continued)

Table 2.5 *(continued)*

FRIDAY				
Hang snatch	**Clean from floor**	**Squat**	**Bench press**	**Incline press**
1 × 6 @ 50-60%	1 × 6 @ 50%	1 × 6 @ 60%	1 × 6 @ 65%	1 × 3 @ 80%
1 × 6 @ 50%	2 × 3 @ 70-80%	1 × 6 @ 70%	1 × 5 @ 70%	1 × 2 @ 85%
4 × 3 @ > 80%	2 × 2 @ 85-95%	5 × 6 @ 80%	1 × 4 @ 75%	1 × 1@ 90-95%
	3 × 1 @ 95-100%			

Do assistance exercises and torso work; basketball is optional on Fridays. Social life is also important.

SATURDAY
Throws
Good weather: Discus (20-30 throws), shot (15-20 throws) Winter: Throw primarily shot and weight (15-20 throws each)
Sprints and Jumps
6 × 40-yd dash (may go up to 10-15 sprints) 6 × 6 hurdles (height and number of hurdles vary by how athlete feels) Depth jumps from 12-in., 20-in., 36-in., 48-in. boxes (no depth jump from 48 in., just jump up to this height from 36-in. box) Medicine ball: Tosses for height (6), chest pass to partner (10), side passes (10 each side)

Nik also likes to do some bodybuilding, and he does extensive torso conditioning. Nik throws from 15 to 30 throws on Tuesday, Thursday, and Saturday. During the winter most of these throws are with the shot and the weight. However, he does throw the discus against a screen at least once per week, or weather permitting, he throws outside. After throwing, he sprints from 5 to 10 40-yd dashes and then does a good stretching program. Nik frequently plays basketball with others twice per week for about an hour.

javelin throwers do, rather than looking at one specific athlete. Most of the world's best javelin throwers do some form of this type of training. There is usually a prime goal for physical and technical training in each period. The main focal points in the fall are to

1. develop a base to build future training on, and
2. correct major technical problems from the previous season.

This is long duration, low intensity (50 to 70 percent of maximum) training that includes running over various distances; throwing medicine balls, weighted balls or javelins, and normal weight javelins; weight training; and a variety of aerobic activities like biking, swimming, and sport games.

The most stressful portion of training takes place during the winter. The intensity is higher and technical work is pushed to higher levels. The physical goal is to improve general and specific explosive power while the technical goal is to make effective use of this new power by way of the technical improvements from the fall. The methods of training used in the fall are still used, but at higher intensity (70 to 90 percent levels), and a lot of jumping is added; horizontal bounding and hopping over hurdles are very important exercises. This is a period of high stress training as the training loads/intensity increase, but there is still a very high volume of training. (When rest periods come they need to be used!)

As you prepare for the competitive season the goals shift again. Physically, the aim is to be elastic and powerful—at the peak of your abilities. Technically, the goal is to have complete confidence that your training has put you in a good position to use your physical ability; you know you can throw far. A lot of short duration but high intensity training takes place—lifts often at 90 to 95 percent of maximum, very explosive jumping, and throws with shots, medicine balls, and various weight javelins. Sprinting and runway work at speed are very important toward blending the technical and physical abilities needed for long throwing. Rest is just as important; this is when you start to compete, so it's good to have "gas in the tank" when you go to meets, not be flat from overtraining.

Training for Athletes in Multiple Throwing Events

General strength conditioning for athletes who may throw any combination of shot, discus, and hammer is the same. The programs discussed in this chapter will work for any of these athletes. To consider specific conditioning for athletes in specific events, refer to the chapters on those events.

Javelin throwers will also participate in the same general conditioning programs that we have discussed. The body contains only so many muscles, and those muscles (groups) are the focus of the programs we have presented. At the collegiate level and above, javelin throwers seldom participate in other throwing events. The specific demands of the javelin throw require a lithe body type that usually has some difficulty competing effectively in the other three throws. Of course, the term *lithe* describes javelin throwers in comparison to other throwers. To put this in perspective, the average height and weight of the top 10 ranked men in the javelin throw over the last 10 years is 6 feet, 3 inches (1.9 meters) and 228 pounds (103 kilograms). However, some javelin throwers have been relatively successful in the weight and hammer throws. The converse is also true; shot, discus, and hammer throwers seldom do well at throwing the javelin.

Conditioning for Athletes in Multiple Sports

Placing a high priority on strength and power conditioning will assure the best result possible when providing a strength conditioning program for a multisport athlete. This situation occurs most frequently at the high school level. All coaches know about the blue chip athlete—the person who is a winner at just about any sport. Such athletes are naturally wanted by all coaches.

What are the conditioning problems for such an athlete? If you have a thrower who is a starter on the football team and a good basketball player or wrestler, how are you and your fellow coaches going to assure that this person gets the best conditioning experience possible over the academic year? The answer is that each coach must believe in the value of a strength conditioning program and incorporate such into the student's weekly training schedule. Most high schools now have strength conditioning classes. Athletes frequently participate in strength training at a time other than during the athletic workout. If this is the case, problem solved. If this is not the case, it is important that the coaches include strength conditioning twice per week as part of the weekly athletic regimen.

Strength conditioning programs are crucial for throwers. There is no one best strength conditioning program, but all programs must include activities that produce strength, power, and flexibility. Agility activities are also essential in a thrower's conditioning program.

Conditioning requires careful thought, hard work, appropriate rest, and a willingness to consider concepts that may be useful. Adequate conditioning programs will help any athlete to perform better.

Shot Put

chapter 3

Written by Kent and Ramona Pagel
With contributions by Jay Silvester

The concept of throwing a heavy, nondescript object such as a rock held no allure for the aesthetic-minded Greeks of the ancient Olympic era, who preferred the elegant lines of the discus and javelin-like throwing events. The organized forebears of the modern day shot-putter were from the Scottish Highlands, where an attraction to ascetic brute force outweighed the desire for the flowing lines and artistic movements found in the Greek athletic ideals. If athletics measures the limits of various forms of human performance, what could be more basic than the simple competition of who can toss a heavy object, such as a stone, the farthest? Its aesthetic value may always be questioned, but the sheer force and physical explosiveness necessary to propel a heavy object within a short space has produced a fascination that has lasted and increased into the modern Olympic era. The shot put is now the most frequently contested Olympic throwing event.

The Scottish "stone," weighing in at 18 pounds or 8.2 kilograms, is the forefather of the modern Olympic shot. Records of athletic competition with various forms of the stone may be found as far back as the 15th century in Scotland and England, and forms of competition using stones can be found on the European continent as early as the 17th century. It is not surprising then that the shot put was included in the first modern Olympic Games in 1896 in Athens, along with the more commonly accepted ancient Olympic Greek throwing events. Throughout the history of the modern Olympics, the Americans have written the majority of the chronicle in the shot put for men. For women, who entered the event in 1948, shot-putting at elite levels has been strictly a European affair; most contestants have been from formerly communist states, particularly Germany and Russia.

Two primary classifications of shot put techniques are used today: the glide, developed by Parry O'Brien, and the spin, developed by many but made famous by Aleksandr Baryshnikov and Brian Oldfield. Other techniques, which may be described as partial movements, have merit as either drills or competitive movements. Normally, only novice athletes would use these movements in competition, but they are frequently part of the training regimen of the more skilled shot-putters. All throws and movements discussed in this chapter are described for a right-handed thrower.

Glide Technique

Parry O'Brien developed the glide technique that is now used worldwide. Most throwers would agree that gliding is less technically complex than spinning. The world record in shot putting is 75 feet, 10 1/2 inches (23.13 meters) held by Randy Barnes, a spinner. The women's world record is 74 feet, 2 inches held by Natayla Lisovskaya of Russia, also a glider. The longest throw by a glider is that of Ulf Timmerman of then East Germany at 75 feet, 10 1/4 inches (23.12 meters). The longest throw in an officiated competition is 81 feet, 3 inches (24.77 meters) with a 12-pound shot (5.4-kilogram) accomplished by Michael Carter—a glider—when he was in high school. It is common to think that tall, strong throwers might be better gliders and the shorter, powerfully built persons might best use the spin.

Grip and Arm Position

Holding the shot is not as complicated as many individuals would like to make it. A simple way to start is to hold the implement in your nonthrowing hand (your left hand if you are right-handed). Hold the fingers of your dominant hand together loosely with your thumb extended out from your fingers. Gently slap the shot with your dominant hand and tip the shot up into your hand (figure 3.1a). The weight of the shot should rest along the ridge of your hand between your fingers and your palm.

The placement of the shot on your neck is mostly at your discretion; choose a position based on comfort. However, your thumb should be down and you should push the shot firmly into your neck (figure 3.1b). Your elbow should be in a position from which it can rotate back behind the shot sometime before delivery.

Learning the Standing Throw

The standing throw from a power position is very important when learning the shot put. Knowing how to make a proper standing throw will contribute a great deal to your success when moving on to the glide or spin technique.

A system of reference is crucial when discussing foot and body positions in the circle. We have found the clock system (figure 3.2) to be very helpful and will use it throughout this chapter.

Figure 3.1 *(a)* Grip and *(b)* placement of the shot against the neck.

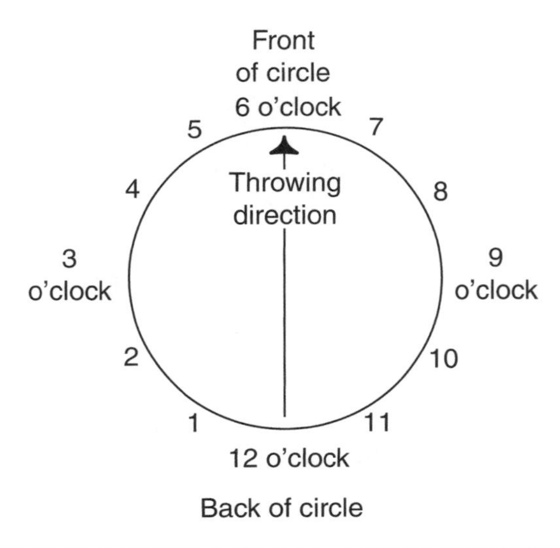

Figure 3.2 Shot circle, with 6 o'clock being the direction of the throw.

Power Position

Stand in a shot circle with your feet parallel and shoulder-width apart. About 60 percent of your body weight should be over your right foot and 40 percent should be over your left foot. Place your right foot near the center of the circle facing toward 9 o'clock, with your left foot closer to the toe board (figure 3.3a).

Hold the shot at your neck with your thumb down and your four fingers pressing the shot into your neck. Rotate your shoulders to the rear of the ring so that there is a relatively straight line from your head to your left foot at the front of the ring, as shown in figure 3.3a. Your left arm should be loose and away from your body to the side. This is the completed power position. This basic power position for delivery of the shot is similar, independent of the style of implementation, spin or glide, and a standing throw should indicate that.

Delivery

To "unwind" and lift out of this position, your initial movement comes from your right foot. Push your heel out and rotate your knee in the direction of the throw to start the unwinding of your somewhat torqued and flexed body (figure 3.3b). This forceful unwinding, lifting, and driving somewhat forward of your torqued body advances up the centerline of your body through your hips, chest, shoulders, and finally to your arm, wrist, and hand, at which time the implement receives the culmination of these rotational, linear, and vertical forces. Your post or blocking left leg at the toe board should give only slightly to the load while you shift the forces to the linear and vertical direction. The blocking side leg resists the rotation so that all forces transfer into the implement, propelling the shot up over your left side through the delivery (figure 3.3c).

Figure 3.3 Standing throw from the power position.

Your right leg pushes your hip plane around and forward toward your left leg, leading the shoulder plane and shot. Because your body has been maximally torqued and flexed before initiating delivery, your left arm begins to sweep out away from your body at essentially the same time your right knee begins rotating. When your left arm reaches a parallel plane with your chest, it rotates with the chest, almost as if you were opening a door with your left arm before moving through it (see figure 3.3b). When your shoulders reach the position facing the direction of delivery, your left arm stops or blocks further rotation of the shoulder plane. To envision this movement, imagine a pole coming up the left side of the toe board; your left hand grabs the pole and holds the left side of your upper body in a solid position while you deliver the shot (figure 3.4). Your head rotates back and locks in place during delivery, again transferring momentum into the implement. Your legs finish their lift and rotation up into the body as the shot is delivered.

Figure 3.4 To prevent further rotation of the shoulders, imagine a pole coming out of the toe board; the left hand grabs the pole and holds the left side of the upper body in a firm position while the shot is delivered.

Follow-Through

Two different finishes may be used for the standing throw: the nonreversing finish, which may be used with a balance step through, and the reversing finish. When finishing with a nonreverse, you may keep both feet in place if you have learned the balance required for this technique (figure 3.5a), or you may switch or reverse your feet *well after the shot is delivered* with your right foot traveling to the toe board and your left leg sweeping up and back for balance. This is known as a nonreverse or late reverse standing throw. The reversing finish involves an aggressive jumping action with both legs driving up into the throw. The shot is delivered as a result of your right side driving forward, up and around into the lifting, blocking left side, where the summation of forces is directed into the implement. Your right foot comes down near the toe board with your left leg reaching up and back toward the center of the ring for balance (figure 3.5b).

Figure 3.5 *(a)* Nonreversing finish and *(b)* reversing finish.

Starting Stance: Full Glide

The concept of the "full" glide is to move quickly and efficiently over the 7-foot (2.135 meter) distance of the shot ring to develop greater momentum than is possible with a standing throw, thereby applying much greater force to the shot and "putting" it much farther (see chapter 1). Begin the glide by facing away from the direction of the throw. Stand with your body weight over your right leg/foot at the back of the circle, with your foot facing 12 o'clock, or away from the landing area (see figure 3.6). You may stand vertically or bend at the hips. We recommend a bent-over or flexed-hip starting position, because by flexing at the hip the thrower lowers the center of gravity, thus becoming more stable or better balanced as the throw begins. Your left arm should hang down, and your left leg should be bent with your toe touching the surface of the circle.

Figure 3.6 Proper starting position for the glide technique.

Drive to the Center of the Circle

The O'Brien glide style shot-putting technique requires the ability to use a single-leg support while maintaining balance and driving backward toward 6 o'clock. Four forces are being applied during the drive out of the back of the ring:

1. Unseating
2. Shoulder lift
3. Right leg drive
4. Left leg drive

For maximum momentum development and transfer to the shot, these movements must be made in a rhythmic, coordinated sequence.

Unseating is the term used in shot-putting to describe moving the body's line of gravity beyond its base of support, the basis of all translation (moving the body from one place to another) of the body on earth. With your body in the bent-over starting position, initiate the rhythm of the movement by lifting your left leg up and then down and bending it while moving it somewhat forward toward your right leg (figure 3.7a). Just before your left leg reaches a full forward position (almost parallel with your right leg), begin the unseating process.

Unseating is the process of shifting your center of mass from a balanced position over your right foot (base of support) at the back of the ring (12 o'clock) to a moving position behind your right foot by causing your hips to slide or sit to the rear. You should feel somewhat of a "sitting" sensation toward the direction of the throw as you begin the glide. The greater the distance behind the heel of the right foot this line of gravity is forced or allowed to shift, the faster you must move to avoid falling on your rear. Too much shift of the line of gravity and you will fall; too little and you will not develop maximum momentum. Many trials of this movement are required to determine the proper speed of movement to enable a successful throw with maximum force development. As you shift the line of gravity rearward from the front of your foot, move your hips down and to the rear and lift your shoulders slightly to allow your right leg to drive your body quickly to the center of the ring. In a move timed carefully with the right leg thrust, kick your left leg strongly toward the toe board (figure 3.7b), producing momentarily the appearance that you are doing the splits with your legs. This rearward kick, if timed properly, adds momentum to the throw, keeps your hips ahead of your upper body, and ensures that your feet will arrive simultaneously at the power position.

Figure 3.7 *(a)* Unseating and *(b)* drive to the center of the ring.

Landing at Midthrow in the Power Position

As your right foot is in the air moving from the start position to the power position, rotate it in the direction of the throw as much as you can, 90 degrees or 9 o'clock if possible. Upon landing there should be a relatively straight line from your head through your torso to your left foot at the toe board. A majority of your body weight, 60 to 70 percent, should be over your right foot in the center of the ring upon landing. From this point the technique follows the power position execution described in the discussion of the standing throw, ensuring that as soon as your foot hits the middle of the ring, you can initiate the rotation.

Delivery

The delivery of the shot is, according to the name of the event, a "put" rather than a throw. In a throw the elbow usually leads the wrist and hand into the delivery, whereas in a put the wrist and hand are always ahead of the elbow throughout the delivery. The rules of shot-putting also state that the implement must be above the shoulder plane and in close proximity to the neck when the delivery is initiated, which would make a throwing delivery difficult as well as illegal. The actual release of the shot should occur with the thumb pointing down and the wrist flexing in a snap with an inside-out movement (figure 3.8).

Figure 3.8 Shot release.

The lifting and release angle of the shot result from good body mechanics that include the lift from the legs and hips; upper-body torque and hip flexion; and shoulder, arm, and hand projection angle. The force produced by the entire body aids in the correct delivery of the shot. The upper body, particularly the chest, throwing arm, hand, and fingers, must be powerful enough to handle the force that the whole body delivers into the implement through the release. The upper-body delivery should simply follow the path through the put that the preceding movements and forces have set up.

Follow-Through

The follow-through for the glide can be extremely varied depending on the athlete and the type of glider he or she is. The two major forms of finish and follow-through for the glide are the nonreverse and the full reverse. The nonreversing finish is often simply that. The forces built up through the glide across the circle meet against a firmly placed left side, and the shot is delivered as a result of a braced or blocked left leg, shoulder, and arm. A small step through may follow for balance, but the feet, particularly the left foot, remain in contact with the ground well after the shot has been released (see figure 3.5a on page 43). A good image for the nonreversing glide is to imagine the body as a door with the hinges on the left side. When the shot is delivered, the right side of the door slams against the frame, which is hinged at the left side of the frame, and the power is transferred to the shot.

The active reverse uses an active left side to transfer the momentum built up during the glide into the delivery. A natural reverse occurs as a result of a powerful drive up with the left leg as the shot is delivered, so much that a jumping action, sometimes quite high off the ground, occurs. The remaining rotation takes the right side into the toe board as the upper body extends into the throwing direction and the left leg sweeps up and back into the circle for balance (see figure 3.5b on page 43). A landing on the heel of the right foot at the toe board is preferred for balance as levers continue to extend and energy not transferred into the shot dissipates. The reverse is also a result of a powerful right side rotation into a lifting left side.

Spin Technique

Every technique in every event has advantages and disadvantages. The major advantage that the spin possesses over other techniques is that both the thrower and the shot travel a much greater distance in the shot ring, thereby resulting in the potential to accelerate the shot to greater velocity than when using the glide. There is also the potential for greater, more efficient use of body levers to accelerate by both the body and the shot as they travel through the circle. The disadvantages are (1) the shot circle is somewhat smaller than the discus circle, and the turn performed must be tighter; (2) the discus, at the end of an extended throwing arm, acts as a counterbalance to the actions of the rest of the body, whereas the shot must remain close to the neck, at the center of rotation, and offers little help in balancing the athlete; and (3) the glide and other techniques are relatively simple in their basic form, while the spin has more movements and shifts from differing support positions, thus requiring more balance and body control. However, the major advantage that the spin offers the thrower is far greater ability to produce speed traveling into the power position, both in the body itself in rotary movement and in the shot itself. If this speed can be controlled and channeled into the delivery, the potential for greater distance is obvious.

As coaches and athletes we recognize that everyone has strengths and weaknesses. That is undoubtedly the reason we see differences in the movement patterns of different throwers. Despite idiosyncratic differences, however, the movements are basically the same: a 540-degree spin through a 7-foot (2.135-meter) circle to deliver the shot with maximum speed at a desired release trajectory and height. Successful world-class spinners range from 6 feet 8 inches tall (2 meters) to well under 6 feet (1.8 meters), and their technique variations relate, at least to some degree, to their size differentials. Since both the shot and the thrower travel so much farther using the spin technique than any other shot put technique, proper summation of forces and balance throughout the movement are crucial to the success of the movement. The more variations of movement that exist within a technique, the greater the possibility of variations within those movements. In other words, while learning or developing a spin technique for the shot put, it is important to keep the movement as simple as possible, since even the most basic technique is fairly complicated.

All throwing motions and drills discussed in this section are described for a right-handed thrower.

Grip and Arm Position

The grip of the shot is the same as when gliding—four fingers on the shot, thumb more or less helping hold it in position. Place the shot where it is most comfortable, ranging from resting high and back on your trapezius to pressed tightly under your chin. Many variations of placement of the shot in the spin have been successful. The most important consideration in positioning the shot on or about the neck is which position allows the thrower to put the farthest. Experiment with higher and lower positions before concluding which is best. Comfort and security while turning through the circle and ease of moving the shot into proper delivery position are important components of position.

Starting Stance

Place your feet at the back of the circle splitting the line or with your left foot on the line. We prefer putting the left foot on the line. Placing the left foot on the line (12 o'clock to 6 o'clock) allows the thrower to drive from the left foot position directly across the circle on a line. The throw (put) should be driven out on an extension of this line. If this is accomplished the thrower has been very efficient in focusing the energy developed in the circle.

Your feet should be spread more than shoulder-width apart. Before beginning the rotation, sit low on the legs in a well-balanced position (see figure 3.9).

Figure 3.9 Proper starting position for the spin technique.

Movement From First Double-Support Phase to First Single-Support Phase

Remember that you should be in a well-balanced, bent-leg, sitting position. As you begin the throw, be sure to follow a rhythmic sequence of movements. You must become very sensitive to the rhythm of the throw, not simply the mechanics. The rotation normally begins by rotating the torso clockwise to a comfortably torqued position. If you are a beginner, it may be best to "wind up" very little as the throw starts and keep the majority of your body weight over your left leg (this is known as "cheating left"). See figure 3.10.

Figure 3.10 Cheating left start.

Many, if not most, coaches would advocate keeping the line of gravity centered between the legs in this "back winding" move. Others, perhaps those of more advanced throwers, might argue that moving the majority of the weight to the right leg (line of gravity moved over to the right side) and then sweeping the body back around to the left offers an advantage. This results in an increase in momentum as the throw is initiated. However, beginners often benefit by hitting positions correctly as opposed to trying to make moves that require fine coordination of complex movements.

Begin the move out of the back wind into the throw with a weight shift to your left side (keeping shoulders level), moving your body weight initially left and toward the direction of the throw as you continue to rotate over your left foot. Your weight should be on the ball of your foot, but with a low left heel that pushes in as your left foot turns out (figure 3.11a). Your line of gravity shifts to somewhere behind your left foot, and your left leg is powerfully loaded (takes the full body weight in a bent, rotating, resisting-of-forces position) as your right foot comes off the circle (figure 3.11b). Your left arm can be helpful in this move if you sweep it in front of and out away from your body to keep you from leaning backward prematurely. Your left arm and left thigh rotate in synchrony in this beginning stage of the movement. As your right leg clears the surface, the first double-support phase ends.

Figure 3.11 Moving out of the back wind into the throw.

Driving Out of the Back of the Circle

At this point of the movement it is absolutely crucial that you become dynamically balanced over your left leg, controlling and focusing your body movement over and around your left leg as you begin the drive into the circle. As the right foot lifts, many throwers delay the swing or sweep of the right leg as the left knee rotates away from the right toward the throwing direction, the right thigh lifts up and the knee bends, the lower right leg rises to a parallel with the surface of the circle position, hanging briefly in air as the muscles of the thigh stretch and the upper body "moves ahead" of the right hip and leg (figure 3.12a). When the muscles are stretched, the right leg is swept down and around the left in a sweeping soccer-like kick (figure 3.12b) that ultimately catches up with and passes the leading upper-body shoulders and right hip (figure 3.12c). As the right leg passes the left foot/leg, it lifts subtly as the left leg thrusts the body into a low jump (flight phase), as shown in figure 3.12d. Other successful throwers do not delay the swing of the right leg. They pick the right leg up high immediately and quickly sweep it around, with the right leg/foot leading the hips through the circle from pickup through landing in the center. Either move with the right leg has proven successful. Make certain that your right leg sweeps around your left, creating some sweeping momentum that adds to the momentum that may be converted to force on the shot.

Flight and Second Single-Support Phases

As your left leg clears the circle (flight phase), your body has initiated the necessary torque between the arms and torso and the hips and legs. The left arm, which has swept around your left side rotating with, not ahead of, your left side, now stalls between 5 and 3 o'clock, putting significant torque between the upper and lower body. This process (torquing) continues through the flight phase and after right leg touchdown (second single support). Maximal torquing appears to be reached somewhat *before* left leg touchdown (second double support).

Figure 3.12 Drive into the circle.

We would be remiss in our discussion of spin technique if we did not include some reference to the technique of 2002 U.S. shot put champion Adam Nelson. Adam sweeps his right leg widely around the left as he begins the throw (as advised). He then drives strongly off his left leg toward the toe board. As the left foot clears the surface (flight phase), it is lifted in a rather high-looping, semistraight leg sweep up, over, and around the grounded, pivoting right leg. This looping sweep of the left leg appears to create considerably more momentum than keeping the left leg low as it moves from 11:30 to 5:30 in the circle. As the left leg sweeps and rotates *counterclockwise,* the right arm and shoulder are swept *clockwise* against the counterclockwise turn of the lower body. These oppositional movements put the muscles and tendons of the hip, torso, and shoulder on tremendous stretch (torque) (figure 3.13b). If this movement can be made without disturbing the rhythm and energy flow, it could add considerably to the potential for long throwing. That being said, however, most world-class throwers follow the more traditional technique shown in figure 3.13a.

Figure 3.13 *(a)* Traditional technique compared to *(b)* the high-looping left leg sweep and oppositional arm movements that Adam Nelson employs.

Right Foot Touchdown

Your right foot should land beyond the center of the circle with your toes pointing between 4 and 1 o'clock. Landing in this position results in a relatively long pivot into the delivery position. This pivot should begin immediately upon landing and end with your toes pointing at about 9 o'clock as you deliver the shot. Many beginners will jump high out of the back and land completely around in a delivery position (toes pointing at approximately 10 o'clock), minimizing or eliminating a pivot on the ball of the right foot. This move, referred to as backing into the throw, results from rotating too long on the left (overrotation) and does not produce as much momentum as the drive forward from the left foot without overrotation. Keep your left leg bent and bring it quickly from the liftoff across the circle to a position slightly left of a centerline and near the toe board, slightly open from the 6 o'clock line, allowing your hips to rotate through the delivery phase.

Delivery

Except for a very few throwers, most rotational shot-putters throw from a narrow base delivery position. The delivery stance should not be more than inside shoulder width (the outside of the feet should not be wider than the outside of the shoulders). A fairly narrow delivery stance is desirable. One of the major problems rotational throwers will encounter if they don't pivot properly through the delivery movement is throwing the shot like a glide thrower with a more linear right-to-left long pull action. The spinner must seek a "lift and rotate" action as the power source. This not only potentially increases force but will also allow the thrower to stay in the circle. The 7-foot (2.135 meter) circle probably limits very powerful throwers from driving as hard as they would like to out of the back of the circle, but by landing at midthrow in a tight stance well beyond the center of the circle with the weight back over the right leg, and by making a well-executed pivot, the thrower can explode upward and throw very successfully off a narrow base.

Lift your head and keep your chin up until you deliver the shot. Begin your left arm strike before grounding your left foot near the toe board. As you begin the counterclockwise turn into the delivery, sweep your left arm around from 10 o'clock to approximately 4 or 5 o'clock and stop it there, arresting the rotating shoulders and hopefully transferring some momentum to your throwing arm (see figure 3.14).

Follow-Through

The basic nature of the "lift and rotate" delivery in the spin technique makes the reverse almost required in the rotational shot put. Reversing is much discussed and unfortunately not much understood in the sense of saving a throw. The reverse, if an athlete does a reverse, should occur naturally as a result of the lifting and rotating forces applied in the delivery (figure 3.15). Teaching an athlete to reverse who does not do it naturally may be difficult; however, in the spin technique some sort of balance assistance in the form of a follow-through is usually necessary after delivery. Most rotational shot-putters are off the ground when the shot is delivered; some are quite high off the ground.

Figure 3.14 Spin delivery.

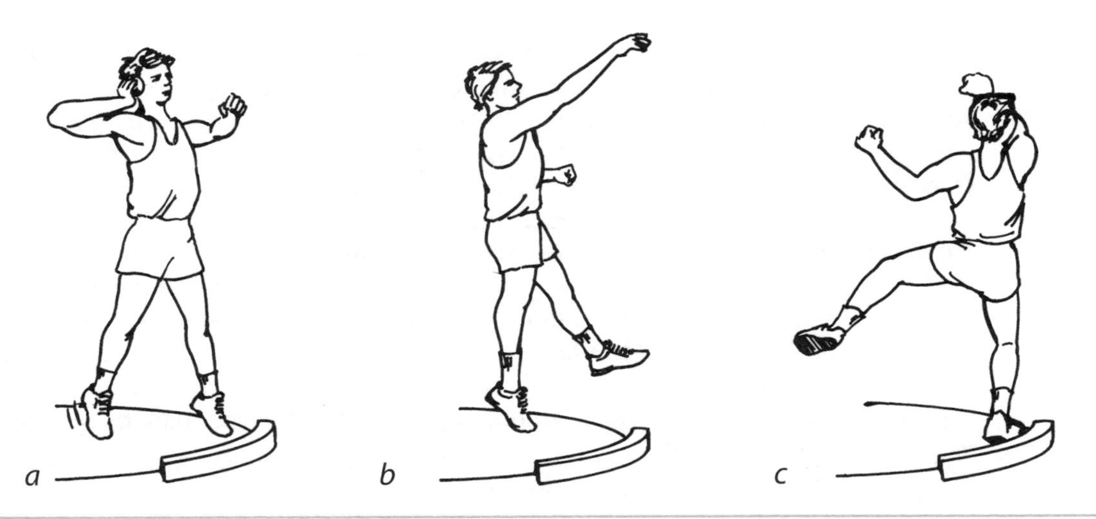

Figure 3.15 The reverse should occur naturally as a result of the lifting and rotating forces applied in the delivery.

While off the ground the left leg moves to the rear and the right leg moves forward to a single right-foot landing at the toe board. How to control the body after the landing in a single support to avoid fouling is a question with various possible answers. The following technique is offered as a way of arresting movement and bringing the body under control without fouling:

1. Land with your right foot turned perpendicular to the direction of the throw, toward 3 o'clock, and flat-footed, not on the ball of the foot. This helps with deceleration and balance.
2. Upon landing, extend your body with your right knee locked out and your right shoulder and arm held high and keep your center of mass tall, thus continuing the energy flow through the delivery.
3. Extend your left leg up toward the back of the ring along with your left arm. This lengthening of levers acts as a stabilizing movement/position for the final recovery.

Technique Drills

A world-class thrower can perform the total movement of the glide in less than one second. Consequently, the throw must become a reaction, a motor pattern executed without thought. Drills and repetition of similar movements are important in establishing proper motor patterns. The sequencing of the shot technique occurs so quickly that breaking it down into individual movements has merit, if the pieces are then put back together in a correct, complete technique.

Drills for the Glide Technique

The following drills are helpful when learning the glide technique.

POLISH STAND DRILL

The Polish stand is a three-part drill that works on the left side of the throw and the concept of delivering the shot as a result of the block. In the first position of the Polish stand, place both feet parallel at the toe board, facing the sector; your knees should be relaxed and slightly bent. The shot is at your neck in a normal carry position. Torque your body rotationally back as far as you can while still keeping balance on the balls of both feet (figure 3.16a). The untorquing action is initiated in the same manner as the standing position throw with your right foot rotating and pushing in, subsequently causing your hips to pull your upper body around. The blocking left side does not move, but rather pushes down, forming a firm, straight line from the left ankle, through the knee, hip, and shoulder. Block with the left arm and hand as described in the standing throw, but focus on holding them longer through the delivery of the shot.

In the second Polish stand position, move your right foot back 12 to 18 inches (30 to 46 centimeters) toward the center of the circle (figure 3.16b) and repeat the action described in the first position. Use greater shot and hip movement, but keep your focus on the left side block.

In the third position, move your right foot another 12 inches (32 centimeters) back toward the center of the circle (figure 3.16c) and repeat the movement again with even greater hip and shot movement. Repeat each position three or four times.

Figure 3.16 Three starting positions in the Polish stand drill: *(a)* both feet at the toe board, *(b)* right foot 12 inches toward the center of the circle, and *(c)* right foot 24 inches toward the center of the circle.

HALF STAND DRILL

The next progression of drills is called the half stand. The half stand works the left blocking leg position with linear force, eliminating a majority of the rotational force from the full stand position. Place your feet in the standard standing throw power position: left foot at the toe board and right foot in the middle of the ring (figure 3.17a). Shift your body weight to the right side and bend the right knee to receive the weight. The left knee is not locked out but rather used in a shock-absorber type of action. Do not rotate your upper body back but keep it perpendicular to the sector. Initiate the throw in the same manner as a standing throw: Rotate your right side in and push your heel out while transferring your weight up your left side (figure 3.17b). This creates a solid line from your ankle through your shoulder, with your shoulders finishing facing the sector with a solid left side block (figure 3.17c). The release point is at your highest position on the left leg. No reverse should occur other than for balance.

Figure 3.17 Half stand drill.

STOP DRILL

In the stop drill you drive out of the back of the ring, land in the power position, and hold the standing throw position. The stop drill is primarily a position- and balance-checking drill. For the athlete it is a method to feel if positions are correct. For the coach it is a method to slow down the movement to see that the athlete is in the correct balanced positions. Initially this drill should be done as a partnership between the coach and the athlete so that the athlete can learn the correct feel and the coach can correct what he or she sees if need be. After the coach and the athlete have established a good understanding, the drill will become more valuable for the athlete to do on his or her own. This drill should be used with care with athletes who already pause or stop in the middle of the circle. If the stopping or pausing is caused by balance problems, this drill will actually identify the problem. If, however, the athlete is simply in a bad habit of stopping, this drill could reinforce that habit.

LONG SHORT DRILL

The long short drill works the movement from the back of the ring to the middle with the right side and also emphasizes the left side block. Start the drill as if you were in a standing throw power position. With your right leg, "overstride" or take a longer step toward the back of the ring and place your right foot approximately halfway between the back and the center of the ring (figure 3.18a). From this position push off with your right foot and pull it under your body while rotating before landing. Your right foot should land rotated up to 90 degrees with your left side not moving significantly except to resist the force applied to it (figure 3.18b). As soon as your right foot touches the ground, push your right knee in and your heel out. Continue pushing up through the hip and begin to pull your right shoulder and shot (figure 3.18c); continue this up-and-around movement through the release.

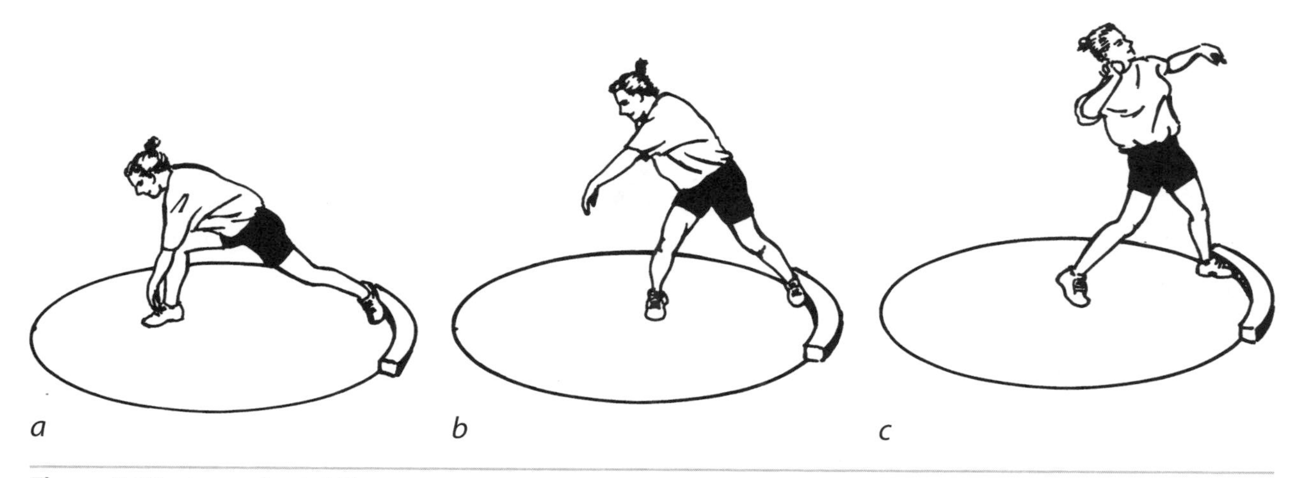

Figure 3.18 Long short drill.

STEP BACK DRILL

This drill can be performed in two different ways. Both methods focus on the shoulders staying in a torqued position and the right foot turning in the middle of the ring. This drill can also be an effective competitive alternative to the glide or the spin for those individuals who are uncomfortable using a single-support method of throwing.

(continued)

Figure 3.19 Step back drill.

The setup for the step back has you facing the back of the ring with equal weight on both feet, knees bent to approximately 90 degrees with shoulders down over your knees (figure 3.19a). To initiate the movement out of the back of the circle, shift your line of gravity toward the middle of the circle until you feel off balance as if you were going to fall into a chair. At this point take a small step with your left foot about halfway between the back of the ring and the middle, while shifting your weight toward the front of the ring (figure 3.19b). It is appropriate to jump subtly up and forward off your left leg as your right foot is pulled in under your body as you move to near the center of the circle. Rotate your right foot medially (in) so that when it lands it is rotated up to 90 degrees (pointing at 9 o'clock) from its starting position (figure 3.19c). Your center of mass continues to shift toward the throwing direction; however, the majority of your weight remains over your right foot until you begin the delivery out of the now established power position (figure 3.19d). Body torque should be at its maximum. Continue to turn your right foot inward and pull your right hip around as your body weight shifts to the lifting, blocking left leg (figure 3.19e) and force is driven from your legs, through your hips and torso, and out through your throwing arm into the implement.

Drills for the Spin Technique

Since movement, balance, and tempo are more important in the spin than simple power and position, drills to establish that moving balance are also more important to learn and practice. When learning drills and full technique, you should practice two basic types of movements. The first is the gymnastic type of drill, in which positions and timing should be the main focus, and body positions should garner the majority of physical attention. The second type of drill focuses on how power, speed, and energy are put into the positions, resulting in an evolving throw. Be sure to establish relatively solid drill positions before putting any real effort into the throwing delivery to establish balance and rhythm. The body learns through repetition, and attention to detail is important. Drills can even be filmed and observed for proper technique. Speed should always be saved for the accomplished learners. A concept of what the throw should look like is important, and it is also crucial to view basic technique, not simply your individual nuances due to your unique physical makeup. Once you have established basic positions in an event, you can then personalize your technique to accommodate your individual physical strengths.

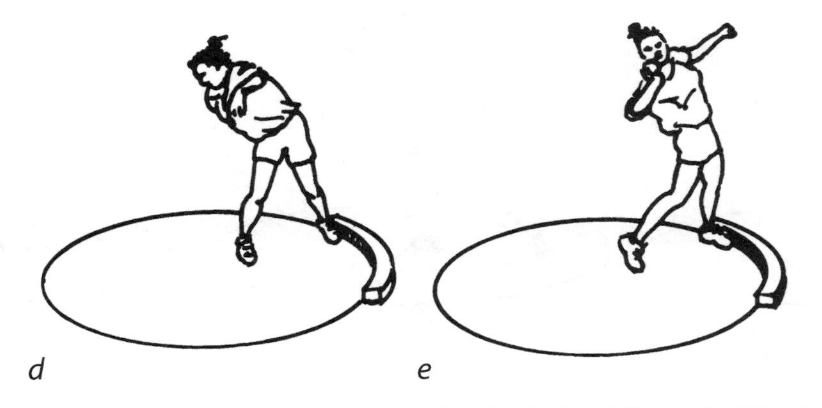

Figure 3.19 *(continued)*

180-DEGREE DRILL

The 180-degree drill, known by various other names such as power pivots or wheels, emphasizes the balanced rotating position over the right leg in the center of the circle. Start in a basic standing throw position with your right foot in the center of the circle, facing 180 degrees opposite the position of a standing throw (figure 3.20a). Pick up your left foot while pivoting on the ball of your right foot (figure 3.20b), and turn your entire body in the direction of the throw until you are in a normal standing throw position when your left foot comes back down (figure 3.20c). There should be no extra movement in any direction, up, down, back, or forward during the turn, and the relative position of your shoulders and hips should remain the same throughout the turn. The motion is accomplished by pivoting on your right foot, pushing your heel counterclockwise, and rotating your knee and hips counterclockwise. The movement of your left airborne leg and foot also contributes to the rotation in sync with the push of your right side. At this point you can either complete the movement with a standing throw (single 180 with throw) or continue into another 180 (multiple 180s with throw). You can perform multiple 180s with a pause in the power position, checking for correct stance, or in a continuous fashion.

Another variation of this drill may be accomplished outside the ring without throwing in a movement known as walking 180s or walking pivots. In this drill you walk in a line with your shoulders and hips in a straight line three steps until your right, or pivot, foot strikes to begin the drill. At that point rotate your right foot and leg inward, or counterclockwise, on the ground to begin the movement while lifting your left leg and tucking it behind your right leg, rotating into the standing throw position. After a brief pause in the standing throw position with your shoulders facing back and your hips parallel to the walking direction, rotate out of the power position and back into a normal straight-line walk preparing for the next 180 turn.

Figure 3.20 180-degree drill.

SOUTH AFRICAN DRILL

The major purpose of this drill is to teach the *linear drive* across the circle. Coaches and athletes should ensure that the footwork proceeds on a line from 12 to 6 o'clock. This drill incorporates most of the movements of an actual throw. One quarter of a turn at the beginning of the throw is eliminated. This drill can be very helpful in teaching the rhythm of the movement from the balanced position in the first single-support position.

The starting position for the South African drill is with your right leg outside the circle behind 12 o'clock, left foot on the line at 12 o'clock (figure 3.21a). Start the drill by rotating your body weight counterclockwise around a well-balanced position on the left leg and driving it across the circle as the right leg swings around the left (figure 3.21b). The left knee drops toward the center of the circle not unlike a sprint start. This is basically the same movement made in doing the South African Drill for the discus (see page 92) except, of course, the distance traveled across the circle is somewhat shorter. The drive is violent, but the right foot must ground down 12 to 18 inches (30 to 46 centimeters) more quickly than in the discus throw South African Drill. This grounding should be from 8 to 12 inches (20 to 30 centimeters) past the center of the circle. The left foot is swung around the right leg and rapidly brought down near the toe board in a relatively narrow stance (figure 3.21c). The delivery proceeds with both legs lifting and rotating into the delivery (figure 3.21d). When done properly, the action of the left leg and hip assist in lifting the body and also block the rotation of the right side as does the left arm just prior to delivery. The starting position of this drill can vary in the position of the right leg and the degree of bend at the hip and knees and the amount of swing of the right leg. Remember, the drill is to teach the *linear drive* and the *rhythm* and *body positions* of the throw. The movements should parallel what the thrower wants to achieve in an actual throw.

Figure 3.21 South African drill.

360-DEGREE DRILL

The 360-degree drill is intended to establish balance when turning in the rear of the circle from double support (two legs) to single support (one leg). It is the bridge movement between the South African and the full spin technique, the segment that allows a rotational movement to be translated into a linear movement. The importance of balance in the spin cannot be overstated, and nowhere is it more crucial than in the rear of the circle. The drill itself is prohibitively simple.

Begin at the rear of the circle with your weight balanced evenly on both feet and your knees slightly bent (figure 3.22a). After a short rotation of the shoulder plane to the right to gain momentum, perform a 360-degree toe turn on your left foot (figure 3.22b), picking up your right leg for balance and placing it back down in the starting position after your completion of the turn (figure 3.22c). Try to stay at the same height with both your hips and shoulders while turning, and try to keep your shoulders and hips in the same relative rotational position, not allowing your upper body to lead the movement ahead of your legs and hips. Imagine a line between your extended left arm and your bent left knee, the length of which should never change throughout the turn.

The value of the 360-degree drill is in learning how to turn in the rear of the circle while remaining in the proper balanced position, and what mechanics actually perform the turn correctly. Speed is also a determining factor of balance, as some athletes may be able to perform the drill quickly, but not slowly. More advanced throwers can maintain the beginning distance between the knees throughout the entire turn.

Factors that you may vary include the method and timing of the opening of your left foot and knee, the amount and force of your weight shift to the left to pick up your right leg, and how to complete the turn when momentum slows down. There are many variations of this drill as well, including multiple repeats and combinations working a 360-degree turn into other drills such as South Africans and full technique turns. If you have difficulty with a complete 360-degree turn, you may break it down into half or

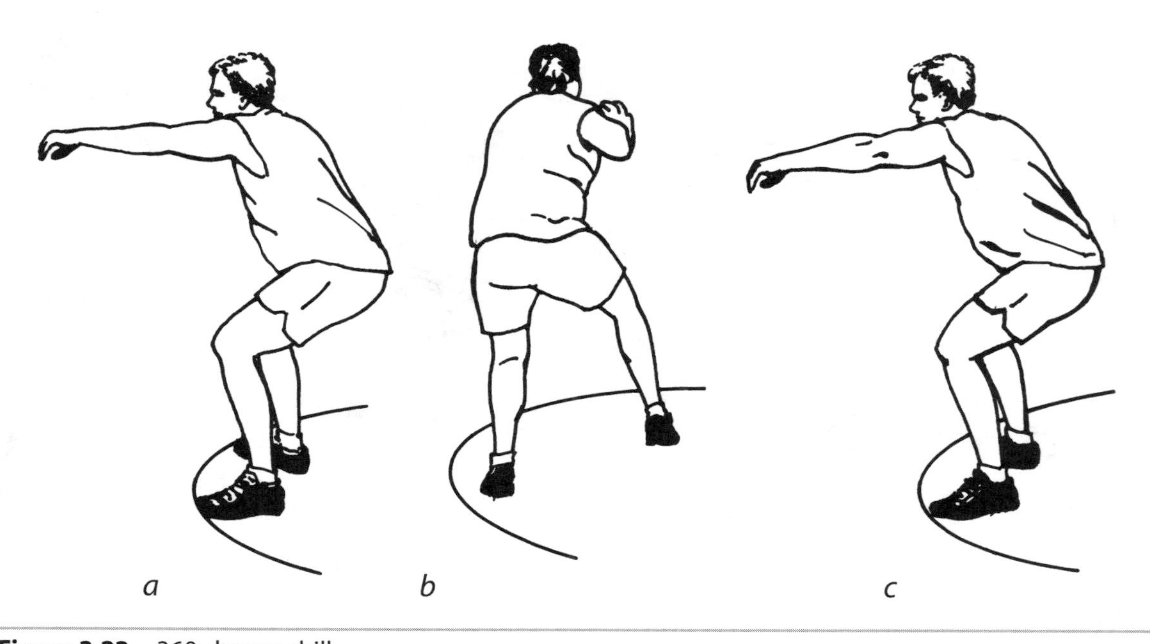

Figure 3.22 360-degree drill.

even quarter turns until you are able to master a complete turn. Once you have mastered this turn, you can then discover the proper positions and timing needed for the correct balanced linear drive into the power position.

Sample Strength Conditioning Workouts

The main objectives for preseason strength workouts include muscular conditioning with light to moderate resistance, and becoming familiar with correct technique. Early season workouts include high-level strength training; this is the "core" of the strength conditioning program. During championship season, strength workouts are low volume and high intensity; this is the peaking of the strength and power phase.

Table 3.1 is a sample weightlifting program for a thrower who may also compete in a fall sport. Year-round single-sport programs would have longer conditioning phases, with sets of 10 to 12 reps and greater emphasis on the technical development of the lifts. Strength development also should follow lines of necessary direction; athletes should spend more time on weaker areas rather than increasing already powerful regions. Flexibility, speed, body control, and injury prevention should be as much a part of weightlifting as strength development.

Sample Training Program

The total conditioning program of a shot-putter is a complex series of challenging activities carefully designed to bring an athlete to a competitive peak. The sample training program outlined in table 3.2 is a framework for developing such a conditioning experience.

Shot-putting has a rich history of crowd-pleasing events that have inspired and excited countless spectators and would be throwers. This chapter has described just what it takes to become a successful competitor. Very satisfying, if not glorious, results will come to those who, with consistent effort and commitment, seek them.

Table 3.1 Strength Conditioning Workouts for Shot Put

PHASE 1: PRESEASON (6-8 WEEKS, 4 DAYS PER WEEK)	
10 reps = 60%, 4-6 reps = 75-85% of a 1 RM lift	
Day 1: Olympic / Leg and Back	
Power clean	5 sets × 4-6 reps
Back squat	5 sets × 4-6 reps
Lunge	5 sets × 4-6 reps
Hamstring curl	3 sets × 10 reps
Knee extension	3 sets × 10 reps
Day 2: Upper Body	
Bench press	5 sets × 4-6 reps
Dumbbell incline press	5 sets × 4-6 reps
Dumbbell bench press	5 sets × 4-6 reps
Lat pull-down	3 sets × 10 reps
Dumbbell lat raise	3 sets × 10 reps
Day 3: Olympic / Leg and Back	
Power snatch	5 sets × 4-6 reps
Front squat	5 sets × 4-6 reps
Leg press	5 sets × 10-15 reps
Straight leg dead lift	5 sets × 10 reps
Day 4: Upper Body	
Incline press	5 sets × 4-6 reps
Dumbbell rows	5 sets × 4-6 reps
Flat fly	5 sets × 4-6 reps
Triceps / biceps	3 sets × 10 reps
PHASE 2: EARLY SEASON (4-6 WEEKS, 3 DAYS PER WEEK)	
5 reps = 80%, 3 reps = 90% of 1RM lift	
Day 1: Power	
Bench press	3 × 5, 3 × 3
Back squat	3 × 5, 3 × 3
Straight leg dead lift	4 × 5
Day 2: Power	
Power clean	3 × 5, 3 × 3
Dumbbell incline	4 × 5
Lunge	4 × 5

Day 3: Speed	
Quick snatch	4 × 5
Quick squat	4 × 5
PHASE 3: CHAMPIONSHIP SEASON (2-4 WEEKS, 2 DAYS PER WEEK)	
Day 1: Power	
Bench press	5, 4, 3, 2, 2, 2
Power clean	5, 4, 3, 2, 2, 2
Back squat	5, 4, 3, 2, 2, 2
Day 2: Speed	
Quick snatch	4 × 5
Quick squat	4 × 5

Table 3.2 Sample Training Plan for Shot Put

	Throwing	Lifting	Running	Bounding	Medicine ball
Conditioning cycle 4-6 weeks	• Drills– several • Easy throws 3K , 3.8K • Technique work • 2-3 × week/event	• High repetitions • Combination lifts • 50-60% • 4 × 10-12 • 3 × week • Focus on large muscle groups	• Circuits • Ladders • Body circuits • 2-3 × week	• Grass bounding • Sand bounding • Linear direction • 2 × week •	• Can be part of circuit • General strength 3-4K • 2-3 sets of 10 • Can be part of drills
Rest/recovery phase 1-2 weeks Testing	• Overhead • Underhand measured	• Clean • Snatch • Squat • Bench press	• 40 m timed •	• Standing long jump • Vertical jump	
Strength phase 6-8 weeks	• Throw 3 × week • 4.2K, 5K, 4K • Vary weights for specific strength • Minimum 25 throws/session • Drill 2 × week • Discus heavy 1 × week • Balls or plates	• Percentage lifting • 80-85% of max • 5-6 reps • Change as the body tells you • No more than 10 lb • Minor lifts 4 × 10-12 • Two per area especially back •	• Body circuits 1 × week • 75-100 m × 6-8 • 2 × week 1 × timed	• 2 × week • 1 × integrated into weight training • 1 × varied direction •	• Upper-body plyometrics • Integrate drills and technique • 2-3 sets of 10
Rest/recovery phase 1 week testing Extra days off	• Throw 4K • 2 × week • Under/over measured	• Clean • Snatch • Squat • Bench press	• 40 m timed	• Standing long jump • Vertical jump •	

(continued)

Table 3.2 *(continued)*

	Throwing	Lifting	Running	Bounding	Medicine ball
Precompetition phase/power phase 6 weeks	• Throw 3 × week • Early season meets count as practice • Increase the amount of throws • Introduce light implements 4.2K, 4K, 3K	• Modified pyramid • 10, 8, 6, 4, 3, 3, 3 to 90-95% • Focus changes to power/moving the weight fast • Minor lifts 3 × 10 • One per area	• 30-40-50-40-30 × 2 • Stadium running • Hill runs	• Multidirection • Stadium • Hurdle	• Upper-body plyometrics • Lighter balls, quicker • Mimic drills • Midsection work
Rest precompetition 1 week just throwing Second week—	• Measured over/under • Throw 4K, 3.8K, 3K • 3 × week	• Clean • Snatch • Squat • Bench press	• 40m timed	• Standing long jump • Vertical jump	
Competition phase 6-8 weeks	• Throw 4K, 3.8K, 3K • Emphasis is technique and speed	• Lifting pyramid • 6, 4, 2, 2, 1, 1 • Minor lifts 2-3 × 10 • One per area	• 1 × week timed emphasis speed	• Reaction—emphasis speed	• 1 × week technique emphasis speed • 10 reps

Resting allows you to recover and reduces the amount of repetitive trauma to the body.
Testing allows you to see progress or lack thereof during the cycle; a 10% reduction in scores is a significant amount and workout should be curtailed to reduce/avoid injury.
For double peaks a modified power phase would be inserted after the competition phase. This can be as short as one week or as long as a regular power phase, depending on the situation and athlete, injury, etc.

Discus

Jay Silvester

© The Sporting Image

The discus throw that we know today evolved from the discus throw that was part of the ancient Olympic Pentathlon, which also included the long jump, javelin throw, stade race, and wrestling.

Myron's classic statue *Discobolus* is a stirring portrayal of the human body in a pose with a discus. To modern throwers, the position depicted in the *Discobolus* statue has some similarities to the "power position" achieved just before the delivery. We know that ancient throwers did not throw from a circle; they used a run-up area similar to that used in the javelin throw. Nor were the weight and size of the discus standard from competition to competition. Disci from 4 to 15 pounds (1.8 to 6.8 kilograms) are on display in Greek museums.

When the modern Olympic Games began in 1896, there were two versions of throwing the discus. One was a standing throw from a sloping platform (ancient style), and the other was a "free style." Gradually the event moved away from the standing throw to throwing from a square area. However, by 1912 the discus throw was contested, as it is today, from a 2.5-meter-diameter circle.

For many years these throwing circles were outlined on dirt or grass. The dirt throwing circles were the favorite because they could be carefully watered and tamped to produce a relatively stable and consistent throwing surface. "Field" shoes with one-inch spikes were the shoe of choice for shot and discus throwers. With such shoes the dirt circles were quickly "chewed up." Throwers spent many hours grooming the throwing circles. In the 1950s circles constructed first with asphalt and then concrete made their appearance. Throwing shoes became spikeless flats. Because of its consistent surface and almost zero maintenance, concrete became the favorite, and that is the standard today. There are still many friction problems with concrete. Circles are frequently either too slippery or too abrasive for the best footing, but throwers make do.

The rules describing the diameter, thickness at various points, symmetry, smoothness of surfaces, and minimum weight of the discus have been the same for many years. However, the material of construction and the rim weighting of the discus have changed. Variable degrees of rim weighting are much tested and researched in modern discus construction.

Table 4.1 lists the world records for men and women since we started keeping such records. It is interesting to note that the world records have not changed since 1986 for the men and 1988 for the women.

To be successful, discus throwers must learn to move through the throwing technique at high velocity, with one or more periods of rapid acceleration, while maintaining precise control of the body and the implement. Great speed and precision are required for success in most, if not all, sports of the 21st century.

The challenge to the thrower is to hit each mechanical position precisely while moving at very high velocity with very efficient rhythm (timing or sequencing of the motion). The challenge in writing this book is to describe the throw in a way that allows you to learn the positions and feel the speed and rhythm.

Rhythm and Mechanics

The emphasis on mechanical positions in this chapter might leave you feeling that a discus thrower is like a robot, mechanically moving from one position to another without fluidity or grace. Nothing could be more incorrect for this or any other throwing event. Indeed, rhythm, or beautifully sequencing the various mechanical actions into a fluidly accelerating whole, is of far greater importance than moving through a throw with precise attention to each body position. In this chapter I hope to impart not only a cognitive understanding of the various positions or phases of the total throw but also ultimately a feel for them as part of a rhythmic whole.

Throwing Keys

There are many "throwing keys" (technical emphases) that an athlete might attend to, perhaps thousands. Each thrower must go through the process of experiencing this myriad of technical focus points, gradually eliminating those that have no lasting positive effect on performance while working hard to make the "golden keys" (those that produce superior performance) part of his or her automatic motor pattern. It is my experience that each individual has only a few throwing keys that will consistently have a significant impact on how far or how well that person throws.

Almost every technical emphasis seems to "feel good" the first time an athlete tries it. However, after the second or third workout most of those technical emphases no longer cause the throw to feel better or fly a bit farther. Over

Table 4.1 World-Record Holders in the Discus

MEN'S WORLD RECORDS			
Record distance	**Record holder**	**Location**	**Date**
47.58m (156' 1")	James Duncan USA	New York, USA	27 May 1912
47.61m (156' 2")	Thomas Leib USA	Chicago, USA	14 Sept. 1924
47.89m (157' 1 1/2")	Glen Hartranft USA	San Francisco, USA	2 May 1925
48.20m (158' 2")	Clarence Hauser USA	Palo Alto, USA	3 Apr. 1926
49.90m (163' 8")	Eric Krentz USA	Palo Alto, USA	17 May 1930
51.03m (167' 5")	Paul Jessup USA	Pittsburgh, USA	23 Aug. 1930
51.73m (172' 0")	Harold Andersson SWE	Oslo, NOR	25 Aug. 1934
53.10m (174' 2")	Willi Schroder GER	Magdeburg, GER	28 Apr. 1935
53.26m (174' 9")	Archie Harris USA	Palo Alto, USA	20 June 1941
53.34m (175' 0")	Adolfo Consolini ITA	Milan, ITA	26 Oct. 1941
54.23m (177' 11")	Adolfo Consolini ITA	Milan, ITA	14 Apr. 1946
54.93m (180' 3")	Robert Fitch USA	Minneapolis, USA	8 June 1946
55.33m (181' 6")	Adolfo Consolini ITA	Milan, ITA	10 Oct. 1948
56.46m (185' 3")	Fortune Gordien USA	Lisbon, POR	9 July 1949
56.97m (186' 11")	Fortune Gordien USA	Hameenlinna, FIN	14 Aug. 1949
57.93m (190' 0")	Simeon Iness USA	Lincoln, USA	20 June 1953
58.10m (190' 7")	Fortune Gordien USA	Pasadena, USA	11 July 1953
59.28m (194' 6")	Fortune Gordien USA	Pasadena, USA	22 Aug. 1953
59.91m (196' 6")	Edmund Piatkowski POL	Warsaw, POL	14 June 1959
59.91m (196' 6")	Richard Babka USA	Walnut, USA	12 Aug. 1960
60.56m (198' 8")	L Jay Silvester USA	Frankfurt AM, W GER	11 Aug. 1961
60.72m (199' 2")	L Jay Silvester USA	Brussels, BEL	20 Aug. 1961
61.10m (200' 5")	Al Oerter USA	Los Angeles, USA	18 May 1962
61.64m (202' 3")	Vladimir Trusenyev USSR	Leningrad, USSR	4 June 1962
62.45m (204' 10")	Al Oerter USA	Chicago, USA	1 July 1962
62.62m (205' 5")	Al Oerter USA	Walnut, USA	27 Apr. 1963
62.94m (206' 6")	Al Oerter USA	Walnut, USA	25 Apr. 1964
64.55m (211' 9")	Ludvik Danek CZH	Turnov, CZH	2 Aug. 1964
65.22m (213' 11")	Ludvik Danek CZH	Sokolov, CZH	12 Oct. 1965
66.54m (218' 4")	L Jay Silvester USA	Modesto, USA	25 May 1968
68.40m (224' 5")	L Jay Silvester USA	Reno, USA	18 Sept. 1968
68.40m (224' 5")	Richard Bruch SWE	Stockholm, SWE	5 July 1972
69.08m (226' 8")	John Powell USA	Long Beach, USA	4 May 1975
69.18m (226' 11")	Mac Wilkins USA	Walnut, USA	24 Apr. 1976
69.80m (229' 0")	Mac Wilkins USA	San Jose, USA	1 May 1976
70.24m (230' 5")	Mac Wilkins USA	San Jose, USA	1 May 1976
70.86m (232' 6")	Mac Wilkins USA	San Jose, USA	1 May 1976
71.16m (233' 5")	Wolfgang Schmidt GDR	Berlin, E GER	9 Aug. 1978
71.86m (235' 9")	Yuriy Dumchev USSR	Moscow, USSR	29 May 1983
74.08m (243' 0")	Jurgen Schult GDR	Neubrandenburg, E GER	6 June 1986

(continued)

Table 4.1 ***(continued)***

WOMEN'S WORLD RECORDS			
Record distance	**Record holder**	**Location**	**Date**
48.31m (158' 6")	Gisela Mauermayer GER	Berlin, GER	11 July 1936
53.25m (174' 8")	Nina Dumbadze USSR	Moscow, USSR	8 Aug. 1948
53.37m (175' 1")	Nina Dumbadze USSR	Gori, USSR	27 May 1951
53.61m (175' 11")	Nina Ponomaryeva USSR	Odessa, USSR	9 Aug. 1952
57.04m (187' 2")	Nina Dumbadze USSR	Tbilisi, USSR	18 Oct. 1952
57.15m (167' 6")	Tamara Press USSR	Rome, ITA	12 Sept. 1960
57.43m (188' 5")	Tamara Press USSR	Moscow, USSR	15 July 1961
58.06m (190' 6")	Tamara Press USSR	Soifia, BUL	1 Sept. 1961
58.98m (193' 6")	Tamara Press USSR	London, GBR	20 Sept. 1961
59.29m (194' 6")	Tamara Press USSR	Moscow, USSR	18 May 1963
59.70m (195' 10")	Tamara Press USSR	Moscow, USSR	11 Aug. 1965
61.26m (201' 0")	Liesel Westermann FRG	Sao Paulo, BRA	5 Nov. 1967
61.64m (202' 3")	Christine Speilberg GDR	Regis Breitingen, E GER	26 May 1968
62.54m (202' 3")	Liesel Westermann FRG	Werdohl, W GER	24 July 1968
62.70m (205' 8")	Liesel Westermann FRG	Berlin, E GER	18 June 1969
63.96m (209' 10")	Liesel Westermann FRG	Hamberg, W GER	27 Sept. 1969
64.22m (210' 8")	Faina Melnik USSR	Helsinki, FIN	12 Aug. 1971
64.88m (212' 10")	Faina Melnik USSR	Munich, W GER	4 Sept. 1971
65.42m (214' 7")	Faina Melnik USSR	Moscow, USSR	31 May 1972
65.48m (214' 10")	Faina Melnik USSR	Augsburg, W GER	24 June 1972
66.76m (219' 0")	Faina Melnik USSR	Moscow, USSR	4 Aug. 1972
67.32m (220' 10")	Argentina Menis ROM	Constanta, ROM	23 Sept. 1972
67.44m (221' 3")	Faina Melnik USSR	Riga, USSR	25 May 1973
67.58m (221' 9")	Faina Melnik USSR	Moscow, USSR	10 July 1973
69.48m (227' 11")	Faina Melnik USSR	Edinburgh, GBR	7 Sept. 1973
69.90m (229' 4")	Faina Melnik USSR	Prague, CZH	27 May 1974
70.20m (230' 4")	Faina Melnik USSR	Zurich, SUI	20 Aug. 1975
70.50m (231' 3")	Faina Melnik USSR	Sochi, USSR	24 Apr. 1976
70.72m (232' 0")	Evelin Jahl GDR	Dresden, E GER	12 Aug. 1978
71.50m (234' 7")	Evelin Jahl GDR	Potsdam, E GER	10 May 1980
71.80m (235' 7")	Maria Petkova BUL	Sofia, BUL	13 July 1980
73.26m (240' 4")	Galina Savinkova USSR	Leselidze, USSR	22 May 1983
73.36m (240' 8")	Irina Meszynski GDR	Prague, CZH	26 Aug. 1984
74.56m (244' 7")	Zdenka Silhava CZH	Nitra, CZH	26 Aug. 1984
76.80m (252' 0"v	Gabriela Reinsch GDR	Neubrandenburg, E GER	9 July 1988

time (after many throws) a few of these technical concepts seem to produce positive results consistently. These are the *golden keys* for that athlete. These keys may or may not be the same for other athletes. The challenge to the coach and the athlete is to find these helpful keys and then work on them until the athlete develops a fluid, technically efficient throw.

Feelings and Feedback

To the athlete everything about the discus throw technique is a feeling. All throwers generally know what a good throw feels like. Although a 120-foot (37-meter) thrower doesn't know how a 200-foot (61-meter) throw feels, he or she knows how a "good" throw feels. A good throw is what coaches and athletes seek.

Athletes *must* have the ability to focus their minds on any body part and feel what happens when they try to make a particular movement. While the athlete can discern whether the movement felt good, it is also important to know where the feet and other body parts were while making the movement as well as whether it looked or felt good from the coach's perspective. Feedback from the coach, other athletes, or videotape can be very important.

Athletes need to know the distance of most throws. The very important test of all technical keys is this: Did this technical key, when executed reasonably well, improve or at least maintain good performance? To summarize, then, throwers are helped by two kinds of feedback:

1. Their own sensations
2. The coach's information, including video, comments on rhythm, feet, and body positions, and the distance of the throw

Coaches need to understand that athletes can normally focus on only *one* throwing key on any given throw. Coaches need to *see* mechanical positions and *feel* good rhythm kinesthetically to teach it. They help athletes by carefully crafting comments, physically showing positions or rhythm, and by using video to consider rhythm and positions in more depth. Coaches and athletes must work together to develop a throw that contains beautiful rhythm and sound technical positions, and feels great.

When an inexperienced thrower throws the discus for the first time, the results will be predictably poor. The process from that point to becoming a competent thrower is one that includes becoming conditioned and learning and refining skills (both physical and psychological). While large leaps sometimes happen in short periods of time, most improvement comes rather slowly. Each small technical or conditioning improvement results in the ability to throw farther.

Many technical concepts are discussed in this book. Each one holds potential for longer throws. How much longer cannot be predicted because results differ among throwers. Technical keys that work well for one thrower may not work as well for another. However, it is true that some positions or movements are common among better throwers. These will be amply emphasized.

Discus Fundamentals

It is possible to discuss technique in the discus throw without addressing the differences in technical movements, or style, among throwers. I could continue referring to the differences among throwers as variations of one general technique as has been done since at least the 1920s. However, after careful consideration I have decided that in this book I will describe two styles of throwing the discus:

1. Reversing technique
2. Nonreversing technique

Describing the techniques in this manner will make it easier for you to learn how to teach or master each. Even so, many characteristics of the two techniques are the same. This section addresses issues that are common to both techniques, including the proper way to grip the discus, the orbit or path of the discus, separation of the upper and lower body, control of the discus at release, and prethrow preparation.

Discus Grip

Most accomplished throwers grip the discus with all fingers rather close together—the first two fingers very close together (less than 1/8 inch apart) and the next two not spread very far, perhaps 1/4 to 1/2 inch. The thumb lies alongside the index finger separated by about 1 inch. See figure 4.1a.

The contact points of the discus and the hand are very important. The discus is held firmly in the fingers just beyond the distal (last) joints. The thumb contacts the discus on the outside of the thumb from the last joint to the end of the thumb. Light to moderate thumb pressure is necessary to produce good flight. If you look carefully at the hand of a good thrower holding the discus, you will see a *cupped* or somewhat *clawed* hand (figure 4.1b). The discus is in contact with the muscle pads around the palm both medial to the little finger and the thumb, but not with the palm or any portion of the fingers other than that already described.

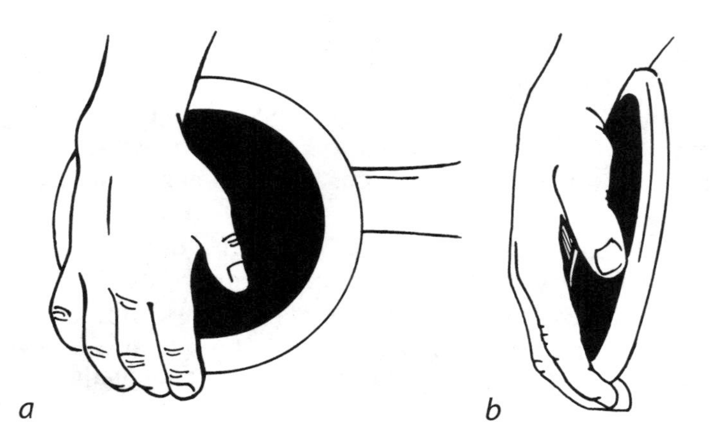

Figure 4.1 *(a)* Discus grip. Notice that the hand is placed on the rear two thirds of the discus. *(b)* Side view of the discus grip, showing the cupped hand and slightly flexed wrist.

The hand of an experienced thrower appears to be placed on the rear two thirds of the implement, as shown in figure 4.1a. Gripping and carrying the discus in this manner helps a thrower develop a release that transfers maximal energy with beautiful flight. Good flight and energy transfer result from a combination of forces and control movements that come together properly at release.

Discus Orbit or Path

The words *orbit* and *path* are used interchangeably to describe the discus movement/positions from the starting stance through delivery. This path will be discussed here at the outset, then again at each stage of the throw.

In the early part of the 20th century, the term *wave* was used to define the movement of the discus as it was carried or moved through the circle from start to delivery. This wave concept is generally applicable today. The major technical unknown is how high and low the discus should move during its wavelike journey from start through delivery. The general answer is that each athlete needs to experiment to find what feels best. However, moderate ups and downs often feel better than extremes. Try both the extremes and more moderate positions of the discus before choosing.

When the discus is in a position directly opposite the throwing direction (12 o'clock), it is carried low (figure 4.2a). This low position occurs twice during the throw, once near the beginning of the movement just after right foot pushoff (figure 4.6e, page 75), and again in the center of the circle in the midstage of the delivery motion (figure 4.6j, page 77).

When the discus is in the throwing direction (6 o'clock), it is moved through a relatively high path (figure 4.2b). This "discus in the throwing direction" happens three times during the throw: first during windup, then in the center of the circle just at the beginning of the power position, and again as the discus is delivered. It is *not* crucial that the discus be carried high during the windup. The most neglected and perhaps most important of these high discus positions occurs at the beginning of the power position in the center of the circle (figure 4.6i, page 76). By expending energy to get the discus *up* at this

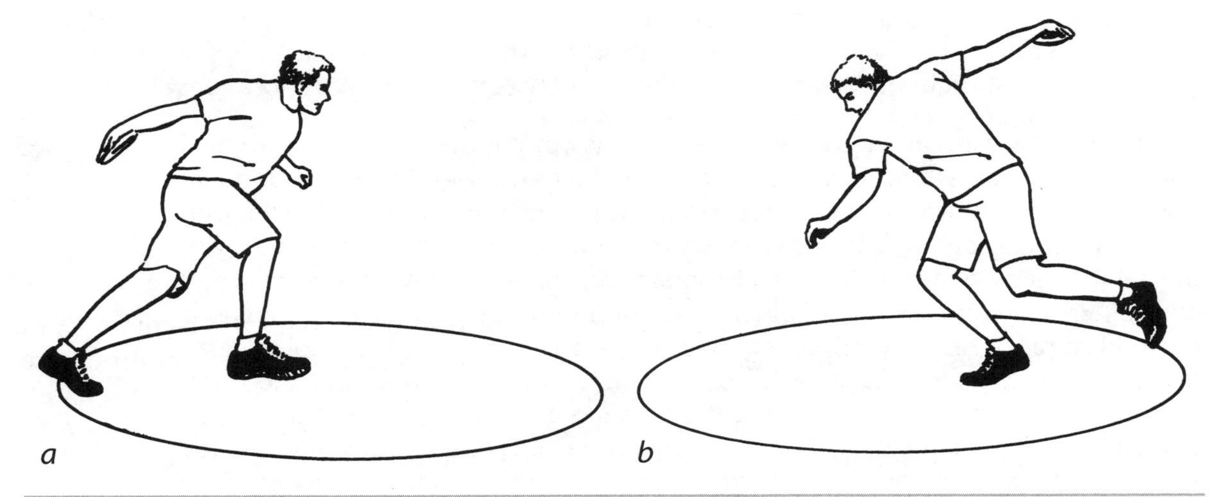

Figure 4.2 *(a)* Discus at low point, directly opposite the throwing direction. *(b)* Discus at high point, in the direction of the throw.

midpoint of the throw, an advantage in acceleration results from gravitational assistance when the discus is pulled down from this high position as the delivery begins. This concept will be treated in greater detail in the discussion of the delivery motion of the throw.

The majority of this high-low movement of the discus is the natural result of the movement of the shoulders; however, purposeful raising and lowering of the discus is helpful and often necessary to teach or learn the best positions.

Separation of the Upper and Lower Body

A state of body and mind is helpful to get the proper feeling when you move through a windup or any other phase of the throw. I refer to this mental state as separation of the lower and upper body. The lower body (hips and legs) is a very active, hardworking entity that drives you around and across the circle, while the upper body (torso, arms, neck, and head), in a very relaxed manner, gets the discus up and back and then waits. The upper body waits (stalls, or slows in its rotation) and relaxes (the left arm, if used properly, is very helpful in this action) while the lower body torques (winds up) the muscles, tendons, ligaments, fascia, and any other elastic tissue as much as possible. (See figure 4.6e-i on pages 75-76 to observe the relaxed torque of the upper body.) Then, at the last possible moment, the torqued body unwinds with a tremendous flow of energy from the lifting and driving up and around legs, to the hips, torso, shoulder, arm, and hand. (See figure 4.6i-l on pages 76-77.) I call this the long pull. The long pull is a marvelous feeling. Approximately 70 to 80 percent of the release velocity is derived from this lifting, unwinding, and driving delivery motion.

Releasing the Discus for Efficient Energy Transfer and Maximum Aerodynamic Efficiency

When delivering the discus, energy transfer and the most advantageous discus orientation for efficient flight in the atmosphere are crucial. The shape of the discus gives it its aerodynamic quality. A discus released with correct aerodynamic orientation will fly farther than one thrown incorrectly. For most situations the best discus orientation for the most efficient energy transfer and best flight at release is with *the outside edge down about 5 to 10 degrees and the leading edge slightly up (2 to 5 degrees),* as shown in figure 4.3. If there is a direct right cross wind (90 degrees from the right), the outside edge should be *level* at release, not down.

Prethrow Routine

You will benefit greatly from having a prethrow routine that settles your nerves and prepares you mentally to make a good throw, particularly in competitive situations. This routine may begin before entering the circle or as you enter, but be sure to develop a comfortable system of preparing to make a throw. The prethrow routine should include the following:

Figure 4.3 The ideal orientation of the discus at release is with the outside edge down about 5 to 10 degrees and the leading edge slightly up about 2 to 5 degrees.

1. Relaxing visualization of the direction and flight of the discus
2. Careful entry into the circle and exact positioning of the feet
3. Preliminary rhythmic windup(s)
4. Windup key that puts the body on automatic

Reversing Technique

In discus throwing, the term *reverse* derives from the action that naturally occurs for most discus throwers when using the side arm sling. The feet *reverse* their delivery positions. For example, a right-handed thrower would deliver the discus with the left foot forward and the right foot back. The violence of the throw (lifting and driving the right hip, shoulder, and arm into the throw) usually results in the right side being driven to the front while the left side rotates to the rear—thus the term *reversing,* which is short for reversing the positions of the feet.

Starting Stance

To properly orient a thrower or coach in the circle, two things are necessary:

1. Clock system imposed on the circle with 6 o'clock as the direction of the throw (figure 4.4)
2. Line bisecting the circle from 12 to 6 o'clock

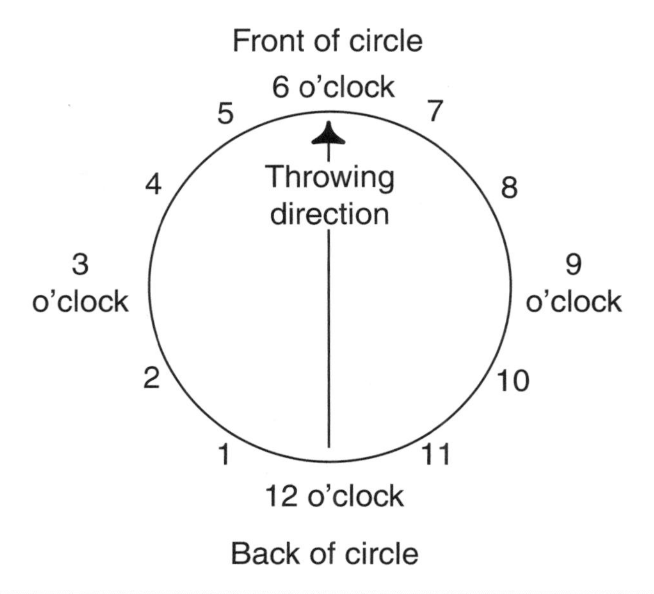

Figure 4.4 Discus circle, with 6 o'clock being the direction of the throw.

To be in the proper starting stance, face 180 degrees away from the throwing direction; your feet should be wider than shoulder width (figure 4.5). Your left foot should be either on the line or slightly left toward 11 o'clock. All phases of the throw are important, but I consider the phases from the start through the end of the first single-support phase as the most crucial. Double support means two feet on the ground. Single support refers to only one foot on the ground. Your feet should be wider than shoulder width for stability and also for the potential to move from the right to the left foot to allow somewhat of a running start. By running start I'm referring to the body mass moving over a range (width of stance) to develop momentum before moving across the circle.

Figure 4.5 Starting stance.

Windup

It is important that you develop a *relaxed rhythm* during this move. Strive to keep your upper body relaxed. In the windup position 60 to 70 percent of your body weight should be on your right foot. Keep your knees bent (figure 4.6a). The beginning movements demand great balance. Stay low or move from high to low to achieve this balance. Your right foot stays planted, but your left foot turns freely with your left knee bending medially. Contact the circle with your left foot on the medial side of the ball of the foot or on the toe of the foot. Because your right foot stays planted, you will feel some torque in your right leg. At the completion of the windup (figure 4.6a) you should be standing with some bend in your legs and hips (about 80 to 90 percent of normal height). *A key for consideration:* Some throwers like to develop a feeling of torque at the completion of the windup that is *very similar to if not the same as the torque developed in the power position.*

Most accomplished throwers take only one windup. I took three. Some beginners take too many. Choose a number between one and three and make it work for you. As your upper body winds back, carry the discus high but not higher than shoulder height. Wind your throwing arm back until your arms are perpendicular to the throwing direction. Some throwers may not go that far and some may go farther.

First Double-Support Through First Single-Support Phase

As you complete the windup and begin turning into the throw, transfer your body weight to your left leg (figure 4.6, b through c). Lower your center of mass and pull your left foot down on the inside ball of your foot (figure 4.6b) and rotate until your foot is pointing at 7 or 8 o'clock (figure 4.6, c through e). Keeping it relatively straight, swing your left arm wide and to the left. Some throwers straighten the left arm, others do not, but all sweep it from about 2 or 1 o'clock around to between 6 and 4:30 o'clock, essentially over the left

(continued)

Figure 4.6 Reversing technique.

thigh. Do not rotate your left arm ahead of your left thigh until perhaps after left foot liftoff. When your left arm reaches approximately the 4:30 position, it stalls to begin assisting the slowing of the upper body necessary to develop maximal torque for the delivery phase.

Most beginners overrotate out of the back of the circle with both feet and their upper body. Associated with this overrotation is throwing the left arm far ahead of the left thigh completely around to a position pointing to the back of the circle—12 o'clock. Coaches should work hard to help beginners *stop the rotation of the left foot at the 7 o'clock position* and keep the left arm over the left thigh as they turn out of the back of the circle.

The right leg is picked up relatively early (beginning the first single-support phase) and swung *wide* and at a *low to medium height* around the left leg (figure 4.6, c through f). Proper use of the right leg is very important in discus throwing. The pickup of the right leg can only occur when the body weight has been transferred to the left (figure 4.6c). Some coaches advocate delaying the right leg pickup as long as possible. Others suggest picking it up early. The difference in timing of either an early or delayed pickup is not large, but the feelings are definitely different. In all cases right leg pickup can only occur as the body weight is shifted to the left leg and the rotating left knee has spread the knees, putting the muscles of both left and right inner thighs on some stretch. The difference in early and late pickup is the degree of inner leg stretch allowed before the right foot clears the circle. If a thrower delays the right leg pickup until the right shoulder passes the right hip (figure 4.7a), there is a necessary "catching up" that the right hip must do to create torque for the delivery. This catching up can easily create a jerk in the throw as the shoulders are delayed or the hips are forcefully driven ahead. Picking up the right foot as soon as possible, thereby keeping the right shoulder slightly behind the right hip from the start, would appear to be the better alternative (figure 4.7b). As the movement proceeds around the left leg and into the circle, the degree of torque between the upper torso and the hips is minimal.

(continued)

Figure 4.6 *(continued)*

Figure 4.7 *(a)* Late right leg pickup, where the discus passes the right hip long before the leg is lifted. The left arm is dramatically overrotated, a common mistake for beginners. *(b)* Early right leg pickup, where the right leg is lifted off the circle before the discus arrives at the right hip. This technique is preferred over a late pickup.

Importance of the Movement Around the Left Leg at the Beginning of the Throw

This section describes how a good discus thrower moves around the left leg and enters the circle. (See figure 4.6, a through f.) *This is arguably the most important movement in the entire throw.* Here are some helpful keys:

- Stay relatively low (bent legs); you can "fall" or "drop" into this low position.
- Sweep the right leg at a low or medium height.
- Sit and lean toward 9:30 (to the left rear) as you *begin* the rotating drive out of the back of the circle.

Figure 4.6 *(continued)*

- Do not let your line of gravity move too quickly toward the throwing direction; move primarily left in the initial stages when going from double to single support.
- Feel that you have moved left primarily by shifting your weight left with only a small degree of rotation; then post your left foot pointing at about 7 o'clock, and swing your right side around it as you lean and drive into the circle.

With your left foot pointing at about 7 o'clock, your left leg becomes somewhat of a post. Swing your body around this post; your natural lower-body lean (shoulders remain rather level) in the throwing direction will place your line of gravity directly in front (toward the throwing direction) of your left foot (figure 4.6d).

Bend your right leg as it clears the circle (figure 4.6e). Be sure to keep your right leg relatively low and out away from your left knee and sweep it wide around to the 10 o'clock area. When your sweeping right leg is at about 12 o'clock, it is quite straight (figure 4.8); then, as you rotate into the throwing direction, flex your right leg again and lift it slightly (figure 4.6f).

Figure 4.8 Right leg at 12 o'clock and straight.

This slight lifting is your right leg's contribution to the subtle jump that occurs as your left leg thrusts your body forward and up, clearing the back of the circle. Additionally, if your right leg did not bend and lift at this juncture of the throw, it would possibly, because of the acute lean of your body, hit the surface of the circle. The discus is carried rather low and behind the right hip around the back of the circle. (See figure 4.2a on page 71.)

Continue the flexed rotation of your left leg until your body begins facing the direction of the throw (figure 4.6e).

At this point you should experience a rapid left leg thrust that is timed with the lower-body lean to drive your body forcefully across the circle with a subtle lift or jump.

Flight Phase

As a result of the subtle lift described in the previous paragraph, you should become briefly airborne. The left leg thrust combined with lower-body lean should produce a powerful *linear drive* in the throwing direction (figure 4.9). It

Figure 4.9 Flight phase and subtle jump.

is crucial that you learn to combine this linear drive from body lean and left leg thrust with a strong rotary force from the sweeping right leg to maximize momentum development. Too much linear drive produces a stalling when your right foot lands near the center of the circle. In this case you must reduce the linear force or increase the rotary force. The latter would be the preferred solution. Most beginners do not experience this problem. Almost all novice discus throwers overrotate or spin through the circle without developing significant linear force.

Creating Momentum at the Beginning of the Throwing Movement

The 2.5-meter (8-foot, 2 1/2 inch) distance across the throwing circle is a run-up area wherein throwers are allowed to develop as much energy or momentum as possible. Following is a list of momentum-developing techniques you can use as you begin the throw:

1. Body mass movement from the right leg to the left leg.
2. Push off of the right leg just before pickup (minimal force).
3. Left foot/leg pulling action as it pulls the body left at the start of the throw.
4. Sweeping left arm.
5. Body lean or moving the line of gravity beyond the base of support. The basis of translation of the human body is moving the line of gravity (a line from directly above through the body's center of mass) beyond the base of support (the outside dimensions of the feet when standing). Body lean puts the mass in motion, which creates a degree of momentum that can be substantial.
6. Sweeping right leg. The wide-sweeping right leg creates greater momentum than the right leg kept close to the left leg. Sweeping the right leg wide is an important momentum-producing move.
7. Thrust of the left leg and foot.

The degree of kinetic energy/momentum derived from these techniques depends on your mass, power, and skill.

Discus Path From Start to High Point

As you move around your left leg into the circle from the first single-support position, *carry the discus slightly behind your right hip, relatively low* (see figure 4.6d). As the discus rounds the left leg and starts into the direction of the throw, it *rises on a sloping path* to the *high point* of the throw (about 7 o'clock) that occurs at or shortly after right leg touchdown (second single support) (see figure 4.6i). Your left arm, which has been actively sweeping in a relatively wide arc around the left side, sweeps to near the 4:30 area, where it slows and may very briefly stop. This stalls your torso while your lower body continues rotating, thereby developing torque between your torso and hips.

Right Foot Touchdown or Second Single-Support Phase

Continuing the technique description, the position following the flight phase is the right foot touchdown or second single-support phase. Because driving out of the back of the circle is so crucial, and because it is most efficient to have a subtle jump rather than a high jump, your right foot should contact the circle with the heel pointing between 8 and 9 o'clock. (See figure 4.6, g and h.)

As the flight phase begins, initiate the torquing process by stalling your left arm and shoulder while your lower body continues to rotate. As the movement continues through right foot touchdown, the torque between your torso and hips that develops significantly in the flight phase increases until you have achieved the predelivery maximal torque position (figure 4.6h). This normally occurs slightly before left foot touchdown (second double support).

Left Arm's Role in Developing Upper-Body Torque

Before the right foot landing and during the initial phase of the right foot pivot after landing, your upper body must stall to develop the torque needed in the delivery phase. As mentioned earlier, your upper body must be very relaxed to achieve this torque-like stretch. *The left arm is a key help in this process.* Holding it back across your chest can be very helpful. (See figure 4.6, f through h.)

Relax your right arm and shoulder and carry them relatively high behind your back. The discus achieves its *high point* during this phase. *Maximal body torque* for most throwers appears to be achieved very near right foot touchdown, which is the beginning of the second single-support phase. Hold this torqued position briefly as you pivot on the ball of your right foot. Shortly before left foot touchdown, initiate the unwinding, very powerful delivery phase.

This single-support initiation of the delivery is perhaps puzzling. However, careful examination of videos of many successful throwers reveals that the unwinding of the torqued upper body *begins* before left foot touchdown. This is not something that is taught. Coaches should not tell their throwers to initiate left arm unwinding before left foot touchdown. Conversely, some coaches tell their throwers to delay the delivery until the left foot is down. My experience with that concept is that it causes an unnatural delay in the delivery that potentially results in a jerk. From this right foot touchdown position the foot should quickly pivot around to a delivery position with the heel pointing at 4 or 5 o'clock.

Left Foot/Leg Action From First Single Support Through Power Position

The left foot/leg sweeps from the push-off position to the front of the circle. Most successful throwers try to keep the knees close together during this back-to-front movement of the left foot to get it down quickly. (See figure 4.6, g through j.)

It is often said that a bent leg travels faster than a less bent leg (in sprinters). However, if you keep your body and your left foot low to the circle during much of the crossing of the circle (as does Virgilius Alekna, winner of the 2000 Olympics), perhaps your left leg need not bend as much as has been common. When the ball of your left foot grounds down in second double support, it should be on line with the arch or heel of your right foot. Both feet should be grounded by the time the discus has approximately 180 degrees of rotation left before release (see figure 4.10).

Figure 4.10 When the left leg touches down, both legs are bent and the discus should have 180 degrees of rotation left before leaving the hand.

Discus Path From First Single Support Through Second Single Support

Move the discus up on a sloping path (not looping) on the *right rear side of your body* to a high point at least head high. As you continue the movement, the rotational velocity of the upper body slows while the lower body rotates as quickly as possible until there is significant torque between the hips and the torso and the discus is positioned relatively high behind your back as the delivery phase begins (figure 4.6i). Getting the discus up to this position requires some energy expenditure. You will gain the following benefits:

- Significant stretching of the muscles across your shoulder and chest
- Increased acceleration of the implement as you whip it down from this high point to the low point before the last phase of delivery (figure 4.11)

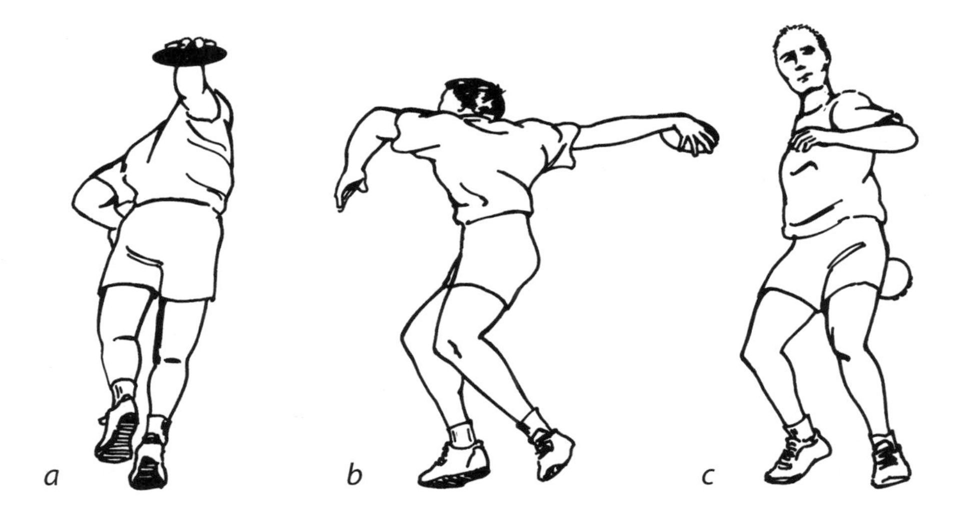

Figure 4.11 Discus as it is whipped down from the high point to the low point before the last phase of delivery.

Delivery

When your left leg touches down, both legs should be bent and the discus should have 180 degrees of rotation left before leaving your hand (see figure 4.10—position between 4.6 i and j). Your right arm should be fully extended and your left slightly bent with both somewhat perpendicular to the throwing direction. Lift and rotate both legs, driving your body around, up, and forward. Lift and block with your left leg while driving around and forward with your right side. Sweep your left arm violently around and fold it against your left side. These actions basically arrest the left side and transfer some rotary momentum to the right shoulder/arm, and ultimately into the discus. Your right arm, after delaying as much as possible by stretching muscles and tendons, is ultimately whipped around by your shoulders. Your right hand, which is fighting to control the angle and attitude of the discus, receives tremendous force in the moment before release. Your hand adds slightly to the force as it guides and propels the discus into the atmosphere.

Discus Path in Delivery Phase

The discus is swept down and around in a wide orbit, reaching the lowest point in its orbit just before being lifted and driven forward with a tremendous force resulting from the long unwinding of your torqued upper body and the driving and lifting of your leg and hip muscles. *Then comes the ultimate moment of the throw, the release.* (See figure 4.6, j through l.) The goal is to transfer a major portion of the developed force from your hand/fingers into the heart of a correctly oriented discus that knifes through the atmosphere on the longest possible flight.

Reversing

As a result of the delivery force, particularly the lifting and driving legs, your body is driven off the surface of the circle while still rotating. As your right foot/leg moves from the rear to the front where it lands, immediately lower your center of mass to gain balance and remain in the circle (figure 4.6m). This switching of leading feet is called reversing (figure 4.12, a through c). It is not forced or practiced. The reverse results naturally from forces developed during the delivery phase. Reversing throwers seldom land and stay on the right foot; instead they usually spin around to dissipate the remaining energy in the body and to regain stability within the circle. Some throwers do not reverse the feet at delivery. We will consider them next.

Figure 4.12 Right leg/foot moves from rear to front of circle as "reverse" takes place.

Nonreversing Technique

The East Germans—both men and women—have used a nonreversing technique very successfully. Among men throwers Jurgen Schult and Lars Reidel have dominated discus throwing for many years. Virgilius Alekna, a reversing thrower, won the Olympics in 2000 and is successfully challenging Lars Reidel. On the women's side, Ilke Wyluda and Martina Opitz-Hellman have won Olympic crowns and have set various world and Olympic records. It is true that more women have used the nonreversing technique than men have. However, both techniques have been and are used successfully by people of both genders.

Starting Stance

There is basically no difference in the starting stances of the reversing and nonreversing techniques. Face 180 degrees away from the direction of the throw, and place your feet wider than shoulder width (figure 4.13a). You may split the 12 to 6 o'clock line (feet equally distant on either side) or position your left foot near or on the line.

First Double-Support to First Single-Support Phase

The first major difference between the nonreversing and reversing technique occurs when the right foot comes off the circle, resulting in the first single support. Note that in the initial stage of moving into the throw after the windup, your weight shifts to your left foot, your upper body rotates, and your knees separate, stretching your inner thighs. (See figure 4.13, b and c.) Rather late in the movement your right leg lifts off (delaying the right leg pickup) (figure 4.13c). As your right foot lifts off the circle, it more or less moves up and stays back as the left side of your body continues rotating left. Rotate your left side away from your right leg, which will significantly stretch the hanging, delaying right leg. Raise your right leg to near parallel with the surface of the circle and bend your right knee significantly (figure 4.13d). When you have developed significant tension, snap your right leg around in a powerful soccer-like kick, straightening as you first face the direction of the throw (figure 4.13, e and f). Straighten your leg when you begin facing the throwing direction (near the 4 to 3 o'clock position), then lift and bend it as you become airborne (figure 4.13g).

Flight Phase Through Second Single Support

Rotate your right foot in the air during the flight phase before landing (figure 4.13g). This rotation puts some torque on your right leg before touchdown. The torquing of the *upper body* during the flight phase (figure 4.13, f and g) is not unlike that characteristic of the reversing technique. The feeling I get as a thrower or coach when performing or observing the right leg action from the beginning of the sweep through the delivery is that the *right leg is the supreme focus of the action.*

The right leg leads all other actions. It appears that all actions are dependent on the completion of the right leg tasks. Once your right foot touches down, bend your right leg slightly at the knee and begin rotating (figure 4.13, h through j). For this to occur, your body must be balanced precisely over your right foot.

(continued)

Figure 4.13 Nonreversing technique.

Delivery

As your left foot comes to touch down, rotate on the ball of your right foot until it spins out onto the lateral aspect of the foot with your right heel lying well to the right of your right forefoot (figure 4.13, j and k). (Recall that most of the torque between your upper and lower body has been developed by the time your right foot touches down; see figure 4.13h.)

The medial rotation of your right knee adds to the rotation of your right foot, which is followed by a "hip strike" rotation that, when executed properly, drives your torso, shoulder, and finally your already-stretched arm around and up into the throw. Your left foot should touch down relatively early with your right arm at about 3 o'clock (figure 4.13i). The delivery is driven by your right leg and hip rotating around (against) the blocking left leg, which is firmly planted on the surface of the circle (figure 4.13, i and j). Rotate your right shoulder until well past the point at which your chest is facing the throw position; at this point, with the muscle and tendons of your arm well stretched, your arm rips forward, unleashing the implement. Before, during, and after the release your left foot should be firmly planted at the front of the circle. Your right foot should also remain in contact with the circle, heel up, toes lightly resting on the circle.

To review—following are the major characteristics of the nonreversing throw:

1. Right leg pickup—As you lean left and rotate toward the throwing direction, raise your right thigh and lower leg up to a "parallel with the ground" position. Bend, drag, and hang your right leg, putting your thigh muscles on preparatory stretch.
2. Develop momentum with your right leg by means of a very strong soccer-style kick from the dragging, hanging position to the center of the circle.
3. The soccer kick causes your right leg to straighten between 11 and 9 o'clock.

(continued)

Figure 4.13 *(continued)*

4. From the beginning of the kick through the delivery, your *active focus* should be on your right foot, leg, and hip, which drive the throw.
5. Do not lift your planted, blocking left leg off the circle until the discus is long gone. Do not reverse.

Technique and Rhythm Drills

Good discus throw technique is a synchronized blending of a series of body movements. Many things need to happen simultaneously. When parts of the whole movement are difficult to produce within the whole movement, devising a drill to work on the parts can be helpful. However, the parts that are drilled need to be incorporated into the whole as soon as possible.

Earlier in this chapter under the heading "Feelings and Feedback," I briefly discussed a concept that is of paramount importance in learning any skill: the ability to focus on a particular body part or a particular rhythmic sensation when making a movement. The importance of being able to focus your mind on a specific body part or rhythmic feeling and thereby sense what is occurring or to cause a specific movement to take place while learning the discus throw cannot be overstated. It naturally follows then that when making the same movement you must be able to sense or emphasize (on separate throws) a variety of body parts. It is difficult if not impossible to focus your mind on more than one feeling or movement on each throw. The drills that follow therefore often address the same technical movement but with a different focus during the movement. The hope of all technique work, including drills, is of course to continue to refine each part of the total movement until the technique is an efficient, fluidly blending, rhythmic whole.

Figure 4.13 *(continued)*

STARTING STANCE DRILL

The circle should have a line from 12 to 6 o'clock. Place the ball of your left foot on the line or slightly to the left; your right foot should be more than shoulder width to the right (figure 4.14a). I emphasize again that with beginners it may be advantageous to cheat left, keeping the major portion of the body weight on the left foot (figure 4.14b).

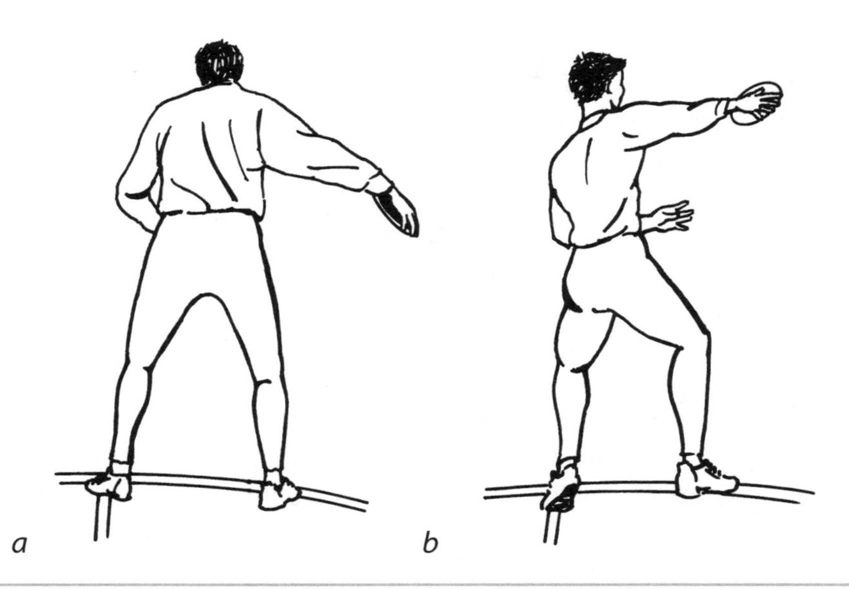

Figure 4.14 Starting stance drill: *(a)* proper position of the feet and *(b)* cheating left.

WINDUP DRILL

As you become more comfortable with the throw, I advocate moving your body weight from your left to your right leg and then back to the left to gain some momentum during the windup, particularly of course in the final windup that precedes the actual throw.

CRUCIAL MOVE DRILL: PART I

Many years as a successful thrower and coach have taught me that the most important or *crucial* phase or movement in the throw occurs from the start of the windup through right foot touchdown. Work hard to master the rhythm and body positions of this very "crucial move." Wind your arms back to at least perpendicular to the direction of throw (figure 4.15a). At this point approximately 80 percent of your body weight should be on your right leg. Your right foot should be pointing at 2 o'clock. Position your left foot with the medial side of the great toe touching the circle. As you begin to unwind, shift your body weight to the left and pull your left foot down on the medial side of the ball of the foot and rotate onto the ball of the foot (figure 4.15b). Sweep your left arm wide around your left leg, which leads the movement in this initial stage of the unwinding and beginning of the throw. As the move proceeds, lift your right foot, keeping your knees spread approximately the same distance as they were in the stance. The lifting of the right foot concludes part 1 of the crucial move.

Figure 4.15 Crucial move drill: part I.

CRUCIAL MOVE DRILL: PART II

Assume a position with your left foot turned perpendicular to the throw direction. Most of your body weight should be on your left foot; your right foot is down (very little weight is on the right foot, which is just touching the circle) (figure 4.16a). Bend your left leg and sweep your left arm wide around the rear of the circle while pivoting on your left foot. Keep your left arm generally over your left thigh until your left leg thrusts you off the circle (figure 4.16, a through d). Some key concepts again are balancing on your left leg/foot, rotating to the left, and pivoting on the ball of your left foot. Pick up your right leg as soon as possible (that is only possible when you have shifted your body weight completely onto your left leg) and sweep it wide around your left leg (into the circle) as your left foot continues rotating until it points to 7 o'clock (figure 4.16, b and c). *Your left foot should stop rotating when the toes point to 7 o'clock. This stop in rotation is to prevent the dreaded overrotation at the start of the throw.* As your right leg starts into the circle (crossing in the direction of the throw—wide)

Figure 4.16 Crucial move drill: part II.

(figure 4.16c), bend and lift your right leg as your left leg thrusts you off the circle and into a subtle jump (figure 4.16d). You should land on the line, balanced on your right foot (figure 4.16e). When your right foot first touches down, your toes should point between 3 and 1 o'clock. Your right arm is of course the important discus-carrying part of this drill. Carry the discus relatively low around the back of the circle and significantly behind your right hip. As you rotate into the direction of the throw, your right arm starts rising on a sloping, not looping, path up to a high point that begins at approximately 7 o'clock, stays high until about 5 o'clock, then descends on a sloping path. The movement of the discus is addressed more specifically in the discus low to high drill on page 91.

NONREVERSING TECHNIQUE DRILL

In this drill pick your right leg up high (until your thigh and lower leg are parallel with the surface of the circle) and fold it into a flexed position at the knee before whipping or kicking it around your left leg and straightening it on the right side. Then lift your leg and entire body while driving to the center of the circle, clearing the ground. While in the air, turn your right leg and foot medially (inward) in preparation for landing. Land on your right foot with your toes pointing between 11 and 2 o'clock and immediately begin rotating. You must be precisely balanced on your right leg at landing. Although you carry the discus perhaps a bit higher at the back of the circle (start of the throw) than in the reverse style, it should still be far behind your hips; you should lift it to a high point at about 5 o'clock and then lower it on a sloping path. Following are the major differences between the nonreversing and the reversing drill:

1. Right leg pickup height and knee flexion (slight delay) (figure 4.17a)
2. Whipping or kicking of the leg on the right side as you face the direction of the throw (figure 4.17b)
3. Significant rotation of the right leg/foot in the air before touchdown by many nonreverse throwers (figure 4.17c)

Figure 4.17 Nonreversing technique drill.

DELIVERY DRILL

The best way to learn this drill is in a static manner, step by step. Once you have the basics down, you can then move into a dynamic practicing mode.

1. Stand with your right leg bent and your right foot in the center of the circle, toes pointing at 11 or 12 o'clock.
2. Place your left foot behind and beyond your right foot on a line toward the direction of the throw (6 o'clock). Only the toes of your left foot should be touching (figure 4.18a).
3. Your discus arm should be up and pointing between 5 and 6 o'clock (high point).
4. Wrap your left arm across the front of your chest with your hand pointing between 6 and 5 o'clock, as shown in figure 4.18a. This position is similar to the position you would be in at the beginning of the delivery, bent at the hips, body torqued, discus up. I recognize that perhaps no thrower gets the left foot down this early, but for purposes of this drill it is down.
5. Begin unwinding by both (a) pivoting on your right foot and (b) swinging your left arm out and away from your body (figure 4.18b).
6. Now lift and drive your body forward as you lift the discus and drive it in the direction of the throw, which should cause you to transfer much of your body weight to your left side as your left arm moves around to the direction of the throw and stalls at your left side (figure 4.18c). The discus should stay up briefly as you begin this movement and then descend on a sloping path to the low point and then back up on the sloping path into the delivery. As this drill concludes, you should be *extended to the right or throwing side as far as possible without losing your balance* (figure 4.18d). Start by moving slowly through this drill paying particular attention to the starting position; then learn to move fluidly through the movement in a dynamic manner.

Figure 4.18 Delivery drill.

SWEEEEP DAH DAH DRILL

This drill is designed to teach the rhythm of the footwork of the throw. Begin by taking the starting stance; then go into the windup. As you move into the right leg sweep at the beginning, pick your right leg up early to medium height and sweep your left arm over your left thigh. At this stage of the movement your emphasis should be on the sweep of your right leg. Pick your leg up to a medium height and sweep around the back of the circle, straightening briefly between 1 and 11 o'clock. This is the sweep (figure 4.19a). The first "dah" is the grounding of the right foot. The second "dah" is the grounding of the left foot. The rhythm is a relatively long sweep followed by two quick dahs. Sweeeep dah, dah. The emphasis is on the rhythmic sweep of the right foot followed by a quick grounding of the right foot (figure 4.19b) followed quickly by the left (figure 4.19c).

Figure 4.19 Sweeeep dah dah drill.

DISCUS LOW TO HIGH DRILL

This drill is to teach the proper path the discus should move on from the low to high point. This path is a *sloping line, not a looping movement.* Stand with your left foot perpendicular to the throwing direction at the back of the circle; your right foot should be outside the circle at about 1 o'clock (figure 4.20a). Carry the discus starting well behind your right hip. Bend your left leg and rotate on your left foot. Now sweep the discus around to the low point (figure 4.20b) and then up on a sloping, basically straight line path (figure 4.20c) from about 11 o'clock to about 7 o'clock (stays high to 5 o'clock), where the discus is at the high point of the throw (figure 4.20d).

Figure 4.20 Discus low to high drill: *(a)* start position, *(b)* entering the circle (first low point), *(c)* midpoint of path to high point, and *(d)* high point.

MODIFIED SOUTH AFRICAN DRILL

This drill is almost a complete throw. It is usually done moving up and down a field, not from a circle. But of course the movement can be made in a circle.

Stand with your right foot perpendicular to the direction of the throw. Swing the discus gently back and forth on your right. Timing your body with the discus, sweep the discus forward then back, and then lift your left leg and drive forward with your right leg (figure 4.21a). The discus, first back, should then swing down and around and up. Ground your left leg down (figure 4.21b) while still driving forward around counterclockwise with the discus and pick up your right leg, *making sure to sweep it wide around the left* as you jump up and forward off your left foot, driving your body in the intended direction of throw. The discus should now be high (figure 4.21c). Land balanced precisely on your right foot with your toes pointing between 1 and 12 o'clock. The discus should be up and back, and your left arm should wrap momentarily across your chest (figure 4.21d). Your left foot should come to rest on line with your right, with your left toes lined up with your right instep or heel (figure 4.21d). Begin unwinding by both swinging your left arm out and away from the body and pivoting on your right foot (figure 4.21e). The actual throw should be crisp and quick—smoothly following the earlier actions. Make a very good release with the discus flying at the proper angle and attitude. As this drill concludes, you should be extended to the right or throwing side as far as possible without losing your balance (figure 4.21f).

Emphasize the following points when performing this drill:

1. Driving into the throw and making a significant linear movement into the throw
2. Getting the discus high (but not too high)
3. Proper rhythm
4. Very good release, with proper flight angle and attitude

Reversing throwers should finish with the reverse. Nonreversing throwers should work hard on rotating the right side and blocking with the left—no reverse.

(continued)

Figure 4.21 Modified South African drill.

STANDING THROW DRILL

This drill emphasizes the following:

- Control of the discus at release (angle and attitude)
- Wide to the right maximizing radius
- Good flight—angle of attack and release into sky

Do both reversing and nonreversing standing throws.

REPEATING DISCUS THROW MOTION PIVOTS

Doing these pivots on a surface with a low coefficient of friction is sometimes enjoyable. Do five throwing movement pivots in succession, emphasizing good balance and foot rotation. Pivot both at the start (left foot and in the delivery position right foot). The emphasis in this drill is on the pivoting, not on the discus path and plane. Learn to pivot on both feet: Pivot on your left foot, take a step, then pivot on your right. Stop; then repeat four more times. Rest briefly and repeat five more times.

In this drill the steps should be short—left foot then right foot—to allow you to emphasize the pivot.

Strength and Conditioning Exercises

Quite honestly, most of the conditioning for the discus is done lifting weights, doing plyometric work, and doing sprinting and agility work. (These areas are covered in detail in chapter 2.) However, following are some concepts that will, if done with intensity and attention to getting the most out of the drill, contribute to your throwing ability.

Figure 4.21 *(continued)*

THROWING VARIOUS WEIGHTED OBJECTS

When practicing with differently weighted objects, use both arms to throw—one throw with the right arm followed by one with the left. Medicine balls, as well as light and heavy disci, can be used. I prefer mostly light disci. Strength and power are gained in the weight room and in performing various jumping and sprinting movements. Some research shows that throwers benefit from throwing both light and heavy implements as long as they don't go more than 20 percent above or below the official weight of the implement. Interestingly, I have seen various throwers throw quite a few heavy implements; not many throw lighter implements.

Many believe that throwers should throw various objects to generally condition the body for throwing. A number of objects have been manufactured and marketed that are supposed to be helpful for throwers, such as cones, puds, balls of many different weights, variable weight discs, many different weights of medicine balls, and iron rods, as well as others. I personally never trained with any of those things. I tried throwing a 10-pound (4.5 kilogram) weight indoors for a few workouts, but I didn't like it. I liked throwing underweight discs during the season. I threw them periodically, not regularly. Medicine ball work can be helpful if done in a variety of ways and with a variety of weights. I never did it, but athletes seem to benefit from this upper-body plyometric work. I am quite firmly of the opinion that athletes must move at high velocities when throwing. Throwing objects that significantly slow the motion are not helpful to long throwing. Obviously you want to do exercises that enable you to throw very far. Strength and power training programs have been proven to do that very well. Many additional activities are still unproven.

In addition to the exercises covered in chapter 2, following are some exercises and ideas that may be helpful to discus throwers.

LOW INCLINE FLY

With the appropriate weight in each hand, first sit and then lie back on the incline bench. Extend your arms directly out from the shoulders, let the weight drop as far toward the floor as comfortable, then do a horizontal shoulder adduction move to bring your hands together above your head. It is not necessary to keep your elbows completely extended. With lighter weight, however, it is desirable to do so.

WRIST ROLLING

Take a cutoff pole vault pole and attach a small rope to the center (tape it on very well). Slip the tube over a straight bar and place the bar on a squat rack. Either tie the rope to a weight or tie some sort of metallic T to the rope so weight can be hung on it. Once you have attached the weight, roll it up, then lower it. Use both wrist flexion and extension in the rolling process.

Something to consider is the statement by 1999 world champion Anthony Washington: "I will never do anything slow in the weight room again." Doing exercises fast *may* increase your power. My experience has been that as long as you include at least one *quick lift* (all of the Olympic lifts/pulls are quick lifts, as are behind-the-neck jerks) in each strength training workout, you will remain powerful and quick. Coaches and athletes must realize that a thrower is always challenging the power mechanisms of the body when throwing, when doing plyometric exercises, and when sprinting. I therefore do not advocate doing each strength training exercise "as fast as possible." When a person lifts 80 to 100 percent of the 1RM resistance in a pressing or squatting exercise, the weight moves relatively slowly. *Reducing* the resistance level or the range of motion to facilitate moving quickly (quickness is obviously subjective) may defeat the purpose of strength training and put the athlete at risk of injury.

Sample Training Program

The objective of a general conditioning program (table 4.2) is to produce a significant amount of strength, power, and anaerobic endurance and to familiarize you with the demands of throwing. Preseason conditioning is directed at causing improvements in speed and power while maintaining a high level of strength. This conditioning emphasis naturally helps you become more effective as a thrower. You train to throw as much as to become very fit. Obviously the competition phase is designed to make you the best thrower possible. The emphasis should be on the throwing, not on conditioning. Conditioning activities are designed to support high-intensity throwing.

Mac Wilkins, a good friend and a great thrower, frequently discusses the mythical "effortless throw." In his view the effortless throw is the most desirable throw. I do not agree with that characterization. I would describe my great throws (world records and a few others) as *very satisfying effort.* When a thrower releases a good or great throw, there is a distinct feeling of completeness or success. The thrower knows immediately whether the effort was "successful." To throwers I say, seek that feeling. I call it very satisfying effort, not effortlessness.

Fortune Gordien, a great discus thrower and a good man, once told me he had only one great throw in his life (he set four world records). I had many. May you who give yourself to throwing also have many, either as a coach or as an athlete.

Table 4.2 Sample Training Plan for Discus

GENERAL CONDITIONING PHASE (3 TO 4 WEEKS PER CYCLE)			
Day	**Throwing**	**Weight/Power Training**	**Running**
Monday		Clean, step-up (low), leg curl, bench press, incline dumbbell press, lat pull-down, abdominal work (Russian twist)	1 hr + of sport games—basketball, soccer, volleyball, racquetball Flexibility for 20 min after game
Tuesday	5-10 standing throws (release and good flight) 6-10 moderate South African drills (get discus "up") 20 full throws (balance on left)	5 × 6 hurdle hops 6 standing long jumps into pit	6 × 100-m buildups
Wednesday		Back squat, behind-the-neck jerks, incline fly, seated bar twist, back hyper, abs	1 hr + of sport games Flexibility, joint mobility after games
Thursday	Heavy discus (10 standing throws) Heavy discus (5 moderate South African drills) Heavy discus (10 full throws and 10 correct weight)	Double-leg stair jumps 6 × 5 hurdle hops Medicine balls (3 exercises ×10)	3 × 20-m, 4 × 30-m sprints
Friday		Snatch, front squat, Russian twist (3×), 15 hanging leg raises, medicine balls (3 exercises × 8)	1 hr + of sport games Flexibility, joint mobility after games
Saturday	Same workout as Tuesday		

Power lifts = sets of 6-8 repetitions; Olympic lifts = sets of 5-6 repetitions; low step-ups = 12-13 inches.
Rank beginners *may* throw every day—not more than 30 throws.

PRESEASON PHASE (3 TO 4 WEEKS PER CYCLE)			
Day	**Throwing**	**Weight/Power training**	**Running**
Monday		Clean, step-up (med), Dumbbell incline press, seated bar twists	2 × 30m, 2 × 50m, 2 × 100m sprints or 1 hr + sport games
Tuesday	Warm up w/ 4-6 standing throws, 4-5 South African drills (always correct release) 25 throws, 5 throws w/light discus	5 × 5 hurdle hops, 5 × 3 single-leg triple jumps (alternate legs)	7 × 100m buildups
Wednesday		Back squat, push jerk front and back of neck, box jumps (20-48 in.), abs (2 × walking weight twist, 30 crunches)	Running drills, cariocas (4 × 50 m: 2 × left forward, 2 × right forward), jump rope 10 min

Thursday	4-5 standing throws, 15 throws w/regulation discus, 10 throws with light discus	3 hurdles followed by jump into sand pit (×10)	None (rest)
Friday		Snatch, jump squat, Russian twist, Roman chair sit-up, back hyper	1 hr + sport games
Saturday	Same workout as Tuesday	Double-leg triple jumps (4 × 3) Medicine balls (3 exercises × 10)	2 × 30-m, 2 × 50-m, 2 × 100-m sprints

Power lifts = sets of 4-6 repetitions; Olympic lifts = sets of 3-5 repetitions; medium step-ups = 14-15 inches.

COMPETITION PHASE (2 TO 4 WEEKS PER CYCLE)

Day	Throwing	Weight/Power training	Running
Monday	No throwing	Snatch, jerk, dumbbell incline press, Russian twist	3 × 20-m, 4 × 30-m sprints
Tuesday	15 throws w/regulation discus 12 throws w/light discus	Double- and single-leg stair jumps (emphasize power not endurance)	5 × 100-m buildups after squats
Wednesday	No throwing	Front squat, step-up (high), incline fly, Roman chair sit-ups, back hyper	Running and agility drills
Thursday	15 throws w/regulation discus 5 throws w/light discus	Hang clean (light), one-arm snatch w/dumbbell, Russian twist	6 short sprints
Friday	Rest and/or travel	Rest	Rest
Saturday	Competition	Rest	Rest

Power lifts = sets of 1-5 repetitions; Olympic lifts = sets of 1-4 repetitions; high step-ups =16-17 inches.

Javelin

Jeff Gorski

Courtesy of Jeff Gorski

The javelin is among the oldest sporting events in history. Spears for hunting and warfare are some of the earliest tools invented, and contests in distance and accuracy were surely part of early competitive efforts. Ancient art shows the use of spears by athletes, soldiers, and hunters. In every area of the world where records were kept, javelins are mentioned frequently. Along with the discus, the javelin was one of the events contested in the ancient Olympic Pentathlon, where it was thrown for both distance and accuracy.

As the 20th century approached and people turned more attention to sport as a means of recreation and challenge, the javelin became popular in many of the European countries that are today's strongholds of the event. The Scandinavian countries, especially Finland, and other countries in central and eastern Europe became centers of activity for javelin throwing as the first modern Olympic Games approached. The javelin had become a distance-only event, and most of the rules that govern the event today were in effect, including the standards of weight and length. While women threw the javelin at "physical culture" schools in Europe, they did not throw the javelin in the Olympics until 1932, which was when the first women's world record was recognized.

While the specifications of the javelin have been consistent since 1896 for the men and 1932 for the women (800 grams and 2.6 meters long for the men, 600 grams and 2.2 meters long for the women), changes in technology have led to improvements in the materials used to make them. The rules state that the javelin can consist of only three parts: the shaft, cord grip, and metal point. Up until the 1950s javelins were made of wood, usually birch, and seldom lasted very long; warping and breaking on impact were common problems. The decade of the 1950s brought the United States into the spotlight of the javelin world with three important happenings:

1. First came the shocking 1-2 finish by Americans Cy Young and Bill Miller at the 1952 Olympics held, ironically, in Helsinki, Finland.
2. The following year Franklin "Bud" Held became the first American to set a world record in the javelin throw, as well as the first person to exceed 80 meters (262 feet).
3. While Held, Young, and Miller dominated javelin throwing in the world, they were also influential in the technology of the event. They worked with Bud's brother Dick to develop the most significant change in the history of the event—the metal shaft javelin, which had a thicker shaft. The new technology added to the distance thrown and the durability of the implement.

Rubberized runways were built in the 1960s, which ended poor footing in wet conditions and gave more consistent results. More systematic training of athletes, especially weight training and support from sport science, helped athletes improve their size and power. By the end of the 1970s, surpassing 90 meters (295 feet) was no longer spectacular. Throwing technique and training were appropriately focused on knowing and using the flight characteristics of the javelin. By 1980 the world record was beyond 96 meters (315 feet), and some wondered whether the event could be safely held inside most stadiums.

The women were making significant progress as well. After World War II the Soviet bloc sport programs started to dominate women's athletic events, including the javelin throw. From 1949 to 1982 only one world record in the javelin throw was set by a woman not from an eastern bloc country; in 1977 Kate Schmidt of the United States threw 69.32 meters (227 feet, 5 inches). The improvement made by the women mirrored that of the men, and rapid improvement as a result of the Held-styled javelins and scientific training brought the record from just over 55 meters (180 feet) in 1954 to over 74 meters (243 feet) in 1982. In the early 1980s excellent athletes emerged from Finland, England, and Greece to challenge the Soviet bloc dominance.

In the 1980s the distances thrown by both men and women took another big leap. Men threatened the limits of the stadiums, and women were regularly beating 70 meters (230 feet). In 1984 East German Uwe Hohn did the unthinkable—he blasted past the 100-meter (328-foot) barrier with an awesome 104.80-meter (343-foot, 10-inch) throw. From 1983 to 1985 he consistently threw well over 90 meters (295 feet). With Hohn and other athletes exceeding 90 meters regularly, the International Amateur Athletic Federation (IAAF) introduced new rules for the javelin to facilitate staging the event safely inside stadiums. The new specifications for men took effect in 1986.

The new rules imposed a significant reduction in the surface area of the javelin and moved the center of gravity forward, dramatically reducing the flight characteristics of the spear. Athletes who were capable of 90 meters with the old javelin struggled to beat 80 meters (262 feet) with the new one. Elite women were throwing nearly as far as the men were. During this time the final great thrower from the eastern sport factory emerged. Petra Felke of East Germany set four records from 1985 to 1988, the final being a massive 80-meter effort.

The period from 1988 to 2000 has seen another period of consistent gains by the men as they learned techniques specific to the new javelin, while the women regressed a bit. The "big three" men javelin throwers emerged in 1988 and have been the dominant throwers at major competitions since. Finn Seppo Raty, England's Steve Backley, and Jan Zelezny of the Czech Republic were head and shoulders above the rest. However, by 1992 Zelezny was in a class by himself. As of this writing eight men have surpassed 90 meters with the new javelin; seven combined have topped 90 m a total of 21 times, while the eight, Zelezny, has more than 75 throws over 90 meters as well as three Olympic and two world championship titles. He is considered the greatest javelin thrower in history. While the women have seen their results drop a bit since their "new rules" javelin was introduced in 1999 to where the 70-meter throw is now something special, their level of athletic ability has improved greatly.

Technique

Consistent in each of the throwing events are three critical factors that influence the distance thrown:

1. Speed of release
2. Angle of release
3. Height of release

The last two are measured with the ground as the reference point. They are prioritized in the order listed; the speed of release is most important, followed by release angle, then release height. It is important to remember that sound technique controls all three critical factors so that as you become more proficient, you will improve in all of these areas, not just one. The throwing technique you use must allow the application of physical ability (speed, power, and rhythm) into all three of these areas. With proper technique you do not "throw" the javelin with your arm alone; rather, you "pull" or "sling" it through the combined effort of your entire body (figure 5.1).

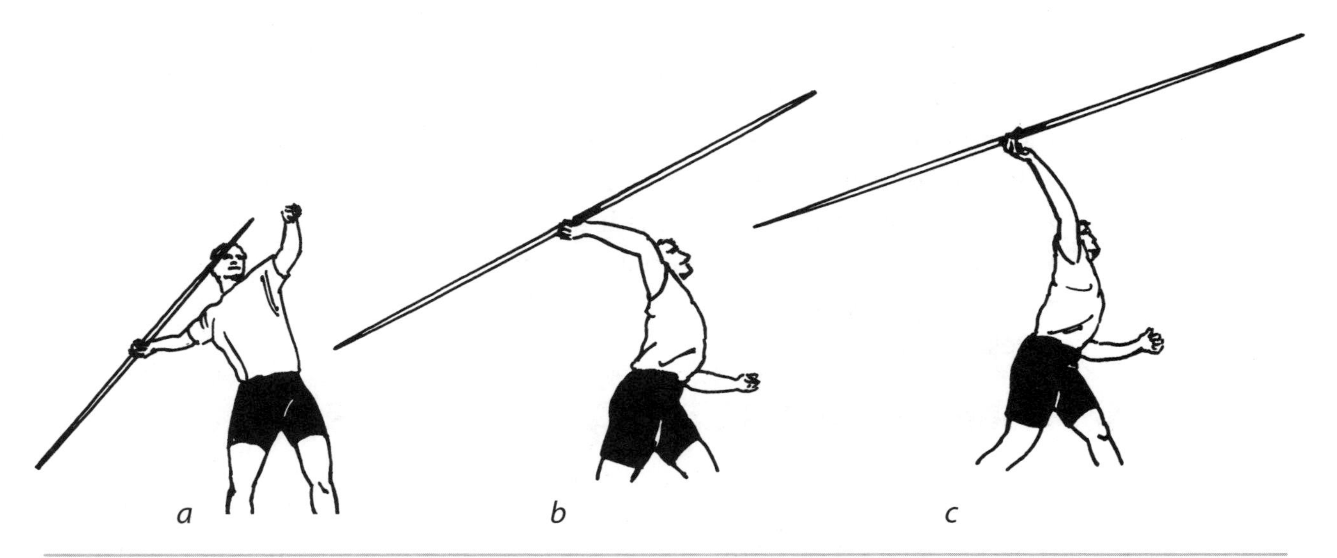

Figure 5.1 "Slinging" javelin release.

The mechanics of delivering the javelin are a summation of forces that begin from the ground and work up the body as energy is transferred from one body part to the next and ultimately into the spear. The analogy of "cracking a whip" is very descriptive of the action of the throw. Basically you want to pull the javelin over as long a distance in as short a time as possible. The movements involved break down as follows (all descriptions are for a right-handed thrower):

1. After a run-up that generates momentum, pull the throwing arm back with your hand at or slightly higher than shoulder height; turn your body somewhat sideways.
2. As you land on your right foot before the throw, bend your right knee—the "soft step"—to allow your body weight and run momentum to continue moving forward without slowing. Keep your throwing arm back and straight while extending your left arm toward the throw direction for balance; extend your left leg forward as well, waiting for the ground contact.
3. Pass your body weight quickly over your right foot and make impact with your left foot. The action of your left side is that of a brace or fulcrum; it anchors firmly to accelerate the right side into the release. Before ground contact turn your right heel out and bring the left elbow over the left foot. These actions are simultaneous and both are complete at the instant of left side bracing.
4. The bracing action causes a series of stretch reflexes that progress upward in your body; first your right hip rotates forward, then stops. That, in turn, pulls your ribs and chest forward, stretching your shoulder as your arm remains behind. Your chest stabilizes and your shoulder is whipped up and over the body, with your arm following.
5. As your arm starts to strike, turn up and bend your elbow, much like a tennis serve, and quickly extend it as your shoulder gives a base to act on. Your arm and hand continue to accelerate after you have released the javelin. The throwing hand often slaps the left thigh as it finishes the throw.

The overall impression of the throwing action is that of an explosive, horizontal movement. Key concepts that coaches and athletes should focus on to refine technique are as follows:

- Maintained or increased momentum from the run-up into the throw
- Backward lean as the legs "run away" from the upper body
- Initiation of the throw from the legs
- Separation of the hip and shoulder axes
- Firm bracing from the left side
- Delayed arm strike

Importance of the Soft Step

A basic theme in all of these actions is the constant forward movement of the center of gravity: the hips and waist. Watch any great thrower and find a reference point behind him or her that is level and parallel to the beltline, such as the horizon or the track/stadium line. As the thrower progresses along in the throw, little or no vertical movement during the crossovers usually results in a long throw (figure 5.2). Keeping the center of gravity moving level and forward is key to long throws, and the "soft-step" action is the key to this happening.

Figure 5.2 During the crossovers, there should be little or no vertical movement, with the hips staying level to the background reference point.

The most critical aspect of throwing technique is the rapid transfer of the body's center of gravity into the braced left side; every other part of the throwing mechanics depends on this foundation movement. Ideally, this is done without losing any speed/momentum from the right leg touchdown to the braced left side during the throwing crossover. The energy is then transferred up the body segments into the javelin during release. Because the "nonaction" of the right leg (soft step) is what allows this weight shift to occur, practicing this skill is very important. There is not a willful drive or push of the right leg; instead, the action is an active turning inward or dropping action of the right knee as the right foot rolls onto the toes and drags on the ground. It's very helpful to think of the right leg "getting out of the way" of the hips (figure 5.3) as they move

Figure 5.3 Soft-step action: The right foot rolls onto the toes and the hips move forward to shift the weight to the braced left side.

quickly into the left. If you feel the right leg working or driving, you have slowed down or stopped. The action of the legs during the entire run-up and crossover pattern must be directed forward and horizontal. Any vertical action by the knees and hips will disrupt the path of the center of gravity and detract from the final delivery position. Throwing the javelin is "long jumping with a stick in your hand," so you must focus on getting the mass (yourself and the javelin) accelerating horizontally into a sudden bracing that transfers the energy of the run into the shoulder/arm/javelin unit.

A good way to visualize the technique is to "leave" the throwing shoulder as far behind you as possible while getting the center of gravity over the left foot quickly. A "drawn bow" is very descriptive of this position; the phrase "reverse C" is also used. This is a position that is extremely powerful as it puts almost the whole body into a stretch reflex, but it is also fleeting—you are there for a fraction of a second. The bracing left side, if done correctly, turns you "inside out," and this contorted position begins a jackknife action that launches your right side, and then the javelin, around and over the left side fulcrum. The plant of your left side is quick, and power transfers quickly into your throwing shoulder if it's done correctly. A good mental picture is to think of the plant as a "trigger" that starts the throw. You will sense a dynamic stretch in your trunk and shoulder followed by a very fast and active follow-through of your right shoulder after release. You get into and out of this "launch" position so quickly that you may only sense the impact position or the "chasing" action after the release. If you can "feel" your body moving through the reverse C, you've lost speed between your right foot and left foot landings as well as important elastic reflex ability. In other words, you're "arm throwing." Using leg action to give speed to your throwing shoulder cannot be a minor focus; it may be the most important part of throwing technique! And it is impossible to do without a fast, level path of the center of gravity into the bracing left side.

With a clear idea of how and why the soft step is the critical part of the technique used to throw the javelin, it will be easier to understand how it works in the entire run-up and delivery action. There are three main parts to the throwing technique:

1. Run-up, which develops momentum and rhythm for the next phase
2. Transition steps, which put the javelin and body in position for delivery
3. Delivery of the javelin

Each of these segments has a specific result that will add to or detract from the distance thrown. The success of one phase has a positive effect on the phase that follows; likewise, a failure in one part makes a good end result very difficult, if not impossible. As mentioned earlier, there will be personal variances in how these constants are performed, but they must work together smoothly to have long throws result from the effort.

Run-Up

The run-up is perhaps the easiest skill to master, yet its importance in producing long throws is often overlooked. Simply put, the run-up is a smooth, accelerated run while carrying the javelin. It is relaxed, without muscle tension, and should develop a rhythm that allows constant acceleration after the javelin is withdrawn.

Length of the Run-Up

The length of the run-up can vary greatly—anywhere from 6 to 20 steps may be used. Usually, the more experienced throwers can make use of a longer, faster run-up. The development of momentum in this part of the throw is essential to the success of what follows. It is much easier to move and contort your body if it is "lighter" as a result of momentum gained in the run-up. Beginners do well with a 4- to 6-step run-up; longer runs of 8 to 12 steps are good for more experienced athletes.

Javelin Grip and Carry

The javelin is carried above the throwing shoulder, roughly parallel to the ground, with a firm yet relaxed grip. There are three generally used grips (figure 5.4) that allow control of the implement as well as a means to direct the power of the athlete into the javelin at release:

1. American grip
2. Finnish grip
3. Fork grip

The three grips all make use of the center groove of the palm as the "cradle" the javelin rests on; how the fingers wrap around the grip and hold the spear are the variables. The first grip is the American, which uses the thumb and index finger to hold the back of the cord (figure 5.4a). The second is the Finnish, which uses the thumb and middle finger to hold the cord with the index finger somewhere along the javelin shaft (figure 5.4b); and the third grip is the "fork," in which the javelin is held between the index and middle fingers (figure 5.4c). There is no "best" way to grip the javelin; world records have been set using all three. Try all three grips and use the one that feels most comfortable to you and allows the best control of the javelin.

You should spend a great deal of time becoming comfortable moving with the javelin. Various running and bounding exercises will help you feel natural moving in a relaxed, athletic manner with the spear in hand. Your grip must allow you to practice these movements without any tension. These exercises are important as they teach you to move lightly and add momentum to the body/javelin unit.

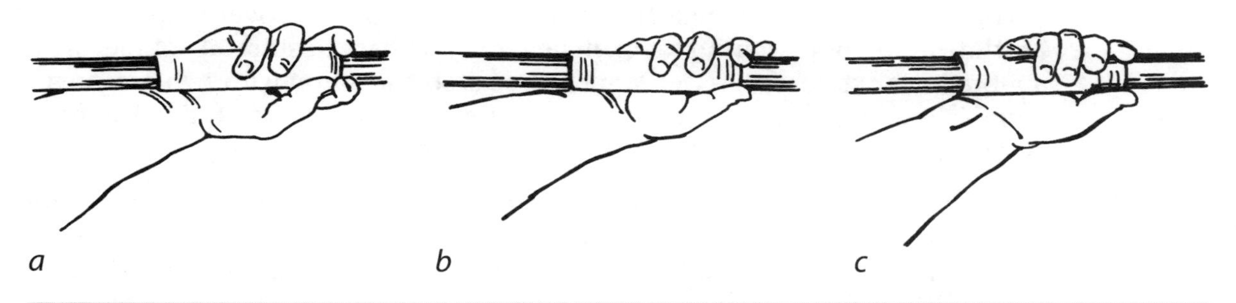

Figure 5.4 Three commonly used grips: *(a)* American grip, *(b)* Finnish grip, and *(c)* fork grip.

Transition

The run-up then carries you into the transition, where you withdraw the javelin into the delivery position while continuing to run in a relaxed and accelerating manner. The withdrawal is another critical phase of the throw where any jerky or tense movements can adversely affect the final effort. During the transition (figure 5.5a-c) your shoulders will rotate somewhat as the javelin is withdrawn while your legs continue to move in an aggressive manner in the direction of the throw. This twisted running posture is quite awkward, and many repetitions are needed to make this unnatural action a "normal" part of the throw. While you want to get the javelin and arm extended back in the "launch" position as quickly as possible, you should not do so in a manner that causes any muscle tension. I find that imagining running away from the javelin or leaving it behind as you run is better than pushing the javelin back. In addition to the positioning of the javelin, the transition also begins a pattern of steps that place your body in the best position to apply the run force into the javelin at release.

Figure 5.5 Transition/withdrawal of javelin.

Most athletes take from two to four "crossover" steps between withdrawal and delivery. These crossover steps are so named because the right leg tends to cross over the left (in a right-handed thrower) with the upper body twisted as described earlier. The final crossover is the one that puts you into position to use the soft-step action so crucial to keeping your center of gravity moving quickly into the delivery of the javelin.

There is some debate over the optimal number of crossover steps and the attitude of the body during them. In general, it is best to start a beginner with a more linear style with fewer steps: a five-step transition with two crossover steps is a good start. As the athlete gains experience, more steps or a more "wrapped" style can be tried. A brief explanation of each style follows:

- *Fewer steps with hips and feet facing the throw (linear crossover).* This more linear approach allows for more speed with a restricted range of motion in the hips and trunk; however, there is also a danger of "blowing past" positions needed to put the run-up momentum into the throw. This style uses a two-crossover-step pattern into delivery (figure 5.6).

Figure 5.6 Linear crossover: Hips and feet face the direction of the throw.

- *More steps with the body turned sideways (wrapped crossover).* This sideways, or "wrapped," position may reduce run-up speed but allows a potentially more powerful range of motion of the body during the delivery. The timing is very sensitive, and there's a greater chance for errors. This "wrapping" style uses seven steps (three crossovers) in the pattern to the delivery (figure 5.7).

Figure 5.7 Wrapped crossover: sideways position during the crossover.

In either style, you must quickly get your legs ahead of your shoulders and develop torque between your hips and shoulders that must be maximized when the soft step takes place and the plant occurs. Just before landing your right foot during the last crossover step (figure 5.8a-c), your left leg passes your right. This occurs because on the final left leg step before the right foot soft step, you "long jump" off your left leg and experience a "floating" phase (figure 5.8c) in which you "wait" for the ground to come to you, keeping your body aligned in the launch position. When your right foot lands (figure 5.8d), the soft step begins the delivery.

Delivery

The delivery of the javelin is the result of a series of elastic reflex contractions of the muscle groups involved; it's a reaction to the sudden stop of the body and the channeling of the energy through the body and into the spear. In extremely simple terms, the human body is like a car: The muscles that make an action happen are the gas while those that oppose the movement are the brakes. When you try to do something with a high level of effort, you step on the gas and the brakes equally. As a result, a lot of energy is expended, but not a lot of positive action happens; you "spin your wheels." This is what happens when you try to throw far, or throw hard—you're spinning your wheels. To use the elastic ability of the gas muscles, you need to be relaxed to avoid stepping on the brakes.

1. Upon landing on the right foot, the soft step takes place. At the beginning of the soft step let your right knee begin to drop, allowing your hips to pass quickly over and in front of your right leg. *This is the critical part of the throw; a poor landing and subsequent improper soft step of the right foot is the most common technical mistake in javelin throwing.* For years coaches have stressed the "drive" of the right leg into the throw. Actually, trying to drive with the right leg causes you to slow down to feel weight and the thrust of the right leg. This results in losing most forward momentum, and the throw becomes a willful action rather than the elastic reflex that comes from carrying speed into the plant.
2. Your hips are "pulled" along by the sweeping action of your left leg as it moves from the "long jump" takeoff to the plant position.
3. Your arms should be extended in a T position, generally parallel with the throwing direction. Your left arm should extend forward, and your right arm should be fully extended to the rear with the javelin parallel to your arms/shoulders at right foot landing.
4. As your right knee drops, "flop" your foot over; lift and turn your right heel out as your foot rolls over your toes. At the same time your left elbow, which has been extended in the direction of the throw, "flows" into your left side under your left shoulder.
5. The left side of your body should be facing the direction of the throw. There is a straight line from left heel to left shoulder that is leaning back from 10 to 20 degrees as you briefly wait for the left leg plant (figure 5.8e).

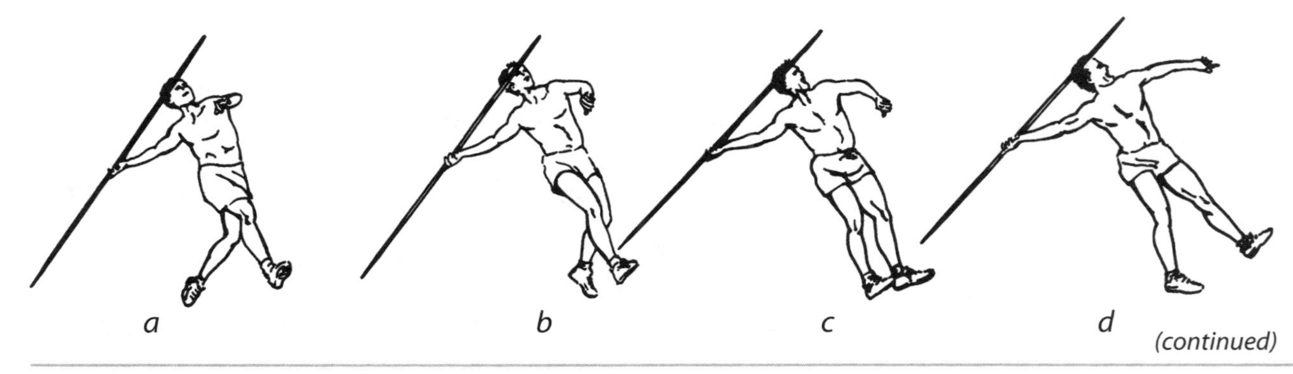

(continued)

Figure 5.8 Javelin delivery.

6. As a result of the soft-step action, your body weight moves completely off your right leg and onto the left, preceding the plant of your left leg; your left side is "pulling" your body forward into the throw.
7. At contact of your left foot a bracing action begins the transfer of energy to the javelin. You will need to work to make the weight transfer/bracing/elastic reflex a natural action. The left side should be firm—a fulcrum that the right side accelerates around and over (figure 5.8f).
8. The plant of your left leg causes your essentially free-floating right hip to whip forward, then stop, pulling your rib cage along with it. As your ribs anchor over your hips, drag and snap your chest/shoulder over and past your hips and stomach.
9. Let your throwing arm stretch and drag behind your shoulder as much as possible (figure 5.8g).
10. As you begin to move your shoulder forward, rotate your right elbow out and up, moving through a striking action similar to a tennis serve (figure 5.8h). Sling your elbow over your shoulder, dragging the hand and javelin, then extend it as it snaps your hand forward (figure 5.8i). This applies the last portion of power into the javelin as you release it into flight.
11. The entire action of your right side is accelerated and anchored against a firm left side and ends in a dynamic "chasing" action of the javelin as your body continues to accelerate after release.

From a biomechanical standpoint, the sequence of a body segment moving then stabilizing is very important. The preceding segment must be a base that the next segment accelerates against, just as the firm left side is the anchor the right works against. If a body segment is still moving, the following segment cannot reach its full potential acceleration. Each successive segment moves faster than the previous one, then stabilizes for the following segment to anchor against as it accelerates. The hand reaches its maximum speed after the javelin is released, because it then has no resistance. A biomechanical force velocity plot of the ideal throw shows a smooth, increasing speed path followed by an abrupt stop for each body segment, with the highest speed just before the stopping action. When throwing is done like this, it feels effortless; these are the "easy" throws that go far. There is little stress on the body, and the potential for injury is very low. Learning to use the "chain reaction" just described is not easy, but it is the best way to have both long throws and an injury-free career.

Figure 5.8 *(continued)*

In terms of technical training, the soft-step or deep knee action of the right leg is something you must practice in high volume to make it a natural part of your throwing technique. Because this action is the basis for the center of gravity movement, it must be performed and practiced with a number of steps (five or more) to add momentum. You must learn how to transfer your body weight quickly and smoothly; this is not a skill that can be mastered by static (standing) exercises or throws. The intensity of the exercises can vary tremendously depending on the speed of the run into the exercise, but they must be done with some steps before the throwing crossover to master the horizontal soft-step, weight-transfer skill that leads to a good delivery position and maximum elastic reflex ability. The elastic reflex that gives the best delivery position comes from the relaxed, "surprise" blocking action of the left side without the loss of any horizontal momentum at the right leg touchdown.

Technique Drills

In terms of physical properties three areas must be addressed in the training of a javelin thrower: technique, flexibility, and power. This section will address methods of developing proper technique; sections on flexibility and power development will follow. All three of these components are equally important; the balance in training priorities is determined by the experience and ability of the athlete. A physically weak athlete with good technical ability, for example, would maintain good throwing movements while improving power capabilities.

A most overlooked but extremely important part of training is the improvement of specific and general flexibility. The light weight of the javelin along with the extreme positions needed to apply force over a long range are often forgotten. The great Hungarian thrower of the 1960s, Gergely Kulcsar, once said, "less strength is often an advantage," meaning that you have to learn good mechanics to throw far; Al Cantello, a former world-record setter, asked, "How strong do you have to be to throw something that weighs 800 grams?"

A large volume of throwing at low intensity is needed to develop the motor skills and timing of the crossovers and delivery; they must flow together smoothly to get the best results. The majority of the throwing exercises need to be done from a step pattern to learn to channel the momentum of the run-up and crossovers into the javelin release. A good start is using a five-step pattern: L-R-L-R-L, in which the athlete has a word cue for each step. I like "1 (L), 2 (R), jump (L) and (R) throw (L plant)" (this is for a right-handed thrower). Standing throws are only good for developing the upper-body strike and throwing power.

The two technical concepts that have the greatest positive influence on how far the javelin will fly are

1. release speed and
2. accelerating path of the center of gravity into a firm block.

You should spend most of your technique development time in these areas. You can work on the release speed aspect in a number of training areas; technique, flexibility, and power training all can contribute to improving release speed. For accelerating the center of gravity, most of the work done will be of a technical nature, with power/release speed improvement being a by-product of throwing while doing the technique exercises. The movement of the center of gravity into the plant without a loss of momentum is difficult to master but has the potential for developing huge release speed. In tests on elite javelin throwers using pressure plates, low readings of right leg activity (no pushing on the plate—a soft step) resulted in both higher release velocities and longer throws than readings that indicated the athlete had "pushed" with the right leg. The elastic reflex that gives the best delivery position comes from the relaxed, "surprise" blocking action of the left side without the loss of any horizontal momentum at the right leg touchdown. You have to develop the ability to move into the blocking action without any tension in the body, especially in the shoulder and arm. Any muscle tension will detract from your ability to get a great stretch and position that would add to the release speed. A perfect throw starts with a near simultaneous landing of the right and left feet, with the right hand as far behind the body at left foot touchdown as possible.

Different parts of the throw can be trained by using various exercises and weights of implements. For example, heavier medicine balls (3 to 4 kilograms or 7 to 9 pounds) and overweight javelins (200 to 400 grams or 1/2 to 1 pound over standard weight) are used to learn the action of the hips and legs in accelerating a heavy resistance, while lighter implements (regular and underweight) are used to train the faster portions of the throw, such as the shoulder and arm strike. It may be helpful in planning technical training to think in terms of generating momentum during the run-up and crossovers and directing this momentum into the javelin during the plant and delivery. The athlete and the javelin must move as a synchronized whole from the start of the run-up through the release.

Medicine Ball, Weighted Ball, and Javelin Throws

Throwing medicine balls (2 to 4 kilograms or 4 to 9 pounds) with two hands from a stand and from a few steps teaches the center of gravity movement and how to channel the power from the hips up into the shoulders and arms. As a general rule, you should work with heavier objects earlier in the training periods and progress to lighter ones as you refine the skill and work at a higher speed. Starting with heavy implements gives you something to pull against and makes feeling the positions of the throw easier. These are awkward positions, and you need to learn how they feel and what is needed to get into them. You have to spend time being "uncomfortable" so you know what it feels like.

Medicine ball throws are followed by single-arm throws with balls (800 grams to 1 kilogram or 2 to 2 1/2 pounds) or heavy javelins, also from a stand and from some steps to more closely copy the actual throw. During any of these exercises you must pay attention to using excellent technique. The movement patterns developed in these exercises are the basis of performance. In all of these exercises, the effort is generated from the large muscle groups and progresses up the body to the shoulder/arm strike.

STANDING MEDICINE BALL THROW

To get the most out of this exercise, keep your arms "long." In other words, don't bend your elbows too much. Do bend your knees, however, to help create a big arch prior to the throw (figure 5.9).

Figure 5.9 Standing medicine ball throw.

WINDUP MEDICINE BALL THROW

In this throw, sweep your arms in a big circle and shift your hips ahead of the ball. Turn the back foot early in the throw (figure 5.10).

Figure 5.10 Windup medicine ball throw.

THREE-STEP MEDICINE BALL THROW

In the three-step throw, strive for a quick right-left landing on the last step, and keep the hips moving forward into the throw (figure 5.11).

Figure 5.11 Three-step medicine ball throw.

Single-Arm Throws

Since the best exercise for a javelin thrower is throwing, much of the technical work is geared toward improving the throwing skill and specific qualities of that skill. Overweight objects such as javelins and weighted balls (100 to 400 grams or $^1/_4$ to 1 pound over standard weight) are used to improve throwing power, to learn the "crack the whip" delivery rhythm, and to improve specific flexibility. These exercises can be done from a standing position and from steps or a run-up. During winter training it is good to throw objects other than a javelin into a net or against a wall so the focus is on learning the pattern of movement without regard to distance thrown—to learn the feel of correct throwing. Javelins are also thrown to ensure that power is applied correctly during the release.

THREE-STEP JAVELIN THROW

In this drill, it's important to keep the hips moving level and actively turn the back foot before the plant (figure 5.12).

(continued)

Figure 5.12 Three-step javelin throw.

Running and Crossover Exercises

Equally important are drills and exercises that teach how to get to the delivery position—learning the run-up and crossovers. Throwing from some steps is one of the best ways to learn this action, and repeated runs and crossovers with the javelin are needed to feel comfortable with the entire action. During any of the running or crossover exercises, the *focus is to move the center of gravity in a path level to the ground.* The main effort needs to come out of your thighs and hips rather than your toes and ankles; think of running with knees bent and pushing/pulling your hips with the thigh action. This is not sprint training; your upper body is being "left behind" by your leg action, so you must not lean forward while doing these exercises. This type of training, along with the throwing exercises, make up most of the work a javelin thrower needs. It develops specific power as well as ingraining throwing technique. *Twice as much time should be spent doing this than any other training.*

Runway drills improve parts of the approach and crossovers that position you to best deliver the javelin. Errors in these phases of the throw should be corrected with individual drills for that phase; then you should move to the entire approach and delivery, putting the entire throw together. Repeated running and withdrawals plus continuous crossovers are excellent ways to improve these areas. On the crossover work include sessions that address specific actions such as the left leg takeoff/right knee drive and both legs working in extension.

Simulation Exercises

Simulation exercises imitate some part of the throw and help in developing specific flexibility. Exercises with elastic tubing, ropes, pulleys, axe or hammer swings, or partner assistance are all good for focusing on a particular

Figure 5.12 *(continued)*

aspect of the throw. These exercises closely mimic the throwing motion with power flowing from the ground up; the legs begin the movement and contort the body into the positions required by the exercise, which ends with the shoulder/arm striking action. Simulating the throwing position by pulling against ropes or elastic tubing, swinging weight plates in the throwing motion, and swinging hammers or axes at an overhead target are very useful exercises.

ELASTIC CORD PULL

Start by dropping the right knee, then roll the shoulder over the hips. This helps practice a smooth transfer of body weight into the braced left side (figure 5.13).

Figure 5.13 Elastic cord pull.

PLATE SWING

Sweep the plate in a big arc as you shift your hips into the left leg plant by dropping/rolling the right knee (figure 5.14). Don't imitate the delivery or arm strike in this drill.

Figure 5.14 Plate swing.

AXE SWING

Make a big sweeping arc as in the plate swing, then roll your shoulder as in the elastic cord pull (figure 5.15). Strike the target over your planted left foot.

Figure 5.15 Axe swing.

Mental Movies

"Mental movies" is a term I like to use to address the psychological aspect of the throw. Technique training must focus on developing a particular throwing technique. While all javelin throwers perform the same actions (run-up, transition, and delivery followed by some sort of recovery), they do not look the same as they go through those movements. All athletes have their own unique style that evolves as they focus on the technique that is best for them.

Watching yourself throw on video or film is especially valuable in helping you correct mistakes; it can give you a blueprint or image of your style. From this basic image you can then spend "practice" time visualizing your perfect throwing technique; you can perform thousands of throws without ever leaving home! This often overlooked area can be very valuable. Knowing what you want to do in training makes the task easier. It's more difficult than it sounds, however; to have the discipline to be totally focused on a mental image for extended periods of time (15 to 30 minutes) requires practice.

Flexibility Drills

Flexibility adds distance to your throw by allowing a greater range of motion over which to pull the javelin. Imitating positions in the throw to gain specific flexibility has a big carryover to technical improvement. These are the simulation exercises discussed earlier. You also need to improve flexibility in body segments most involved with the throw. The greatest range of motion possible is essential for good results.

Throwing Simulation Exercises

Throwing simulation exercises that use elastic cord, rope, javelins, or pulleys to "hold back" the throwing arm/shoulder while "pushing" the hips into the plant are among the best training actions. When doing them, start the action from your legs and actively move your lower body forward; *try to get as much distance as possible between your plant foot and your throwing hand.* In addition to the simulation exercises listed in the "Technique Drills" section, stretches with the javelin are shown here. Some exercises can also be done with a partner who can help with proper positions and carefully add stretch in these exercises.

HIP AND SHOULDER LUNGE

Drop or roll your right knee to put your hips over the "plant." Use the javelin to keep your shoulder back (figure 5.16).

Figure 5.16 Hip and shoulder lunge.

PARTNER PULLOVER STRETCH

In this exercise, a partner holds both wrists, then leans forward and pushes against your lower back to create the stretch (figure 5.17).

Figure 5.17 Partner pullover stretch.

PARTNER SINGLE-ARM STRETCH

In this stretch, keep your hips stable by kneeling. Hold your left shoulder firm as the right shoulder is pulled back (figure 5.18).

Figure 5.18 Partner single-arm stretch.

Specific Flexibility Exercises

Specific flexibility exercises are done to improve range of motion in the body segments most involved in the throw. Special attention is paid to the elbow, shoulders, lower back, ankles, and groin, which are the areas of highest stress during the throw. Partner exercises are also an important part of the flexibility routine and copy the extreme positions that occur during the delivery. In addition to those listed earlier, exercises to stretch the elbow, chest and shoulders (with a partner), hips, and back are shown here.

ELBOW STRETCH WITH JAVELIN

Lift the tail of the javelin to add stretch (figure 5.19).

Figure 5.19 Elbow stretch with javelin.

PARTNER CHEST AND SHOULDER STRETCH

Lie on your stomach, put your hands behind your head, and have a partner lift your elbows to create a stretch in the chest and shoulders as well as the lower back (figure 5.20).

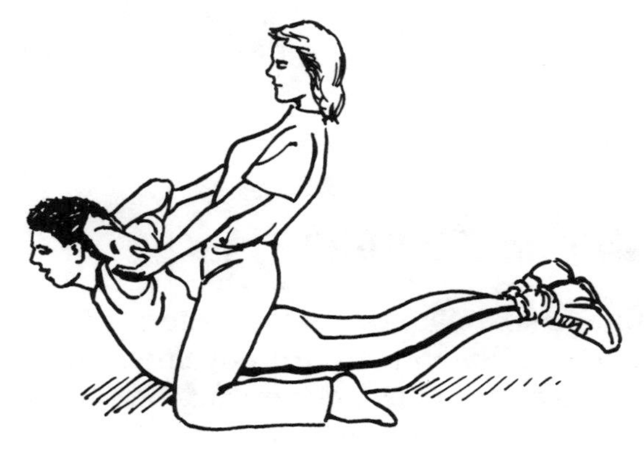

Figure 5.20 Partner chest and shoulder stretch.

BACK ARCH

Lie on your back, with your knees bent and hands by your head. Push up into a back arch; push your hips high to feel the stretch (figure 5.21).

Figure 5.21 Back arch.

SHOULDER STRETCH

Push your hips forward to help feel the stretch (figure 5.22).

Figure 5.22 Shoulder stretch.

General Athletic Flexibility

General athletic flexibility refers to a general method of improving elastic ability. It usually involves some sport movement that requires good range of motion. Swimming and gymnastic exercises on rings and bars or on the floor are excellent choices for this area.

Power Training Drills

As with flexibility training, there are different methods of power training. Specific, general, and athletic power are all important for throwing farther. All of these areas are important; the makeup of the athlete will determine the amount of training done in each. The most return for time invested comes from specific power training, since it also involves technical training. General power is one area that is overused by javelin throwers; they often have higher power levels than their technique allows them to use. This situation usually leads to injury.

Specific Power

Specific power training involves imitating the throw by throwing heavy objects. Exercises that involve throwing overweight implements are discussed in the "Technique Drills" section; exercises that train the throw using resistance are excellent to correct a problem and ingrain an important technical movement. Exercises using pulleys, elastic cords, or axe/hammer swings also do a great job in developing specific power. Some specific power exercises that are very useful copy some portion of throwing technique or improve explosive ability, both of which are helpful in throwing farther. Pull-overs, twisting exercises with plates and barbells, and cleans and snatches all directly improve specific power and, consequently, throwing ability. Explosive jumping such as hurdle hops, bounding, depth jumps, and standing long and triple jumps all should be included in the training of any javelin thrower. These jumping exercises should closely copy the rhythm of the javelin itself: The foot contacts the ground for a very short time, but a lot happens while it is there. "Bare feet on hot coals" describes what you want in jumping work. The goal of training is to throw the javelin farther, so when planning the training sessions, always ask, Will what I'm planning to do help me (or my athletes) throw farther?

PLATE TWIST

Keep your knees bent to "lock" the hips; twist your shoulders, plate, and head as a unit from the waist (figure 5.23).

Figure 5.23 Plate twist.

DEPTH JUMP

Drop from an elevation of 18 to 36 inches (46 to 91 centimeters) and rebound quickly off the ground, moving forward (figure 5.24).

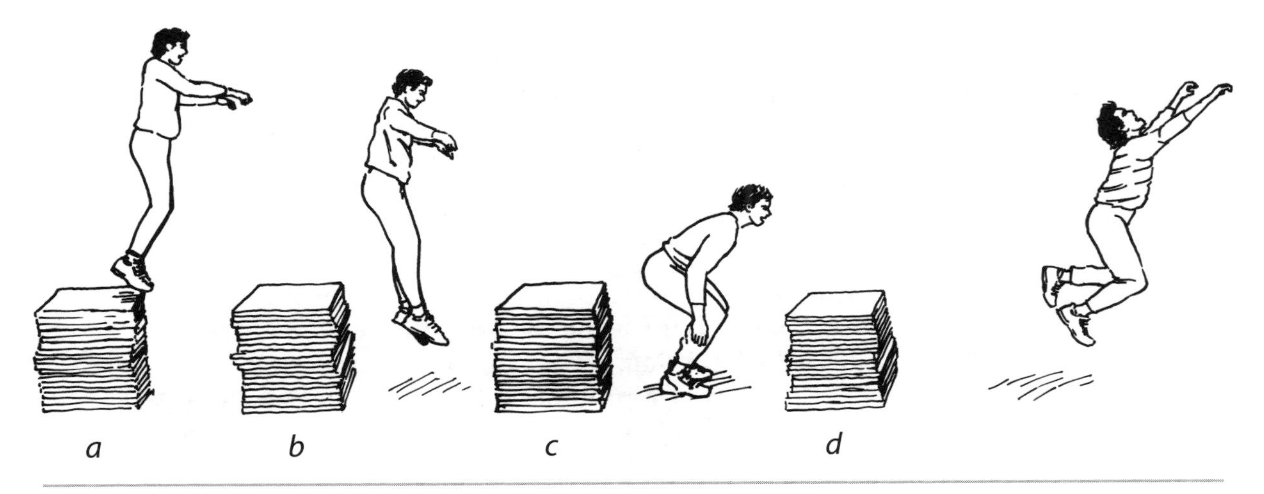

Figure 5.24 Depth jump.

PULL-OVER

Keep the arms "long" by bending the elbows only slightly. "Pull" the bar from the ribs and chest, not the shoulders (figure 5.25).

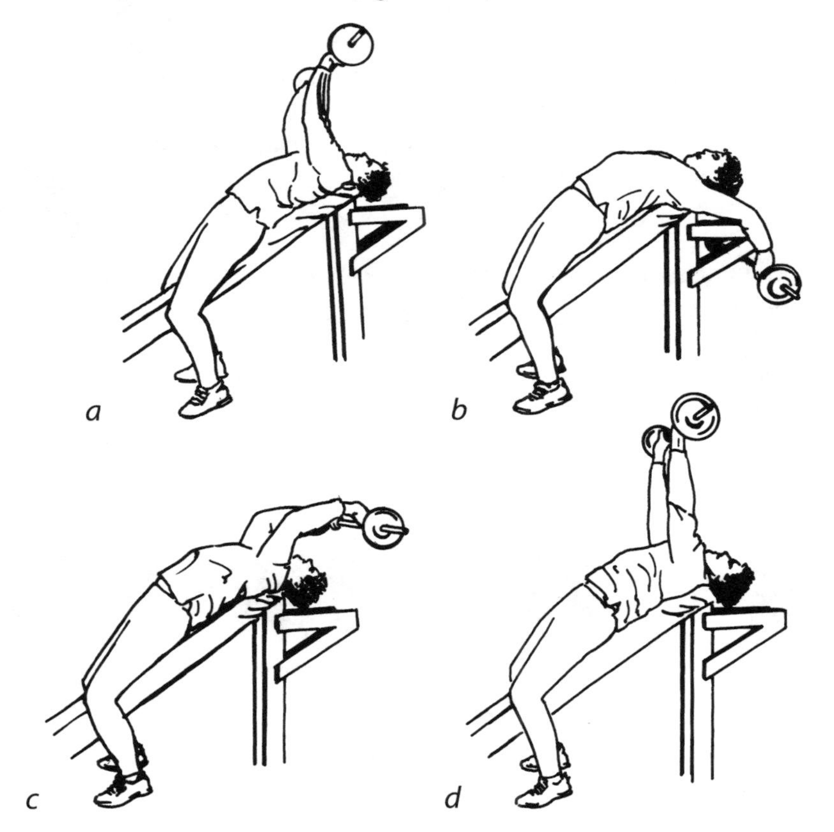

Figure 5.25 Pull-over.

General Power

General power is developed by weight training, which is further broken down into power, Olympic, and ancillary lifting. Power lifting includes the traditional lifts—squat, bench press, military press, pull-over, dead lift, and lat pull or row as well as high pull, jerk press, lunge, or step-up. The Olympic lifts are quite athletic; distance thrown often improves as athletes lift more in the snatch and clean. The ancillary lifts are specialized to the javelin thrower and are important in strengthening any of the "weak links" in the chain of the throw. Those that are most useful are plate swings with one and two hands, hip snatches, and "skin the cat" snatches. Weight training sessions can have great variance; you can combine lifts from different groups in one session or just one area. The sets/reps and intensity are discussed in the training cycle section, but as the season draws closer, you should increase the speed and decrease the weight.

TWO-HAND PLATE SWING

Same idea as the medicine ball throw; the arms make a big circle while the hips move forward (figure 5.26).

Figure 5.26 Two-hand plate swing.

HIP SNATCH

With the bar at the hip/thigh joint, bend over at the waist to start. Get the shoulders "clear" as you move the bar straight up (figure 5.27).

Figure 5.27 Hip snatch.

"SKIN THE CAT" SNATCH

Place your hands on the bar in a wide grip. From a hanging start, move the bar smoothly overhead to a deep arch in back, then pull back to start. This is an advanced exercise and should only be done by throwers who are already at a high level of conditioning (figure 5.28).

Figure 5.28 "Skin the cat" snatch; then reverse sequence.

Athletic Power

Athletic power training is where you learn power application. Explosive sport movements make up this training; jumps and hops over objects, shot and weight throws, sprinting, and gymnastics are part of this training. This starts as sport games, such as basketball, but from winter to the season dynamic training is needed and more power movements are used. Hopping over hurdles, sprints and crossovers uphill, floor exercise, work on the rings and high bar, and throws with shots in many directions develop power and rhythm—the ability to channel forces in sequence toward an end result. This training also develops "relaxed speed," which will help you to accelerate quickly without losing your elasticity.

Sample Training Program

Regardless of your level, there are three different phases or cycles of training to consider: conditioning, preparation, and competition. They can range in time from months for the Olympic-level thrower to weeks for the high school athlete. As the names indicate, each of these periods of training has a primary goal. During the conditioning phase the primary goal is to develop a base for future training to build on as well as to correct any weak areas in throwing technique. The goal of the preparation phase is to gain a higher level of both physical and technical ability that will translate into longer throws. The competition phase is geared to bringing peak technical and physical skills together at the important meets in the season.

Conditioning Cycle

The level of training during the conditioning cycle is broad-based with low intensity and large volume. The training loads during this time are typically about half of maximum effort and are performed for long periods of time.

Table 5.1 offers an example of what can be done in this training phase; it gives an outline of the variety of training needed at this time. Feel free to make adjustments to this program to suit your needs and the amount of time you have available to train in this cycle. If time is short—say, a high school preseason situation—it would be best to spend most of the time doing throwing drills and crossover work at low levels of intensity with high numbers of reps to condition yourself and start to groove the throwing movement pattern. Technical movements at this time must be done correctly and repeated many times to ingrain a pattern of movement that will serve as the core of higher-intensity technique work in the following cycles. A high volume of correct movements helps to erase poor habits and groove the new pattern of throwing. Your goal in this cycle is to become a well-conditioned athlete with a firm grasp of your throwing technique.

Table 5.1 Conditioning Cycle Workouts

Monday	Tuesday	Wednesday
15 standing throws w/ overweight javelin 20 three-step throws w/ overweight javelin 5 × 600 m @ 2:30 min	3 × 15 throws w/medicine ball: soccer style and w/three steps 3 × 20 twisting medicine ball exercises 4 × 15 reps weight training: squat, snatch, pull-over, rows 1/2 hr swimming	1½ hr sport games: basketball, soccer, volleyball, or handball 1/2 hr special flexibility

Thursday	Friday	Saturday	Sunday
5 × 100-m crossovers 6 × 100-m hill runs Medicine balls as on Tuesday 3 × 10 shot throws: backward, overhead, and forward from squat	Same workout as Monday	Rest day	Weight training: 4 × 12-15 reps of squat, clean, lat pull-down, incline dumbbell press, pull-over, plate twist 25-min jog

Preparation Cycle

During the preparation cycle you will increase training intensity to further condition your body for the rigors of the competitive season. The volume (number of activities and repetitions of each activity) of overall training will drop as the intensity increases; stress on the body and spirit is considerable. At this point you are preparing to compete. In fact, the psychological factors involved in dealing with the stress of training and the higher expectations that go with intense sessions help you adjust to the stress of the competitive season. These more challenging sessions require that you include more rest in the planning of training to avoid injuries and burnout. The technical training is done with more speed and more steps to mirror the full throw; the physical training is also raised to a higher level. The running is over shorter distances but faster, the weights lifted are heavier, the jumping is more explosive, and the throwing is more aggressive. Table 5.2 shows how a weekly training schedule for this cycle differs from the weekly training schedule for the conditioning phase.

The level of this training is much more demanding than in the conditioning cycle. Be sure to rest between sets in the runs, lifts, and throws to assure a nonfatigued level of effort during the entire training session. Variations in training depend on experience and physical ability; there is a fine line between challenging work and overtraining. Your individual needs will influence the structure of the training routine; for example, if you are a strong and powerful athlete, you will do less work in the weight room and spend more time improving technique. This is the time to address your weaknesses and improve them. It is important that all physical and technical abilities be as balanced as possible. During this cycle you develop the proper mix of speed, power, flexibility, throwing technique, and "warrior" attitude to prepare you for the coming competitions.

Table 5.2 Preparation Cycle Workouts

Monday	Tuesday	Wednesday
15 standing throws w/ overweight javelin 2 × 20 three-step throws w/ overweight javelin 2 × 12 five-step throws w/ overweight javelin 6 × 300 m at 45 sec	4 × 20 medicine ball throws: soccer, three-step, and five-step 5 × 20 twisting medicine ball exercises 5 × 8-10 reps weight training: snatch, squat, pull-over, row 1/2 hr swimming	25-30 min simulation exercises w/weight 20 min jumping/bounding 15 min special flexibility

Thursday	Friday	Saturday	Sunday
8 × 60-m crossovers 8 × 75-m hill runs Same medicine ball exercise as Tuesday: 2 × 15 reps 2 × 10 shot throws: backward overhead and forward from squat	Same throwing as Monday 1/2 hr aerobic activity: jog, cycle, or swim	Rest day	Weight training: 5 × 8-10 reps of squat, clean, pull-over, lat pull-down, incline dumbbell fly, plate twist 6 × 100-m strides

Competition Cycle

During the final or competition cycle, training exercises are performed at a very high level of intensity, with rest between sets and hard training sessions to allow proper recovery. This is the time to compete; all the work to get you ready physically and technically should have been done by this time. Training is done to hone the "razor edge" for top results in important meets. Speed is most important now, and training activities are generally done at high speed levels. The weekly cycle in table 5.3 shows the focus of training.

The focus of this cycle is to be ready to throw far. Make adjustments according to your ability/experience and the level of competition: Pay more attention to technical perfection before major meets. Along with the physical peaking of the competition cycle, you should also be working on sharpening your mental focus so you are healthy and excited to compete. The psychological aspects of this time period cannot be overlooked; you should be confident that all the previous work was correct and useful and that your throwing technique is the best possible. It is important that you enter important meets with high levels of confidence in your conditioning and technique.

Table 5.3 Competition Cycle Workouts

Monday	Tuesday	Wednesday
10-15 throws w/overweight javelin from stand and steps 10-15 throws w/javelin from jog into step pattern 6-10 throws from full approach w/regulation or light javelin 20 min jumping/bounding	3 × 12 throws w/medicine ball from three to five steps 6 × 60 m over hurdles 6 × 60-m crossovers 20 min runway drills Weight training 4 × 4-6 reps squat, snatch, pull-over, plate swing	15-20 throws w/overweight javelin or ball from steps 15-20 throws w/underweight javelin from short and full runup 6 throws w/full run-up w/normal javelin; meet simulation 80-90% efforts 15 min jumping 10 × 50-m sprinting

Thursday	Friday	Saturday	Sunday
Weight training 3 × 5 squat, clean, pull-over, lat pull-down, plate swing 15 shot throws: backward from squat and soccer-style throw-in 20 min swimming	Light training; pre-meet warmup 15 min runway drills 10 min non-throwing arm throws	Competition	Rest day

This chapter has addressed the many aspects of technique and training involved with throwing the javelin. While you must perform basic foundation movements to throw well, you can (and should) tailor these basics to meet your specific needs and abilities. The goal of this chapter was to teach you these basic movements, show how they relate to good results, and explain how to apply them in your training. Knowing what has to happen and when is an important part of developing your maximum ability in any skill event; how these are accomplished and in what style is where your unique ability plays a hand. A better understanding of the event and what is required for success will help you plan your training and ensure your improvement. While I have put forth a number of accepted and successful methods of training and technical improvement, there are many ways to train successfully. By knowing the important technical and physical aspects of training, you can address your individual needs more readily and with better results. The underlying question for any routine should always be, Will this help me throw farther? If the answer is not a firm yes, there is reason to question that routine.

Because of the unique nature of the javelin delivery, you should devote a great deal of time to becoming comfortable with the movements that position your body for the "launch." This is especially important in the U.S. culture where throwing sports stress the upper body only in the throwing motion and neglect the concept of delivering the javelin as a result of running into a sudden jolt. Rhythm, relaxation, and elastic ability are more important for success in this sport than brute power. Remember that the javelin only weighs 600 to 800 grams ($1\frac{1}{4}$ to $1\frac{3}{4}$ pounds).

Throwing a variety of implements at different intensities and step patterns is the best way to improve both technique and throwing power and build confidence in your skill. Other types of training are useful in improving certain physical abilities that aid in correct throwing movements; weight training, plyometrics, gymnastics, and jumping event training all are excellent for this.

The violent nature of the elastic reflex delivery that results from planting requires that you be well conditioned to handle that stress and channel the energy you created into the javelin. A well-balanced training program that addresses your needs will give good results in both distance thrown and freedom from injury.

Hammer

chapter 6

Don Babbitt

Courtesy of the University of Georgia Athletic Association: photo by Aaron Jollay

The hammer throw is one of the most dynamic and complex events contested in the realm of athletics. Its origins have been traced back to Ireland and Scotland, where the first competitions were recorded during the 16th century. The throwing of the "sledge" was a regular part of the Scottish Games in the early to mid-1800s. Early hammer throwers threw wood-shafted working hammers that weighed between 9 and 15 pounds (4 and 7 kilograms). In the late 1800s the Scottish throwers threw the 16- and 22-pound (7- and 10-kilogram) hammers from a standing position. Donald Dinnie was considered the greatest thrower of that time and is given credit for developing the wind to give the hammer extra speed before it was thrown. Today the hammer can still be seen in its pure form in the Scottish Highland Games, where contestants throw a rounded sledgehammer.

The hammer throw was included in the Olympic Games in 1904 as an exclusively men's event. The "Irish-American Giants" or "Irish Whales" such as John Flanagan, Matt McGrath, and Pat Ryan dominated Olympic competitions through the 1920s. During the 1930s and 1940s no countries dominated, and the progression of the world record was slow, hovering in the 58- to 59-meter (195-foot) range. During the 1950s and early 1960s there was steady progress in hammer throwing technique and training as throwers such as Mikhail Krivonosov of the Soviet Union, Harold Connolly of the United States, and Gyula Zsivotzky of Hungary pushed the world record past the 73-meter (240-foot) mark.

Starting in the late 1960s the Soviet Union began to dominate the hammer. Beginning with Anatoly Bondarchuk's gold medal in the 1972 Olympic Games, the Russian hammer throwers went on to win almost three quarters of the medals available at the Olympic Games and world championships between 1972 and 1992. Bondarchuk went into coaching and developed the current men's world-record holder Iouri Sedykh, who threw an astounding 86.74 meters (285 feet) in 1986. Sedykh and other Soviet greats such as Sergey Litvinov, Juri Tamm, and Igor Nikulin have become the models for what is now considered modern hammer throwing technique. In 2000 the women's hammer was added to the Olympic program. Seventeen-year-old Kamila Skolimowska of Poland won the first Olympic gold medal for this event, at 71.16 meters (233 feet). Mihaela Melinte of Romania holds the current women's world record at 76.07 meters (250 feet).

Technique

All descriptions in this chapter will be for the right-handed thrower; the left hand will be considered the glove hand. The different sections of the ring will be identified according to the degrees of a circle, with 0 degrees being the back of the ring and 180 degrees being the front of the ring, as shown in figure 6.1.

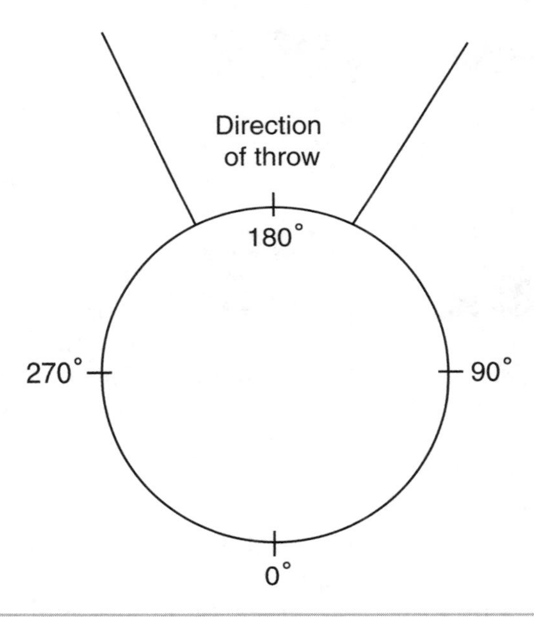

Figure 6.1 Hammer ring, with 0 degrees being the back of the ring and 180 degrees being the direction of the throw.

Grip

A proper grip and smooth, rhythmical winds are essential in establishing a good throwing rhythm and tempo. You must be comfortable with both of these technical elements before advancing to the complete throwing movement. To establish the grip, hold the handle of the hammer at the second metacarpal with your glove hand. Then place the fingers of your right hand over the fingers of your left hand so that your palms are lined up against each other (figure 6.2). Some elite throwers grip the handle using only three fingers on the glove hand to increase the radius of the hammer.

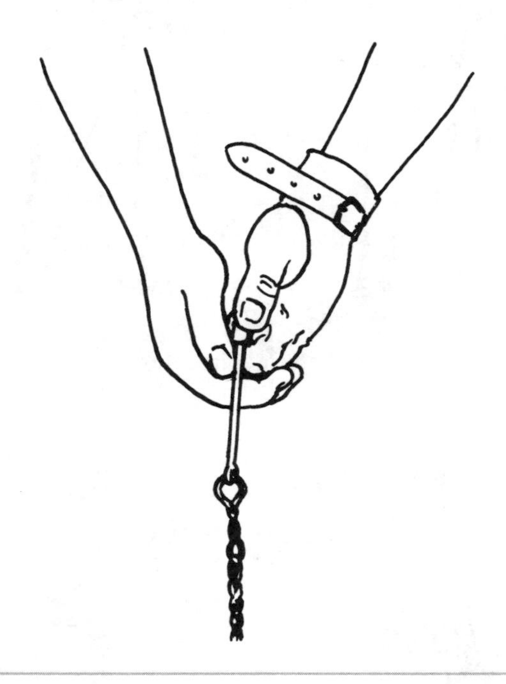

Figure 6.2 Hammer grip.

Preliminary Swings

The initiation of the preliminary swings, which precede the winds, can take place in many different ways. What is most important is that you remain in a balanced and controlled position as you transition from the preliminary swings into the winds. Perhaps the easiest way to start the preliminary swings is to hold the hammer with both hands and keep the handle just above your waist while letting the hammer head hang straight down. From this position, you can rock the ball back and forth under your body twice before casting it out *straight away from your body* (toward 0 degrees) and then back to your right side (toward 210 degrees) before pulling the ball around counterclockwise (left) to begin the first wind. (See figure 6.3.) This type of beginning may be well suited for the beginning or intermediate thrower since it allows a more gradual and controlled acceleration of the hammer at the beginning of the wind start. The rhythmic swings also help set up the rhythm for the winds and turns that will follow.

In a more advanced version of this start you use only your left arm to swing the hammer between your legs once before casting the ball straight away from your body (toward 0 degrees) and then back around to your right side (toward 210 degrees). As the ball moves back toward the apex of the backswing, put the right hand in position on the handle before the hammer begins to move forward into the first wind (figure 6.4).

Figure 6.3 Preliminary swings for beginning/intermediate thrower.

Figure 6.4 Advanced version of the preliminary swings.

Static Start

You can take a more straightforward approach to setting up the winds by placing the ball inside the ring off your right heel. From this position, pull the hammer forward (toward 0 degrees) into the first wind, as shown in figure 6.5. This static wind start eliminates much of the rhythmic swinging of the more dynamic start, allowing you to move into the winds without executing preliminary swings. While the static start may appear to be the simpler of the two types of starts, you should know that this start may cause you to make the mistake of winding primarily with your arms and shoulders. This fault is more likely to occur because this start requires a sudden acceleration of the hammer to initiate the first wind. This rapid acceleration is deceptive; it feels easier because it is accomplished primarily by the upper body. To maximize your throwing distance, however, you must ensure that your hips and legs are the driving force of the winds as well as the entire throw.

Figure 6.3 *(continued)*

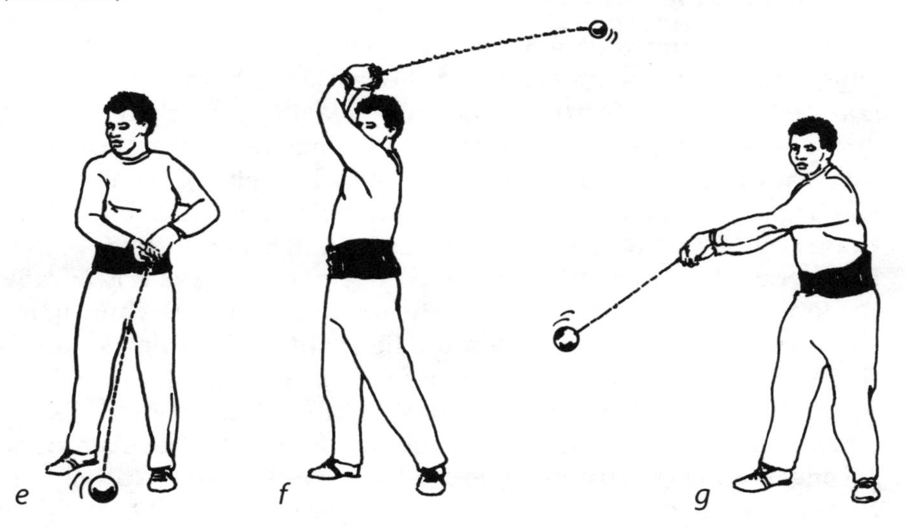

Figure 6.4 *(continued)*

Figure 6.5 Static wind start.

Winds

Proper execution of the winds and entry are critical to setting up a successful throw. Traditionally, throwers use two winds before entering into the first turn. It should be noted, however, that more than two winds have been employed by successful international-level throwers (for example, Heinz Weis, the 1997 world champion, and Karsten Kobs, the 1999 world champion). It is very important that you be in a comfortable and balanced position with the hammer under control when you transition from the winds into the first turn. Therefore, it might be argued that you should use whatever number of winds are necessary to feel comfortable and balanced. However, keep in mind that the greater the number of winds, the more complicated the winding and entry process becomes. For this reason the vast majority of throwers use only two winds.

Winding Mechanics

Both the dynamic and static wind starts can be performed with a "step-in," which occurs at the beginning of the last wind before the entry. With either start, when using the step-in, begin by placing your right foot back from the circle edge. The amount of right foot displacement from the edge of the circle may vary from 10 to 45 centimeters (4 to 18 inches). From this position, you can begin the winds with either the static or the more advanced dynamic start. Upon completion of the first wind, as the ball is about to move in front of you, bring your right foot forward to the edge of the ring so it is parallel with your left foot. (See figure 6.6, c and d.) The distance between your right and left feet (the base) during the winds should be slightly more than shoulder width (70 to 80 centimeters or 28 to 31 inches). Your legs should be in a quarter squat position, which allows greater trunk mobility during the winds.

When you perform the winds, the hammer head travels around you in an "orbit." The plane of the hammer's orbit during the winds will vary from thrower to thrower, but it is generally 37 to 40 degrees in relation to the ground. During the winds you should rotate your shoulder axis in relation to your hip axis to facilitate "winding with the body" as opposed to "winding with the arms." (See figures 6.6, c through f.) If you do this properly, you will turn your trunk until your chest is facing 300 (270 at most in pictures) degrees while the hammer travels back toward 180 degrees. (See figures 6.6e and 6.7c.) Your chest will then be turned back to face 0 as the ball moves in its orbit toward 0.

Rhythm of the Winds

The pace of the winds is generally one of gradual acceleration. After the preliminary swings are used to gain momentum for the hammer, the first wind is used to set up the proper orbit and plane. The orbital plane of the first wind is relatively flat, and the pace should be comfortable and not rushed or hurried in any way. The second wind is used to further establish the desired orbital plane and to speed up the ball in preparation for the entry. Most of the ball speed upon entry into the first turn is produced from the preceding winds.

Establishing a good winding rhythm is critical. If you produce too much ball speed on the first wind, you may tighten up your body in an effort to control the ball during the second wind. Conversely, if the hammer is moving too slowly after the first wind, you may try too hard to speed up the ball on the second wind, which will again lead to tightness and result in your not being "lined up" properly against the ball at entry. Both of these faults in winding rhythm can negatively alter the plane of the hammer orbit.

Entry

The transition from the winds into the first turn should be smooth. As the hammer head completes the last wind and moves around in front of you (0 degrees), your feet should begin moving. Once the hammer head is directly in front of you, you are said to be "lined up" with the hammer. (See figure 6.6g and 6.7 e and f.) This "lining up" is crucial for subsequent turns. If you start turning *before* lining up the hammer, you will "drag" the hammer into the first turn by leading the hammer with your left shoulder, a significant technical error. As the hammer moves through 0 on around toward 90, keep both feet on the ground turning together (whether performing a heel or a toe turn) until the hammer has reached 70 to 90 degrees. At this point pick up your right foot and begin the first single-support phase.

As you enter the first turn, the plane of the hammer's orbit should be much flatter than that of the orbit during the winds. The orbital plane is also usually flatter when making a toe turn than when making a heel turn. Generally speaking, the angle of inclination for a toe turn (for a four-turner) is about 15 degrees upon entry (figure 6.6g), whereas the orbital plane is closer to 20 degrees (figure 6.7e) for a heel turn entry (for a three- or four-turner). The low point of the orbit should be around 0 upon entry into the first turn (see figure 6.7e).

The variations on this point have much to do with individual technique. The most common approach is to set up the low point at 0 (between the right and left feet), but elite throwers have tended to have the low point a little to the left of 0 (in front of the left foot). This variation is usually successful for fast throwers who are able to keep up with the hammer and not let it "run away" from them during the turns. Slower throwers may favor setting up the low point a little to the right of 0 (in front of the right foot) so they are able to "catch" the hammer at or around 270 degrees in the following turns. Starting the first turn with the low point off the right foot was very common in the 1950s through the 1970s. Putting the low point this far to the right allowed throwers to "drag" the hammer, which does not allow the degree of acceleration of the implement that is possible with the modern hammer technique.

First Turn

The first turn can be a heel turn or a toe turn. The toe turn is usually used for the first turn for a four-turn throw (figure 6.6g) because it allows for a smoother transition into the three heel turns that will follow, and it reduces the travel across the circle caused by the heel/toe turn. The orbit of the hammer is usually flatter during a toe turn (when compared to a heel turn), and the hammer is usually not traveling as fast as it would in the first turn of a three-turn throw. A heel turn may be used as the first turn of a four-turn throw. However, heel turns are employed almost exclusively to start throws of three turns or fewer. (See figure 6.7f.) Heel turns allow a faster acceleration of the hammer than toe turns because you can better counter the hammer on your heel as opposed to the toe of your left foot.

Figure 6.6 Four-turn throw.

Proper Footwork During the First Turn

In the case of both the heel and the toe turn, do not start turning your feet until the hammer has reached 0 degrees and they are "lined up" with the hammer. (See figure 6.7e.) As the hammer makes its way to 90 degrees, turn your feet with the movement of the hammer. During the turn, your left foot should be facing the direction of the hammer head.

Toe-turn throwers pivot on the ball of the left foot, keeping the toe in the direction of the orbiting hammer head (figure 6.6g). The heel turn is started by turning on the left heel while keeping the left forefoot pointed toward the hammer head (figure 6.7f).

When the hammer approaches 90 degrees, pick up your right foot to begin the single-support phase of the turn. At this point, the mechanics of the toe and heel turn become very similar. As the hammer head travels around you through 180 degrees, bring your right leg in close to your left leg as you pivot on the lateral aspect of the ball of your left foot. (See figure 6.6h and 6.7 g through h.) During the single-support phase of the first turn, your left foot will pivot about 180 degrees (from approximately 90 to 270 degrees) before your right foot touches down to start the next, double-support phase.

At the end of the first single-support phase place your right foot on the surface of the circle somewhere between 210 and 270 degrees. Bring your right foot to the surface with the help of your left leg, which bends rather acutely (figures 6.6l and 6.7h) as you bring your right leg in and around your left leg during the first single-support phase. The bending of your left leg, which keeps much of your body weight on this leg during this phase, occurs rather naturally in response to the centrifugal force generated by the hammer head. Bal-

Figure 6.7 Three-turn throw.

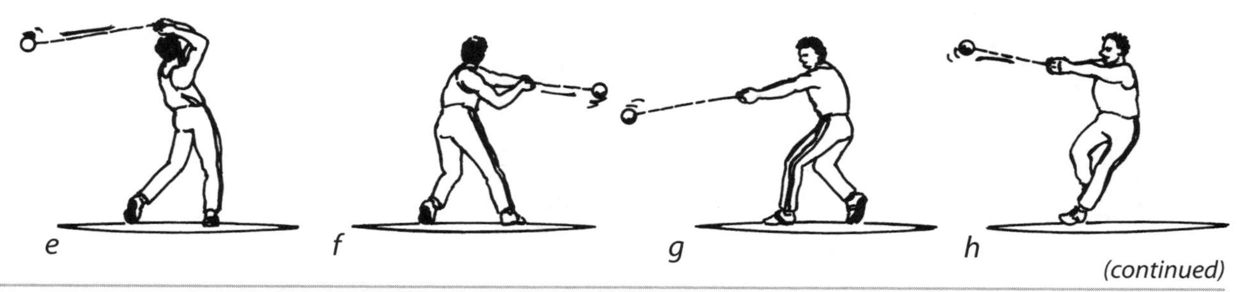

(continued)

Figure 6.6 *(continued)*

ance and stability are enhanced by bending your legs, thereby keeping your center of mass low. This move counters the hammer that wants to pull you up and out of the circle. Once you are back on double support, your center of gravity should be located between both legs with perhaps a little more weight on your right foot. From this position pivot on the balls of both feet back toward 0 as you move toward the entry into the second turn (see figure 6.7i).

Three Turns Versus Four Turns

The decision to use three or four turns requires some careful thought and experimentation. The four-turn technique may be advantageous to a smaller athlete who is perhaps lacking in strength because it includes one more turn that can be used to accelerate the hammer. Throwers who are slow to develop speed in the first couple of turns may also benefit from an extra turn. With three turns the hammer obviously does not travel as far as with four turns, but similar distances have been achieved with both methods. The key question in considering any technique is, How can I achieve the greatest speed of release with the necessary control (release angle consistency and ability to stay in the circle)? Iouri Sedykh's 86.74-meter (285-foot) world record was set using three turns.

While it is up to you to decide which technique will be most effective, control should be considered paramount. For this reason I suggest that you use four turns only when it will allow you to achieve better results than with three turns. Obviously such a determination requires a reasonable amount of time and work. It is a given among accomplished hammer throwers that three turns are the minimum number of turns for maximizing distance. Knowing that three

(continued)

Figure 6.7 *(continued)*

Figure 6.6 *(continued)*

or four turns are the ultimate goal, beginning throwers will often be more successful in competition using one or two turns. Beginning with one and two turns and building up to three is recommended over starting with four turns and then reducing to three because of control and rhythm problems.

Turning Rhythm and Mechanics

The development of the hammer's velocity during the throw is not steady; rather, it goes through a series of accelerations and decelerations from turn to turn. (See figure 6.8 on page 143.) From the beginning of the throw until the release, the hammer head will travel a path of well over 30 meters (98 feet), which gives you a lot of time to develop release velocity. Acceleration of the hammer occurs during all the double-support phases (when both feet are on the ground), while some amount of deceleration usually occurs during the single-support phases.

High-level hammer throwers are able to maximize their double-support phases and minimize their single-support phases by

1. gradually increasing the amount of time spent in the double-support phase in relation to the time spent in the single-support phase while progressing from turn to turn, and
2. effectively reducing the actual amount of deceleration that occurs during the single-support phase.

Turning mechanics begin once the hammer head goes through the low point at the conclusion of the second wind as you enter the first turn. The mechanics of the second, third, and possibly fourth turns will be similar to those of

Figure 6.7 *(continued)*

(continued)

Figure 6.6 *(continued)*

the first turn, with the following technical adjustments, which occur in response to the hammer's acceleration:

- With each successive turn, pick your right foot up earlier (figure 6.6, g, j, m, and p). Pick your foot up when the hammer is at about 90 degrees on the first turn, and between 70 and 80 degrees on the following turns.
- With each successive turn, locate your center of gravity more evenly between your legs and less toward the right as you land back on double support. (See figure 6.6, i, l, o, and r and figure 6.7, l and p.)
- The orbit of the hammer will get steeper and steeper with each successive turn, and the low point will drift slightly to the left with each turn. Four-turn throwers begin with the hammer at about a 15-degree angle in the first turn and finish with the hammer reaching an ideal release angle of about 42 to 44 degrees. Three-turn throwers begin with a steeper orbit (of about 20 degrees) because there are fewer turns to adjust the orbit to the ideal release angle (42 to 44 degrees).
- Make your base during the double-support phase smaller with each turn (see figure 6.6, i, l, o, and r). This will help make the duration of the single-support phase shorter with each turn, which will allow a greater proportion of the throw to take place while both feet are in contact with the ground. More double-support time allows more time for acceleration of the hammer.

Acceleration of the hammer actively causes your shoulder axis to catch up with and align with your hip/foot axis in the frontal plane while you move through the double-support phase. All the while you should maintain a 90-degree angle between your shoulder axis and the wire of the hammer throughout the course

(continued)

Figure 6.7 *(continued)*

Figure 6.6 *(continued)*

of the throw. At the conclusion of the first single-support phase, when you have landed in double support, your shoulder axis should be behind your hip/foot axis. Elite throwers can have up to a 50-degree difference between the hip and shoulder axes. As you turn through the double-support phase, bring your shoulder and hip axes together and line up in the frontal plane before entering the next single-support phase. (See figure 6.7j.) During the double-support phases your arms, shoulders, and torso counter relatively hard against the hammer, accelerating it, while your hips, although still rotating, tend to slow and provide a base for your torso to work against. Failure to resolve the angle between your hip and shoulder axes before the next single-support phase begins causes the previously discussed "dragging" of the hammer and the loss of the "isosceles triangle" necessary in maximizing hammer acceleration.

Delivery

You must be in a balanced position with your trunk almost perfectly vertical when your right leg comes down in double support to begin the delivery and release phases. (See figure 6.7p.) Extend your legs strongly as the ball passes through 0 degrees and continues through the release (figures 6.6, s through v, and 6.7, q and r). Release the hammer when you have accelerated the ball as much as possible. This normally happens as the ball climbs back up to shoulder height very near 90 degrees. (See figures 6.6u and 6.7r.) No special setup or impulse should be used during the delivery and release phases, which should be thought of as continuations of smooth acceleration, blending fluidly with the prior turn.

Figure 6.7 *(continued)*

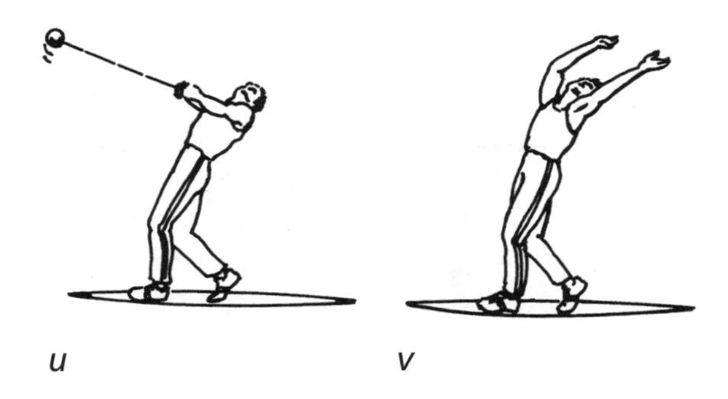

Figure 6.6 *(continued)*

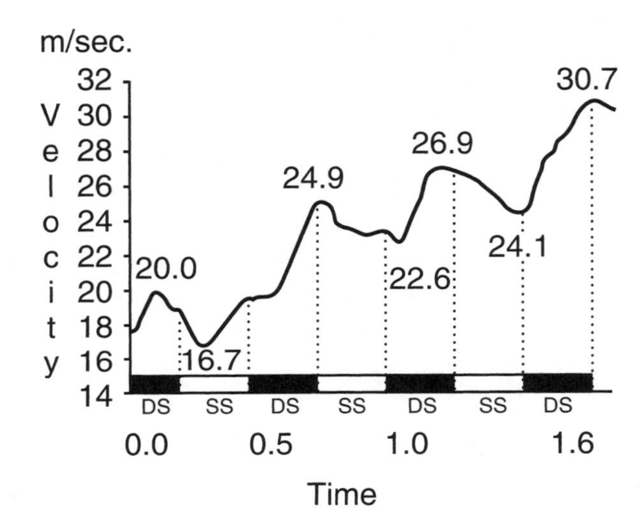

Figure 6.8 Velocity curve of the hammer during the three turns and in the release phase of a throw by two-time Olympic champion Yuriy Sedykh.

Reprinted, by permission, from R.M. Otto, 1992, "NSA photo sequence 22-hammer throw," *New Studies in Athletes* 7(3): 51-65.

Technique Drills

Technique drills are an integral part of developing a hammer thrower's technique and can serve many purposes. They can be used to isolate and improve certain elements of technique during the course of a training session, or they can be used as warm-up drills as a prelude to full throws. It is not unusual for practices early in the training season to consist entirely of throwing drills. Technique drills can teach you the proper throwing rhythm and positions; the greater the number of drills coaches have in their arsenals, the more effective they will be.

ONE-HANDED WINDING DRILL

To teach the wind, start with a one-handed winding drill. This drill can be done with either the right or left hand. These are excellent drills to teach the beginning thrower how to make the arm feel like an extension of the hammer wire. It is also very hard for throwers to "muscle" the hammer through the winds using this drill because they are only using one arm. To start, the thrower can begin the wind with either the static or dynamic start as previously described. The thrower can then perform anywhere from 5 to 10 winds at a steady and even pace.

When performing the right-arm winding drill make sure to

- straighten out your right arm and "catch" the hammer at 270 degrees at the end of the backwind and
- keep the low point of the hammer's orbit in one place during the winds.

When winding with the left arm (see figure 6.9),

- make sure to keep your left arm bent at a 90-degree angle as you are winding the hammer back over your head and
- bring your left elbow close to your left hip as you bring the hammer out of the backwind and begin to push it from 270 toward 0 degrees.

Once you are comfortable with winding with either arm, you can start winding the hammer with only the glove hand (left) for a couple of winds, and then place your other hand on the hammer handle and start a regular double-arm wind. This progression allows you to build up a loose winding rhythm with one arm, and then continue that rhythm with both arms.

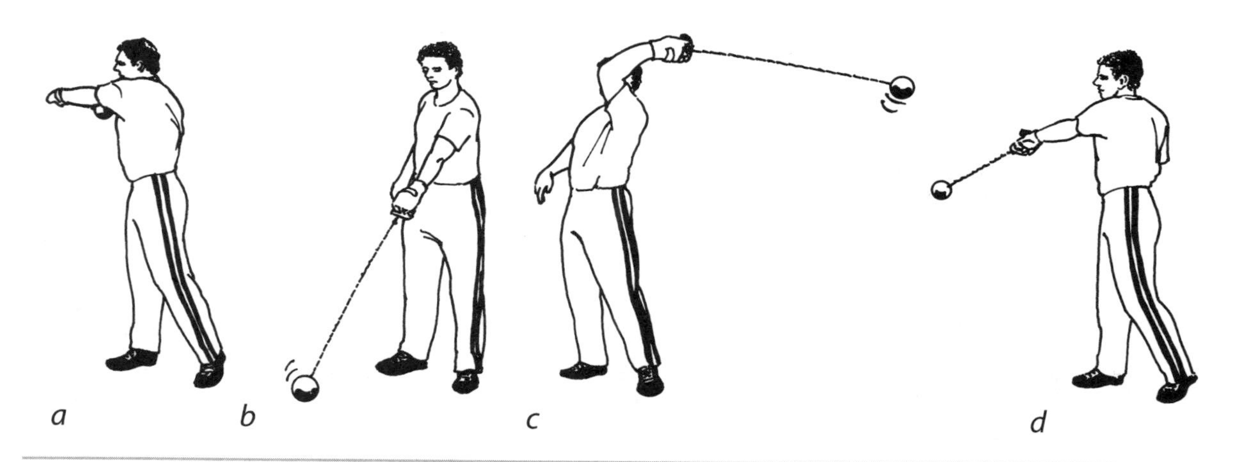

Figure 6.9 One-handed winding drill.

WIND AND RELEASE DRILL

After you are comfortable with winding, you can progress to the wind and release drill. Line up with your back facing the direction you will be throwing and begin to wind. Perform two to three winds before bringing the hammer around and releasing it. Pivot on the balls of both feet while executing the delivery. This will keep you in a balanced position during the release. You can also perform this drill with light hammers on a short wire while using either the right or left arm only.

WALK AROUND DRILL

This drill is designed to help you "line up" or "counter" against the centrifugal force generated by the hammer as you move through a number of turns. While holding the hammer, begin turning in place on the balls of your feet (counterclockwise if you are right-handed). Try to rotate at increasingly faster speeds using very tight steps, keeping your feet close together (figure 6.10). As your rotational speed increases, greater centrifugal force is generated by the hammer. The major objectives of the drill are to "sit back" and relax your arms in response to the pull of the hammer, thus learning how to hold a proper position when rotating with the hammer.

Figure 6.10 Walk around drill.

ONE-TURN AND RELEASE DRILL

Once you can do the proper footwork and perform a wind and release, you can put these two technical elements together in the form of a one-turn throw. The focus of the one-turn throw is to keep the hammer in a proper orbit (with the low point around 0 degrees and the high point around 180 degrees) and to work on coordinating the mechanics of the entry, turn, and release without having to deal with the complexities of a series of turns. This drill can be done with a heavy hammer on a short wire to work on moving your feet while staying with the hammer during the throw.

180-DEGREE STEP DRILL WITH TWO HAMMERS

While holding a hammer in each hand, rotate in place while taking small, tight steps (figure 6.11). When you are turning at a comfortable rate, pick up your right foot and step over in front of your left foot so that your right foot lands facing 180 degrees opposite the direction it previously faced. Then immediately begin turning about in place again and repeat this footwork drill over and over. The purpose of this drill is to introduce beginners to the right foot rhythm during the single-support phase without having to deal with the complexities of the complete footwork timing and technique.

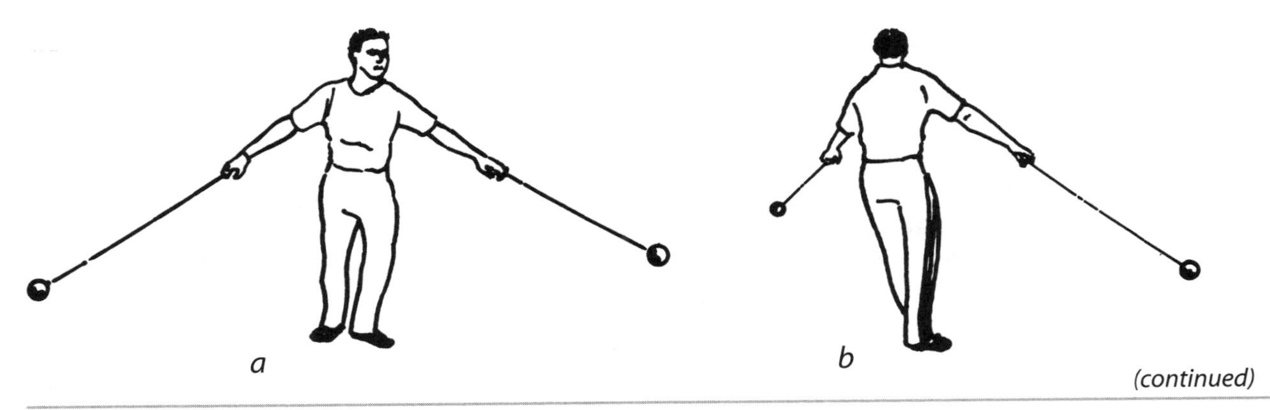

(continued)

Figure 6.11 180-degree step drill with two hammers.

MULTIPLE TURNS WITH TWO HAMMERS

While holding a hammer in each hand, begin to turn about in place using small, tight steps. Once you are turning at a comfortable rate, align yourself at 0 degrees and begin a series of turns using hammer footwork. This is a good drill for refining footwork because you don't have to worry about maintaining an orbit.

THROWING OR TURNING WITH REVERSE GRIP DRILL

You can perform either a series of turns or a full throw using a reverse grip, in which you place your left hand over your right (if you are right-handed). This grip will make you much more aware of "dragging" and will force you to be patient on the delivery since leading with your left shoulder will cause you to lose your grip much more easily than with the traditional grip.

TOE-TURN DRILL

This is an advanced drill that works on balance. It can be done with either one or two hammers. You can start the hammer moving by either winding if you have only one hammer or turning your feet in place if you have two hammers. Once the hammer(s) is moving, perform a series of alternating toe turns between your right foot and left foot (figure 6.12). Carry this drill out at a steady pace using a flat orbit and keep your emphasis on balance and keeping the hammer–thrower system together.

(continued)

Figure 6.12 Toe-turn drill.

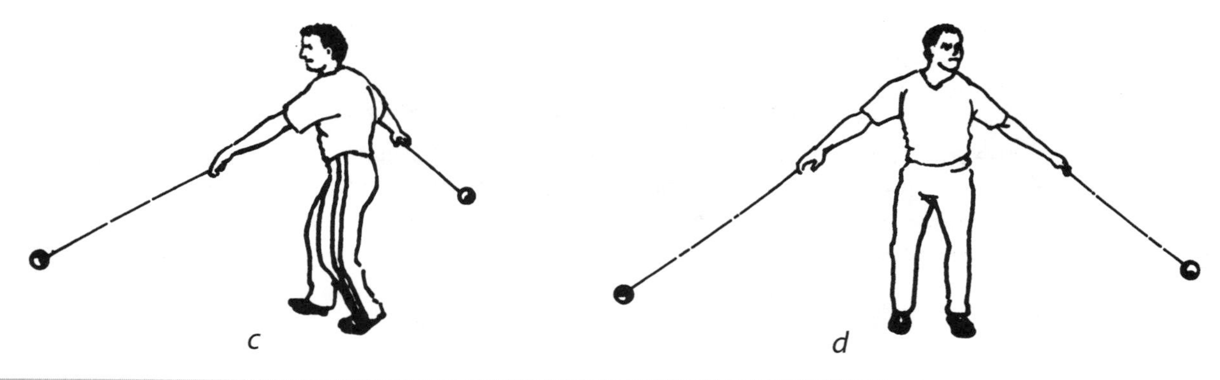

Figure 6.11 *(continued)*

MULTIPLE-TURN DRILL

You can perform a series of turns ranging from 2 to 15 turns (provided there is room) to work on footwork and turning rhythm. Multiple-turn throws (using up to six or seven turns) can also be performed. These can be done while holding the hammer with either one or two hands. One variation of the multiple-turn drill requires you to do your winds and the first two turns while holding the hammer with only the glove hand. After two turns, put your right hand on the handle and accelerate the hammer through two to four more turns before releasing.

This drill can help throwers who start to drag the hammer during the first few turns. By starting the turns with only the glove hand, they become very aware if they are ahead of the hammer (dragging the hammer) as they add speed during the first couple of turns. Throwers are less likely to start dragging the hammer if they accelerate it through a couple of turns before placing both hands on the handle.

TURNING DRILL WITH BROOM OR STICK

A broom or stick can be substituted for a hammer when initially introducing the footwork to beginners. Start first by breaking down the turn into three distinct steps. Step one starts with you facing 0 degrees and holding the stick straight away from you as you would a hammer (figure 6.13a). Turn to 90 degrees by pivoting on the heel of your left foot and the ball of your right foot while holding the stick in place (figure 6.13b). In step two, roll on the ball of your left foot while simultaneously picking up your right

Figure 6.12 *(continued)*

foot and stepping over your left foot. This action will cause you to pivot on the ball of your left foot while your right foot steps over the left and down to the surface, toes pointing toward 210 degrees (figure 6.13c). Once you have completed this step, pivot both feet around to bring your body and stick to again face 0 degrees (figure 6.13d). When you have mastered each step, start combining steps and ultimately put together a controlled series of turns without stopping. In addition, you can also add a steeper orbit for the broom or stick to get a feel for where the hammer should be during each part of the turn.

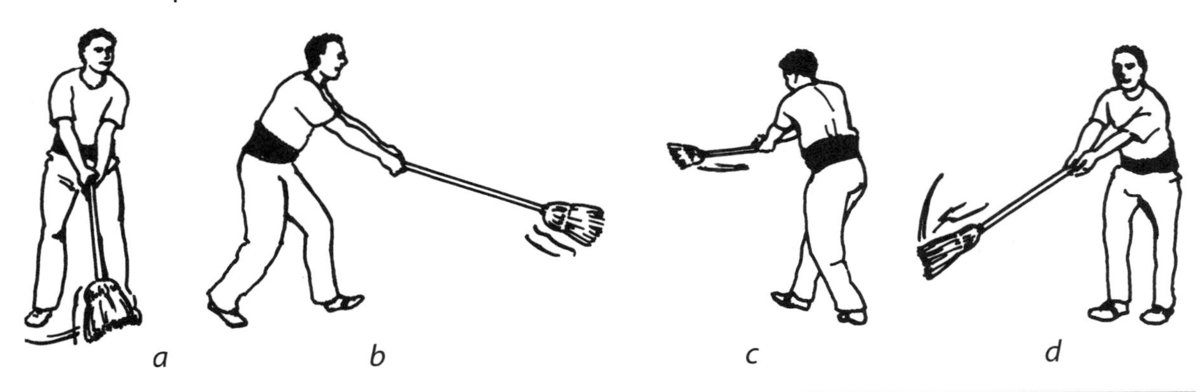

Figure 6.13 Turning drill with broom.

SINGLE-ARM TURNING DRILL

Using only one arm, you can perform two winds to get the hammer moving and then proceed into a series of turns (figure 6.14). This can be done with either the right or left arm. Once you begin turning, the orbit should start out relatively flat; you should focus on keeping with the hammer and executing smooth footwork. When you are comfortable doing this drill with one arm and you are not "dragging" the hammer, you can move on to the multiple-turn drill on page 147.

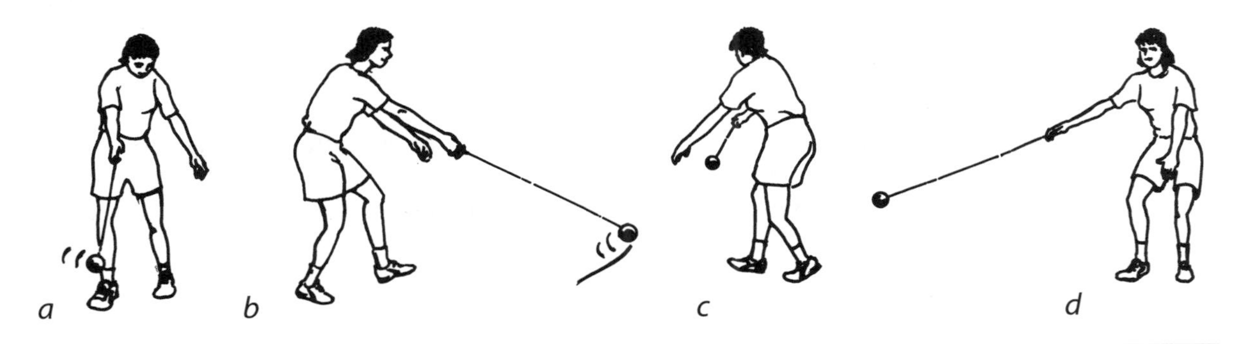

Figure 6.14 Single-arm turning drill.

Throwing Drills

Throwing hammers of various weights can help you work on specific speed (with light hammers) or specific strength (with heavy hammers). How and when to incorporate these hammers into the training regimen will depend on the type of thrower you are and where you are in the training cycle. Generally speaking, use heavy hammers in the early part of training when you are working on developing general strength as well as specific hammer strength. Use light hammers later during the competitive season when you are working on speed development.

Heavy hammers build specific strength and range in weight from 18 to 20 pounds (8 to 9 kilograms) for collegiate and open throwers, to 14 to 16 pounds (6 to 7 kilograms) for high school throwers, to 10 and 11.2 pounds (4 to 5 kilograms) for female throwers. The throwing differential between hammers is roughly 6 meters (20 feet) per kilogram once the thrower has established the technique and timing for that weight of hammer. (See table 6.1.) If you are throwing many different weights of hammers in succession during the same workout, you may not be able to establish this differential right away. As a bit of anecdotal evidence, Iouri Sedykh mentioned that his differential from the 20-pound (9-kilogram) to the 16-pound (7.26-kilogram) hammer was almost invariably 43 feet (13 meters), but that his differential from the 18-pound (8-kilogram) to the 16-pound (7.26-kilogram) hammer would range between 13 and 26 feet (4 and 8 meters) depending on his technique and timing.

Throwing light implements works on specific hammer speed. Light hammers for a collegiate or open thrower are 11.2 to 14 pounds (5 to 6.35 kilograms),

Table 6.1 Training Differential Between Hammers

MEN'S HAMMER DIFFERENTIALS				
12 lb	14 lb	16 lb	18 lb	20 lb
48.00 m	44.00 m	40.00 m	36.00 m	32.00 m
55.00 m	50.00 m	45.00 m	41.00 m	36.00 m
60.00 m	55.00 m	50.00 m	45.00 m	40.00 m
65.00 m	60.00 m	55.00 m	50.00 m	45.00 m
72.00 m	66.00 m	60.00 m	54.00 m	48.00 m
77.00 m	71.00 m	65.00 m	59.00 m	53.00 m
83.00 m	77.00 m	70.00 m	63.00 m	57.00 m
88.00 m	82.00 m	75.00 m	68.00 m	62.00 m
95.00 m	88.00 m	80.00 m	73.00 m	66.00 m
WOMEN'S HAMMER DIFFERENTIALS				
3 kg	3.5 kg	4 kg	10 lb	5 kg
47.00 m	43.00 m	40.00 m	37.50 m	34.00 m
52.00 m	48.00 m	45.00 m	42.50 m	39.00 m
58.00 m	54.00 m	50.00 m	46.50 m	43.00 m
63.00 m	59.00 m	55.00 m	51.50 m	48.00 m
68.00 m	64.00 m	60.00 m	56.50 m	53.00 m
73.00 m	69.00 m	65.00 m	61.50 m	58.00 m
78.00 m	74.00 m	70.00 m	66.50 m	63.00 m
83.00 m	79.00 m	75.00 m	71.50 m	68.00 m
88.00 m	84.00 m	80.00 m	76.50 m	73.00 m

while high school throwers will use the 11.2-pound (5-kilogram), 10-pound (4.5-kilogram), and 8.8-pound (4-kilogram) hammers. Female throwers use the 7-pound (3-kilogram) and 8-pound (3.6-kilogram) hammers for speed training. As mentioned earlier, the differentials between the lighter weights will get increasingly larger per kilogram dropped. The inability to reach these differentials with light implements is usually an indicator that the specific hammer speed is not high enough; you may need to adjust your training to address this weakness.

Another way to train for speed is to throw hammers with shortened wires. For men, this means using short wire hammers of 18, 20, or 22 pounds (8, 9, or 10 kilograms) at lengths of 3 feet (1 meter) down to 31 inches (79 centimeters). Lawrie Barclay, the coach who developed Debbie Sosimenko of Australia, suggests that women use short wire hammers of 12 pounds (5.4 kilograms) at 3 feet (1 meter), 14 pounds (6.35 kilograms) at 31 inches (79 centimeters), and even 16 pounds (7.26 kilograms) at 30 inches (76 centimeters). A regulation hammer on a slightly shortened wire can be used for speed work during the season as well.

Incorporating light and heavy hammers into the workout can be done in a number of ways. It is usually a good rule to start with heavier hammers at the beginning of practice and drop down to lighter hammers as fatigue sets in. The order or succession of various weights can depend on the focus of the workout and should also be based on your strength, quickness, learning capacity, and experience. The following are some examples of ways to set up a workout with various hammers:

- Heavy, standard, and light
- 5 heavy and 1 standard
- 10 heavy (9 kg or 20 lb), 10 heavy (8 kg or 18 lb), and 5 standard (7.26 kg or 16 lb)
- 10 light and 1 standard
- 10 light, 10 standard, and 10 heavy
- Light, standard, and heavy

Young throwers should not use heavy hammers for full technique until they have achieved a certain level of technical mastery. A thrower whose personal best is less than 50 meters (164 feet) who uses a hammer that is more than a kilogram heavier than his or her regulation hammer may suffer technical development problems. This could cause the thrower to alter his or her regular hammer technique to throw the heavy hammer better, which develops what Barclay has described as "heavy hammer" technique. *Young throwers should learn the full technique and throwing rhythm first with a light implement and then gradually increase the weight up to the regulation implement while keeping the rhythm, speed, and technique constant.*

Strength and Conditioning Exercises

There are a great variety of ways to train the body for better hammer performance. The area of strength and conditioning for the hammer can be broken down into the following disciplines: running, jumps, event-specific exercises, and weightlifting. The emphasis on each of these conditioning activities may vary depending on the time of the year. It is good to have a wide variety of exercises to train with so that your training routine does not become stale and to ensure that you are developing overall athleticism. Many different types of training will be presented in the section. Make sure that you perform each exercise with the highest quality. Start out performing simple exercises and only move on to more advanced exercises when you are comfortably able to do so. Advancing too fast can lead to injury and overtraining. Be careful to stay within your limits.

Running Exercises

Running exercises to improve speed and strength should be kept fairly short to focus on quick explosion and acceleration. Exercises that fall into this category are short sprints over distances of 20 to 50 meters (or yards). Stair sprints and hill sprints can also be incorporated to provide a little more resistance. One-hundred-meter/yard buildups can also be helpful. For the first 20 meters/yards, run at about 30 percent of your maximum speed and then gradually increase your speed over the last 80 meters/yards until you reach 80 to 90 percent at the end of the run.

Plyometric Exercises

Jumps are a very important part of the physical conditioning program for hammer throwers. You can perform jumps over hurdles, up stairs, on boxes, or on the ground. Jumps into a sand pit such as the standing long jump or multiple jumps (either single- or double-legged), which finish with the last jump into the sand, are good beginning jumping exercises. In the case of all multiple jumps, you should keep the time spent on the ground during each jump (amortization phase) to a minimum to allow for a quick, springlike motion. You can also perform multiple jumps in place for height. A good rule of thumb is to perform multiple jumps in groups of 10 or fewer. Too many jumps in succession will lead to poor technique and quality in the last few jumps, which defeats the purpose of the exercise.

STAIR JUMPS

Stair jumps can be performed with either one or two legs. As you become more efficient at jumping up stairs with two legs, you can progress to single-legged stair jumps. Spread your double-legged stair jumps out gradually over a larger number of stairs per jump as your fitness level increases. The same can be done for the one-legged stair jumps as soon as you can perform these jumps in smooth succession. When performing any stair jumps, make sure to stay on the balls of your feet and not let your heels touch the ground between jumps. Ascending stair jumps can also be combined with descending stair jumps. Descending stair jumps are performed by jumping "down" a set of stairs; land on the balls of your feet at the completion of each jump and attempt to land as softly as possible. Descending jumps work the legs eccentrically, whereas ascending stair jumps combine both concentric and eccentric contractions of the leg muscles. When jumping on stairs, always remain in control so you do not become fatigued and fall.

HURDLE HOPS

Hurdle hops and box jumps can be the most advanced of the jumping exercises. Hurdle hops are done in succession. Again, make sure you are performing these jumps on the balls of your feet and not breaking at the waist at the beginning of each jump, which will not allow you to get full hip extension as you begin to leave the ground. When just beginning this exercise, you can add a small rhythmic hop to get your balance between hurdles if you are having trouble clearing each hurdle in succession. Once you are proficient in hurdle jumps at one height, raise the hurdles to the next height. You can also set up hurdles to become gradually higher within a given set (for example, in inches, 33, 33, 36, 36, 39, 39). Hurdle hops should be done in sets of five to eight to avoid having too many jumps in succession. Elite-level hammer throwers (e.g., Tibor Gecsek) have been known to perform sets of hurdle jumps at 42 inches (107 centimeters) or more.

BOX JUMPS

Box jumps can be done in a variety of ways. Rhythmic box jumps are an easy way to get good leg conditioning work in and are exercises that even beginning throwers can handle. These types of jumps consist of front box jumps, side-to-side box jumps, and double-legged box jumps, and are performed with a relatively low box, about 12 to 16 inches (61 to 122 centimeters). You can also perform explosive jumps from the ground onto a tall box. Boxes for these jumps will range from 24 to 48 inches (30 to 40 centimeters) depending on your height and jumping ability. Try to land as softly on the box as possible.

Event-Specific Exercises

Success in the hammer throw relies primarily on event-specific speed and strength. For this reason it is important to train using many different types of event-specific exercises.

TRADITIONAL TRUNK EXERCISES

Traditional sit-ups and twisting variations (such as Russian twists) can be used in conjunction with plate twists and bar twists for total trunk conditioning. The use of the Roman chair, glute-ham raise, or scorpion bench for these exercises is very helpful. As with all trunk exercises, perform an equal number of abdominal and lower back exercises as well as rotational exercises in opposing directions for the purpose of muscular balance. Exercises that complement each other (work opposing muscle groups) are as follows: back hyper/Roman chair sit-up, Russian twist facing up/down, and oblique leg roll from side to side. In addition to these major trunk exercises that can build core development, countless other abdominal exercises and their variations can be done using either a Swiss ball or Roman chair, or just the floor.

MEDICINE BALL AND SHOT THROWS

Medicine ball and shot throws, which train very similar movements to the previously described trunk exercises, can also allow for a bigger range of motion and a more dynamic movement. While traditional trunk exercises such as sit-ups and twists allow you to work a muscle group through a certain range of motion, the amount of actual acceleration is limited because of the constant acceleration/deceleration pattern used as a result of your needing to change directions during a set. With ball throws, the ball steadily accelerates until it is released with no deceleration phase. This makes these exercises very similar to an actual throw.

The following are examples of a few medicine ball exercises and their equivalent exercises with a plate or some other form of resistance:

Hammer throw release—plate twists

Prone Russian twist release—prone Russian twist with weight

Underhand ball throw from Roman chair—back hyper

You can throw shots of various weights either from an underhand position or overhead position to enhance overall body coordination and timing for throwing. The underhand throw result will usually be 1 to 2 meters/yards less than the overhead result in a well-trained athlete. Among open athletes, men usually use a 7.26- or 6.4-kilogram (16- or 14-pound) shot, and women usually use a 4-kilogram (9-pound) shot. Elite hammer throwers have posted some very good results with these types of throws in relation to throwers from other throwing events. For example, Hristos Polihroniou of Greece has a best of 21 meters (69 feet) with the underhand shot throw and a best of 23 meters (75 feet) with the overhead shot throw using a 7.26-kilogram (16-pound) implement.

PUD THROW

Puds are probably the most event-specific form of training for the hammer other than throwing the hammer itself (figure 6.15). Puds, which can be thrown in a variety of planes, can weigh anywhere from 15 to 56 pounds (7 to 25 kilograms). Each pud throw should be counted in the same manner that a hammer throw is counted in the training/throwing volume, meaning that a pud workout should be considered a throwing workout. The weight of the pud will depend on your strength and the type of pud

Figure 6.15 Pud throw.

throw you are performing. The heaviest puds are used in the underhand throw for height. Lighter puds are used for the one-armed throws and overhead and underhand throws. The volume of one-armed throws should be performed equally in either direction. Pud throws were a very important part of current American record holder Lance Deal's training.

PLATE AND BAR TWIST

Plate twists and bar twists are excellent exercises to develop the muscles in the trunk. The trunk is a difficult area to hit with traditional weightlifting exercises, so twisting exercises are a great way to condition this part of the body that is so crucial in holding the hammer–thrower system together. Plate twists can be done in a wide variety of ways and within a wide range of planes (figure 6.16). Winds with a plate can also be included in this area of conditioning. Repetitions should be performed equally in each direction to ensure muscular balance and can number anywhere from 8 to 20 per set. The weight of the plate can also vary depending on a number of variables (size of thrower, type of exercise, etc.) but is usually between 5 and 25 kilograms (11 and 55 pounds). You can do bar twists either standing or seated; follow the same protocol with the bar twists as with the plate twists with regard to repetitions and sets.

Figure 6.16 Plate twist.

Weightlifting Exercises

The key components in weightlifting for the hammer throw involve exercises that work the legs and back. The "core" exercises that work these muscle groups are the clean, snatch, and front, back, and jump squat. (See chapter 2 for a complete description of these lifts.) The close-grip snatch is a great variation of the traditional snatch because it makes you generate a longer pull on the weight you are lifting over your head. This is very similar to the pull on the hammer at release. The front squat is preferred by some as the main squatting exercise for hammer throwers because the torso must be kept more erect than with the back squat. This position of the trunk is considered to be more like that seen during the actual throw.

Other auxiliary lifts that work both the back and legs can supplement the core lifts very well and can also be used to address specific weaknesses in certain areas. Leg exercises such as lunges, step-ups, one-legged squats, leg curls, hip raises, and ankle bounces can be inserted into the basic weightlifting regimen to provide supplementation to the leg workouts. Lunges, step-ups, and one-legged squats can be done with fairly heavy weight once you have reached good base levels of lifting fitness. Leg curls using a machine or hip raises on a box work the hamstrings and the other opposing muscle groups to the quadriceps and the muscle groups worked primarily by the squats, lunges, and step-ups. Ankle bounces are a dynamic exercise for the gastrocnemius and lower leg muscles that can be performed with no resistance or with small resistance in the form of weighted vests, hand weights, or bar weights.

The majority of exercises that are used for the back have been described in the event-specific exercise section. Strict weight training exercises for the back consist of the dead lift, Romanian dead lift, and good mornings. The dead lift and Romanian dead lift can be performed with heavy weight and are good for developing general back and hip strength. Good mornings are a more specific back exercise that isolates the lower back a little more. All of these exercises can be used in the preseason competition phase to address any back weaknesses. The training load of a hammer thrower is generally very hard on the back, so these exercises may not be necessary during the competitive season unless you have a major weakness or instability in your lower back.

Sample Training Program

The training program described in this section and presented in detail in table 6.2 consists of three phases:

1. General conditioning phase
2. Preseason phase
3. Competition phase

General conditioning phase—This is a cycle or group of cycles whose purpose is to build general fitness and work on correcting technical problems in the throwing technique. Lifting and conditioning are more general in nature during this phase, and the intensity is lower while the volume is kept high. Throwing is usually geared more toward drilling and/or heavy hammer work for specific strength development.

Preseason phase—This phase has an increase in both throwing and lifting intensity as you prepare for the upcoming competition season. Fewer heavy hammers are used as you focus more on perfecting your throwing rhythm with the regulation implement. Lifting intensity increases while the volume begins to decrease. Lifting exercises also become more specific and dynamic in this phase.

Competition phase—In this phase training is based around the competition schedule. Throwing intensity is very high with the major emphasis on regulation and light hammers to refine speed. Lifting is tapered down with an emphasis on quickness and explosion. Lifting volume is brought down significantly so you can be fresh for throwing sessions. Short sprints and jumps are also emphasized in training to help stimulate the nervous system.

Table 6.2 Sample Training Plan for Hammer

GENERAL CONDITIONING PHASE (3 TO 4 WEEKS PER CYCLE)			
Day	**Throwing**	**Weightlifting**	**Running**
Monday	5 180 step-in drills/5 turns 5 left arm drills/5 turns 5 right arm drills/5 turns 10 full throws	Clean, step-up, leg curl, 3 hammer-specific exercises (×2)	None
Tuesday	Pud throws (×24)	Front squat, front jerk, seated bar twist, back hyper	6 × 100-m buildups
Wednesday	5 wind and releases 7 one-turn throws w/short, heavy hammer 8 full throws w/9 kg (5 kg for women) hammer 9 full throws w/8 kg (10 lb for women) hammer	Rest	Double-legged stair jumps
Thursday	Rest	Snatch, narrow grip snatch, lunge, 2 hammer-specific exercises (×2)	3 × 20-m, 4 × 30-m sprints
Friday	5 winding drills 5 left arm turning drills/7 turns 5 turning drills w/both arms (8 turns) 8 throws with 8 kg (10 lb for women) hammer 8 throws with 7.26 kg (4 kg for women) hammer	One-legged squat, Russian twist, hanging leg raise, 2 hammer-specific exercises (×2)	8 × 5 hurdle hops

Power lifts will be sets of 6-8 repetitions, and Olympic lifts will be sets of 5-6 repetitions during this phase.

PRESEASON PHASE (3 TO 4 WEEKS PER CYCLE)			
Day	**Throwing**	**Weightlifting**	**Running**
Monday	5 left arm drills 10 full throws w/8 kg (10 lb for women) hammer 8 throws with 16 lb (4 kg for women) hammer 5 throws w/6 kg (3.5 kg for women) hammer	Clean, step-up, seated bar twist, 2 hammer-specific exercises	2 × 30-m, 2 × 50-m, 2 × 100-m sprints
Tuesday	Pud throws (×24)	Front squat, box jump, push jerks, 2 hammer-specific exercises (×2)	7 × 100-m buildups
Wednesday	7 one-turn throws w/short wire (8 kg) 7 five- to seven-turn drills without release 15 throws w/regulation hammer	Rest	Running drills, cariocas, rhythm skipping
Thursday	Rest	Hang snatch, narrow grip snatch, lunge, 2 hammer-specific exercises	3 hurdles followed by jump into sand pit (×10)

PRESEASON PHASE (3 TO 4 WEEKS PER CYCLE)			
Day	**Throwing**	**Weightlifting**	**Running**
Friday	8 left and/or right arm throwing drills 10 throws w/regulation hammer 10 throws w/light hammer	Jump squat, Russian twist, back hyper, 2 hammer-specific exercises	8 short sprints

Power lifts will be sets of 4-6 repetitions, and Olympic lifts will be sets of 3-5 repetitions during this phase.

COMPETITION PHASE (2 TO 4 WEEKS PER CYCLE)			
Day	**Throwing**	**Weightlifting**	**Running**
Monday	15 throws w/regulation hammer 12 throws w/light hammer	Snatch, jerk, 2 hammer-specific exercises (×2)	3 × 20-m, 4 × 30-m sprints
Tuesday	Rest	Front squat, step-up, back hyper	5 × 100-m buildups after squats
Wednesday	10 throws w/regulation hammer 15 throws w/16-14-12 hammer	Rest	Running and agility drills
Thursday	20 throws w/regulation hammer	Hang cleans (light), one arm snatch w/dumbbell, Russian twist	6 short sprints
Friday	Rest and/or travel	Rest	Rest
Saturday	Competition	Rest	Rest

Power lifts will be sets of 1-5 repetitions, and Olympic lifts will be sets of 1-4 repetitions during this phase.

Hammer throwing is a sport of repetition; it takes many throws before you can achieve a high level of technical mastery. When developing your hammer technique, pay attention to establishing both rhythm and positions during the course of the throw. Hitting positions without smoothly connecting the movements from turn to turn will inhibit you from reaching your top potential release speed. Conversely, if you are able to move smoothly and rhythmically without maintaining solid positions, you may be able to generate a lot of speed, but you will lack the necessary control. Both speed and control are necessary to be successful.

Bibliography

Agachi, T., Y. Bakarynov, L. Barclay, G. Guerin, B. Rubanko, A. Staerck, S. I. Sykhonosov, and E. Szabo. 1997. "NSA Round Table: Hammer Throw." *New Studies in Athletics* 12 (2-3): 13-27.

Babbitt, D. 1995. "Training With Hammers of Various Weights." *USA Thrower* 2 (4): 16-17.

Babbitt, D. 1996. "Field Testing for Throws." *USA Thrower* 3 (3): 16-19.

Bantum, K. 2000. "Hammer." Pp. 265-277 in *USA Track & Field Coaching Manual.* Edited by J. Rogers. Champaign, IL: Human Kinetics.

Barclay, L. 1998. "Basic Concepts for Training in the Women's Hammer Throw." *Modern Coach and Athlete* 36 (3): 15-17.

Bartoneitz, K., G. Hinz, G. Lorenz, and G. Lunau. 1988. "The view of the DVfL of the GDR on Talent Selection, Technique and Training of Throwers From Beginner to Top Level Athlete." *New Studies in Athletics* 3 (1): 39-56.

Bartonietz, K., L. Barclay, and D. Gathercole. 1997. "Characteristics of Top Performances in the Women's Hammer Throw: Basics and Technique of the World's Best Athletes." *New Studies in Athletics* 12 (2-3): 101-109.

Bondarchuk, A. 1985. "Modern Trends in Hammer Throwing, The Throws." 3d ed. Edited by J. Jarver. Mountain View, CA: Tafnews Press, pp. 123-126.

———. 1987. "Selection and Training of Youth and Junior Hammer Throwers." European Athletic Coaches Association XIV Congress. Aix-Les-Bains, France, January 13-17, pp. 105-108.

———. 1987. "Modern Technique in Hammer Throwing." European Athletic Coaches Association XIV Congress. Aix-Les-Bains, France, January 13-17, pp. 109-117.

———. 1990. "Long Term Training for Throwers." Australian Track & Field Coaches Association Development Programme Publication Book 2, Rothmans Foundation, Sydney, Australia, pp. 1-21.

Deal, L. 2000. "Notes From Lance Deal Hammer Clinic." From: hammer clinic at University of Georgia, Athens, Georgia, November 4, 2000.

Gaede, E. 1990. "Model Technique Analysis Sheets for the Throwing Events, Part V: The Hammer Throw." *New Studies in Athletics* 5 (1): 61-67.

Judge, L.W., and R. Hurst. 1993. "Using the Dynamic Start in the Hammer Throw." *Track and Field Quarterly Review* 93 (3): 4-7.

McGill, K. 1989. "Hammer." *Track and Field Quarterly Review* 89 (3): 27-47.

McNab, T. 1980. "Hammer." Pp. 156-161 in *The Complete Book of Track & Field.* New York: Exeter Books.

Otto, R.M. 1992. "NSA Photosequence 22—Hammer Throw." *New Studies in Athletics* 7 (3): 51-65.

Pedemonte, J. 1985. "Hammer." Pp. 237-262 in *Athletes in Action: Official IAAF Book on Track & Field.* Edited by H. Pain. London: Pelham Books.

Prokop, S.R. 1989. "Hammer Technique Keys." Cal State Los Angeles Track and Field Seminar, Los Angeles, CA, October.

Romanov, I., A. Bogdanov, and Y. Vrublevsky. 1998. "The External Structure of the Hammer Throw." *Modern Athlete and Coach* 36 (3): 8-11.

Romanov, I., and Y. Vrublevsky. 1998. "Women and the Hammer—Some Technical and Kinematic Characteristics." *Modern Athlete and Coach* 26 (4): 35-37.

Saat Ara, M. 1993. *Analysis of the Hammer Throw Technique Progression.* Unpublished manuscript, pp. 1-18.

Sedykh, I., and P. Farmer. 1996. "The Hammer Throw." Pp. 148-149 in Proceedings of the International Track and Field Coaches Association XIV Congress. Edited by G. Dales. Atlanta, GA, July 22-25.

Index

Note: The italicized *t* and *f* denote tables and figures, respectively. The italicized *tt* and *ff* denote multiple tables and figures, respectively.

About the Editor

L Jay Silvester was a six-time world-record holder in the discus and competed on multiple U.S. national teams. He was also a member of four Olympic teams ('64, '68, '72, and '76); he won the silver medal in Munich in 1972. He has coached five NCAA discus champions. Silvester is a recently retired professor from the department of physical education at Brigham Young University, where he coached throwing events for 20 years. He has also written two books (*Modern Drills for Track & Field-The Throwing Events* and *Weight Training for Fitness and Strength*). Since 1985, Silvester has served as USA Track and Field's discus throw chairman and was the Olympic throws coach for Team USA 2000.

About the Contributors

Jeff Gorski was a two-time All-Atlantic Coast Conference performer in the javelin at the University of North Carolina (where he set five school records) as well as a two-time U.S. national finalist. While serving as the throws coach at UNC (1982-86, 1988-91), he coached 23 All-ACC athletes, seven All-Americans, four conference record holders, and all UNC record holders in every throwing event. In 1993, Gorski founded Klub Keihas (Finnish for *javelin),* a throwers-only athletic club that supports and promotes the throwing events, especially the javelin. Through his coaching efforts in Klub Keihas, many of the nation's best throwers sought out Gorski and his club for his coaching ability and support. In February 1999, Gorski was selected as chairman of men's javelin development for USATF.

Don Babbitt has been the throwing coach at the University of Georgia since 1996. While at UGA he has coached 21 Southeast Conference Champions, 21 All-Americans, and 4 NCAA Champions in the throwing events. Before coaching at Georgia, Don was an assistant at California State University at Los Angeles from 1988 to 1996. He built Cal State LA's throwing program into the strongest at the NCAA Division II level, producing 39 All-Americans and 15 NCAA Champions. Babbitt is also a personal coach to several world-class throwers, including current U.S. Champions Adam Nelson, Breaux Greer, and Teri Steer, as well as Canadian shot put record holder Brad Snyder. An avid writer and clinician, he has also written several articles and chapters on the throws and has presented at clinics in eight different states, Canada, and Puerto Rico.

Kent Pagel is currently an assistant coach at Louisiana State University and is the throwers' coach. Before joining the Tigers' staff, Pagel was the throwers' coach and associate program director at Radford University. He has extensive coaching experience working with throwers at Kent State University, California State University at Long Beach, San Diego State, and San Diego Mesa College. Well respected on the international level, Pagel has served on coaching staffs at major international competitions in Japan, Switzerland, Sweden, and England.

Ramona Pagel was ranked one of the top two Americans (including a number one ranking) in the shot put for 11 straight years, and she was a four-time Olympian. She holds the American women's indoor and outdoor shot put records. Ramona also threw the discus and was ranked as high as number two in the United States in 1986 and 1988. Ramona coaches American Record Holder and National Champion Kim Kreiner in the javelin, is the National Women's Shot Put Coordinator, and has been the U.S. national coach for the World Championships, Pan-Ams, and World Cup.

PENN STATE
897
EASTERN ILLINOIS
ILLINOIS